# *The Secrets of Hartleyvale Farm*

Catherine Crawford, a young qualified school-teacher, applies for a position as house-keeper/governess to three small children living on a dairy farm in the Natal Midlands, in the Republic of South Africa. The old farmhouse is said to be haunted and to hold hidden secrets. Their father, Neil Middleton, is unpopular in the district, unapproachable and is known to have a filthy temper. Catherine goes to help him for the children's sakes and wonders what she has let herself in for!

Also by Una Halberstadt

## *Sally's Story*

*A group of four related novels telling the story
of a young girl growing up in the last century,
set in Kwa-Zulu Natal, South Africa*

Book 1 - 'Those hotel years!'
Book 2 - 'Sally at College 1941'
Book 3 - 'Sally and the Professor'
Book 4 – 'The Marriots of Ridge View'

Stories for Luke          First Edition 2006
Stories for Luke          Second Editions 2008

Acknowledgement

My grateful thanks to my son
Michael Halberstadt
whose professional guidance
and computer skills
have been of enormous value
in the publication of this book

# The Secrets of Hartleyvale Farm

Una Halberstadt

Except where actual historical events and characters are described for the storyline in this novel, all situations described in this publication are fictitious and any resemblance to living persons is purely coincidental.

No part of this publication may be reproduced, stored in a retrieval system, or transmitted in any form, by any means electronic or otherwise, without prior written permission of the Copyright owner.

Copyright © 2012 by Una Halberstadt

ISBN: 978-1-105-63555-7

*To dear Jane*
*for your wonderful friendship and laughter*

One

Ruth Crawford

'Please help me! My mother has collapsed and I can't lift her!'

Cathy ran out of their cottage into the garden of the big house, called Chelmsford House, their former home, shouting for Elijah, the gardener, or anyone who could help her. She had returned home on Thursday afternoon from the local school where she taught a primary class of eight-year olds to find her mother slumped in her wheelchair, her eyes closed and her mouth open. She seemed to have fainted. Elijah, the Zulu gardener came running from the big house.

'What's the matter, Miss Cathy? I was in the tool-shed when I heard you shouting for help.'

'It's my mother, Elijah. Come inside quickly, and help me lift her out of her wheelchair. I think she's fainted.'

He hurriedly pulled off his old garden shoes and followed her inside to the sitting-room where they found her mother practically falling out of her wheelchair, her frail body held up only by the waist strap, her head and arms hanging down. Cathy ran to her side, undid the strap and together they lifted her to the sofa, setting her down carefully amongst the cushions.

'Where's Daisy? Why isn't she here? She should be with her.'

'I saw her in the kitchen making the madam's afternoon tea.'

'Stay with her, Elijah, while I phone for Dr Walters.'

She prayed he'd still be in his surgery in the city. She shouted for Daisy as she ran through to the hall where the telephone stood on an oak table. Daisy, their trust-worthy Zulu maid, had worked for them for some twenty years, ever since Cathy was a little girl. She came running to the sitting-room, holding up her arms and crying when she saw Mrs Crawford lying in a sort of dazed state on the sofa.

'Hauw! My madam! What has happened to you?' she cried kneeling down beside her and clutching her arms. She rubbed her hands together and patted her face, but there was no response or sign of recognition from her madam. Cathy put down the phone and ran to her mother.

'She's fainted, Daisy. I found her half falling out of her chair. I've phoned Dr Walters and he'll be here as soon as he can. Bring me a cup of water and we'll try to revive her.'

They tried to sit her up and make her take a sip of water, but it was no use. She couldn't sit up on her own and her head lolled from side to side. She didn't seem to be breathing or to understand what Cathy was saying. Cathy tried to feel for her pulse, but she couldn't find it and if there was one it was very weak. She shook her by her shoulders, desperate to get some response, but she flopped back on the cushions. By this time she was extremely agitated and worried. She knelt beside her, holding her hands and rubbing them again.

'Daisy, I don't know what else to do! Where is Dr Walters? He should be here by now!'

At that moment in the drive they heard a car door suddenly slamming and Dr Walters came rushing into the room. He was at her mother's side, his hands on her wrist, feeling for a pulse; then he opened his bag, quickly took out his stethoscope, searching her chest and back again and again for her heart-beat. In the end he shook his head. There was nothing. He looked sadly at Cathy. She was still kneeling beside her mother, a very worried look on her face.

He took hold of Cathy's hands.

'Cathy, my dear, she's gone. I'm so sorry. There's nothing more I can do. I believe she's had massive heart attack. Her heart has been a worry these past months, as you know, and she has been taking medication which I prescribed. It must have happened before you found her, I estimate some twenty to thirty minutes ago.' Cathy looked dazed. She had gone quite pale. He took hold of her arm and pulled her up.

'Come, sit down on the sofa with me. We can do nothing more for her.' He turned to the maid who was on her knees, weeping softly beside the wheelchair. 'Daisy, get up. Your madam has gone. Make us some tea, please, and bring it here.'

Cathy fished inside her pocket and found a handkerchief and began to wipe away the tears that had gathered in her eyes and were now spilling down her cheeks.

'Is your brother at the office?' Cathy nodded her head.

'Give me the number. I must talk to him.'

The doctor dialled the number and got through right away.

'Garth, it's Dr Walters. I'm at the cottage with Cathy. She called me when she got home and found your mother slumped in her wheelchair. This will come as a shock to you and Julia. I'm so sorry to tell you she was dead when I arrived. There was no heartbeat and there was nothing I could do. I believe it was a huge heart attack. It would have been very quick and she wouldn't have suffered.'

There was silence for a minute then the doctor heard Garth's worried voice.

'This is such a shock! We knew her heart had begun to be troublesome, but I had no idea there was such cause for concern. I'll come over right away. How is Cathy?'

'She's very upset and shocked. I'll give her some tablets and stay with her a while.'

'Thank you, Doctor. I'll be with you in fifteen minutes.'

He put down the phone and went back to Cathy. She was crying and sobbing softly, wiping away her tears.

'Poor Mum. She was always such an active person and hated being confined in a wheelchair. She has missed Dad so much since his death last year. They were devoted to one another.'

'Here's the tea, Miss Cathy.' Daisy came in with the tray and put it down on the coffee table. 'I'll pour it out for you.'

'Thank you, Daisy.' Dr Walters handed Cathy her tea-cup and two tablets which he had taken from his bag.

'Take these now, Cathy. They'll make you feel easier. I'll write out the death certificate while I wait for Garth, then get back to the surgery as there are two patients I must see before I do my late afternoon hospital rounds.'

He drank his tea and went to the dining-room table to write out the certificate. Cathy swallowed the tablets down with gulps of sweet tea. It was such a shock. To lose both one's parents within eighteen months was a hard blow for anyone to accept.

They heard a car coming up the drive, a door slamming and her brother walked hurriedly into the room. He saw his mother lying on the sofa and went to touch her cheek. 'Dear Mum,' he whispered as he kissed her forehead and her face before sitting beside Cathy and putting his arms around her.

'I'm so sorry, Cath.' He kissed her cheeks still wet with tears. 'It's quite a shock. I had no idea her heart was so bad, did you? Julia and I will help you. Don't worry. We'll see this through together. I handled the arrangements after Dad's death and I know what to do. Would you like to come to us for a few days until the funeral is over?'

'Garth, thanks for coming so quickly.' Dr Walters came in with the certificate, interrupting them. 'We meet again in sad circumstances. I'm so sorry for you both. She was a good wife to Brian and a good mother to you children. You'll miss her, and it will take time adjusting to another new situation, but you are both young and strong. Life has to go on, and Julia will have her baby in a few month's time. You will have a new life to love and spoil.'

He gave Garth the certificate. 'Phone me if there's anything more I can do. I've phoned the hospital for an ambulance. An autopsy will have to be done to confirm her death. Phone your relatives and go ahead with the funeral arrangements. You'll feel better when it's over.' He looked at Cathy. He had known her since her pre-school days. 'I'll pop in and see you tomorrow, my dear.' He put a small packet of tablets in her hand. 'Take two tonight and you'll have a good night's sleep. Will you stay on in the cottage on your own?

'Yes, I want to stay here. This is my home and Daisy will be here to help me. There's only another fortnight before the final school tests and I must see my children through their year's work. Thank you, Doctor, for coming so quickly. It's hard to accept that both our parents have left us and it will take time to get over her death and adjust our lives. I'll be glad to see you tomorrow.'

With that, he nodded and took his leave. He knew her to have a strong character. She had been a source of strength to her invalid mother when her father had died, and had quickly taken over the running of Chelmsford House, attending to all the financial matters. As Bank Manager of the local bank her father earned a steady salary and together with money and property he had inherited from his father, they were considered to be 'comfortably off.'

However, it soon became evident that to keep on Chelmsford House and the extensive garden for just the two of them without her father's income was not a possible proposition. They decided to let Chelmsford House and live in Hibiscus Cottage on the property which long ago had been used as a home for the manager of the extensive estate.

It was a sensible move.

Garth stood up and walked over to his father's cabinet and poured himself a stiff whiskey. He hadn't expected to hear this news and he found he was shaking.

'I'm phoning Julia, Cath. She'll be so sad. She loved our Mum.'

He was three years older than Cathy, a tall man with fair blonde hair like his sister's. She was of medium height, a slim, attractive, quietly-spoken girl. He had studied hard and when he became a chartered accountant he joined a firm of accountants in the city. He had met Julia at a friend's birthday party and they became engaged a year later. His father took ill with pneumonia during a severe Pietermaritzburg winter and although he was weak he insisted on attending their wedding. It had been raining and cold the two previous days and much against the family's pleadings he had got up and dressed to be at his son's wedding. It was foolish – he caught another chill and his condition deteriorated. He had been a cigar smoker all his married life, and this added to his breathing problems. His condition worsened and he died a few days later.

Ruth and the family were grief-stricken.

'You know you're welcome to stay with us a few nights, Cath. You can come back to the cottage after the funeral.'

'No, Garth, thank you for the offer but I'd rather be here on my own. I'll phone Miss Thomas and tell her about Mum. I'll stay home tomorrow and return to school on Monday. We should see Father Clements and arrange a date for the funeral, Garth. Let's do it now and then phone the family.'

Suddenly there was a fluttering noise inside a bird-cage standing on a table near the window. It was Peter, her mother's pet budgie. He had been with her for several years and since Brian's death and her own illness she had enjoyed his companionship all the more. She would ask Daisy to take him out of the cage and he would either sit on her shoulder or on the arm of her chair, nibbling tiny pieces of biscuit or seed while she chatted to him. She had taught him to say several words. Cathy had forgotten about him completely in all the worry about her mother.

'Hello, Peter,' she called to him.

'Hello, hello! ........ Cheers!' he answered. This is what Ruth said before she took a sip of her nightly glass of gin and tonic. 'Cheers!' she replied. realising she would have to look after Peter now that her mother had gone. He would miss her voice and her companionship.

Father Clements was free to see them later that afternoon. He was a middle-aged priest who knew the family well and often visited her mother since she had been confined to her wheelchair. He met them at the Rectory door, shook hands with Garth and took them to his study. It was a cheerful, spacious room furnished with his desk which to the despair of his wife, Margaret, seemed to be permanently cluttered with books and papers. Book-cases crammed with books and files lined the wall behind his chair. On the walls were photographs of past rectors and a picture of the original wood and iron church built in 1860 by early settlers and later destroyed by fire. He waved his arm at two old leather armchairs in front of his desk.

'Please sit down and make yourselves comfortable. I'm so sorry to learn of your mother's death. I've often called to see her at tea-time and enjoyed a chat with her. She was a brave woman, but a lonely woman since your father's death. She missed him so much. I would be pleased to take her funeral service and help you in any possible way. Shall we arrange a date to suit you? My diary should be here somewhere on my desk.' He moved some papers around and found it next to his telephone. 'Ah, here it is!'

After consulting his diary the funeral was fixed for the following Tuesday afternoon at three o'clock. He asked about the family members who would be speaking of her at the service, and made suggestions about the bible readings and hymns. Garth said according to her wishes, she would like to be buried beside her husband in the family plot in the city cemetery. The committal would take place at the grave-side.

They thanked him and returned to the cottage.

Garth arranged for notices to be placed in the local newspapers. Cathy phoned their aunts and uncles in Durban, other family members and their friends, who were shocked and saddened to learn of her sudden death. Their remaining grand-mother lived in a retirement home in England and sadly would be unable to be present at her daughter's funeral.

'I'll phone Granny now, Garth. It's a good time to talk to her before their supper-time. She'll be very upset and sad that she won't be here with us at this time.'

Garth kissed her Goodbye. 'Are you sure you'll be all right?'

'Yes. Daisy's here with me. I want to phone Claudia now and tell her. Give Julia my love.'

He drove home and she was left alone in the cottage.

Two


A new beginning


Miss Thomas had been a headmistress at the Waverley Junior School for many years. She had welcomed Cathy on her staff when she was appointed there after her graduation from College and knew her to be an enthusiastic and sympathetic teacher, committed to training her young pupils. She was sad to learn of her mother's death and wanted Cathy to take more leave to attend to her mother's affairs, saying she could apply for a replacement. However, Cathy politely refused. She knew she would feel better at school occupied with her pupils than crying and moping at home. She wanted to be with them for the final revisions and to see them through their examinations. Finally Miss Thomas accepted her decision.

That evening she phoned her friend, Claudia Dean to tell her the news. Claudia lived in Estcourt, the Natal Midlands town on the way north to Johannesburg. She had met her at the Natal Teachers' Training College at Pietermaritzburg when they had both started their teaching careers five years previously. Claudia had a room at a boarding-house in the town quite near to the College. They sat together for their lectures and became great friends. Cathy had spent a few weekends with her family and knew them well.

'Cathy, I'm so sorry to hear about your Mum! What a shock for you, Garth and Julia so soon after your father's death. Mum, Dad, and the boys will be upset to hear this news. I'd like to come for her funeral but next Tuesday is impossible. It's mid-week and we're in the middle of exams. I'll come this weekend by train if I may. What can I do to help you?'

'Just to have you here with me would be wonderful. Please come. The telephone is already ringing, and I know flowers and neighbours will be arriving over the weekend. You would be a great help. I'll meet your train. Is it the late afternoon one on Friday?'

'Yes, it gets in around six o'clock. See you then, Cath.'

What a great friend she was! A lovely, friendly girl, full of life and fun. She was a brunette with greeny eyes, a tall, athletic girl who loved sport. She played an exceptional game of tennis and recently had won a small junior golf tournament held at their local club. Her brother David had given her several lessons when she was at high school and she found she had a natural flair for the game. Cathy on the other hand loved swimming and riding.

Daisy prepared her room and Cathy was there to meet her when the train steamed into the station. She waved at her with a large bunch of garden flowers.

'Cathy!' she called when she saw her on the platform. 'Mum insisted I bring these for you, knowing how much you love her garden flowers. There's also her fruit-cake, scones and biscuits. You know how she loves to bake! How are you?'

'I'm feeling better. I slept well. Getting used to the idea of life without Mum. The house is so quiet, even Peter is less noisy.'

'He'll recover. He's bound to have missed her voice and wonders where she is. You must keep talking to him.'

'I do. Daisy's very good with him, too. Have you got everything? Let's walk to the car-park.'

It wasn't far and it didn't take long to load up 'Pixie,' the Renault her parents had given her for her 21st birthday. Cathy drove to Hibiscus Cottage while Claudia told her of recent happenings at her junior school.

The weekend proved to be a busy one, with callers coming to pay their respects, bringing home-made cakes and meals, and stopping for a cup of tea and cake. Friends came with their condolences. Garth and Julia came for supper. Before they knew it, it was time for Cathy to take her to catch the train home.

'Thank you for coming, Claudia. It was good to have you here with me. You were a great help. I'll be all right now.'

There were more people at the funeral than she expected and the little St Stephen's Church was three-quarters full. Their aunts, uncles and cousins drove up from Durban; her parent's bank, bowling and bridge friends were present, besides her father's golfing friends; her riding friends and Garth and Julia's young friends were also there. It was comforting to know that they had remembered her. Father Clements spoke of her devotion to Brian, her love of gardening and of her uncomplaining years spent in a wheelchair.

Her children were happy to see her back at school after the funeral.

'We missed you, Miss Crawford,' said Jimmy, one of the brighter pupils, 'and we're sorry about your mother. Who will look after you now? You could come and stay with us. We have an empty guest-room, but my cat, Fluffy, sometimes sleeps on the bed.'

'I have Daisy, our maid, who will cook for me and clean the cottage. Thank you for thinking of me, Jimmy. I'll be fine.'

Patricia brought her a bunch of flowers. She was a timid child who Cathy had encouraged to become more self-reliant and confident.

'I picked these for you from our garden, Miss Crawford, and I brought a vase to put them in. It's so sad to lose your mother. I hope my mother lives for a long, long time. I'll look after her.'

'I'm sure she will, Patricia. Thank you for the flowers. My mother loved her garden, the shady trees and the beautiful flowers, especially her pink and red roses.'

'Who will Peter talk to now? He'll be so lonely without your Mum,' said Alan. They all knew about Peter and once when they had worked on a project about their pets, Cathy had taken him to school to show him to them.

'I'll put his cage in the kitchen where he can talk to Daisy while she's cooking for me and I'll take him out of his cage when I get home. He won't be lonely, Alan.'

The children made little sympathy cards to give her. She was so touched. They wrote their final test papers, enjoyed the school Christmas concert and nativity play, made Christmas cards for their friends and small decorations for the Christmas tree that Cathy had put up in her class-room. Miss Thomas came to watch the parade of Christmas paper hats and crackers they had made and to judge the winners. It was such fun! She gave them a party and said Goodbye to them. She had loved her year's teaching with them. She packed up her books, said her Goodbyes to the staff and Miss Thomas, and drove home to Hibiscus Cottage.

'What will you do during the holidays?' asked Julia when she had supper with them one evening.

'I see there's a short art course which the well-known artist Marissa Allen, is giving in December. It's called *'The joy of painting with oil paints.'* It's for all abilities and the price includes a basic start-up kit of paints, brushes and canvas. I thought I'd join the class. I've always wanted to learn more about oil painting.'

'What a good idea!' said Garth. 'You've always liked drawing, Cath, and I imagine you'd do well. You used to like your art classes at school.'

Claudia's mother, Iris, phoned her after the schools had broken up.

'Cathy, what are you doing during the holidays, and more specifically, what are your plans for Christmas? Will you be with Garth and Julia?'

'No, they'll be with Julia's parents at their beach cottage at the coast. They arranged this holiday with them some months ago. I'm joining an art course until the sixteenth and have nothing in mind for Christmas.'

'Cathy, we'd love to have you with us for Christmas if you'd like to come. There'll be the six of our family, and Guy has invited his friend, Stephen Mitchell, as well. He's a journalist and works with him on the newspaper. He's on his own as his family are overseas. You'd like him. Guy often asks him to come for the odd meal. He has an apartment in town near the offices. Please say 'Yes.' Claudia would love you to come and I can't bear the thought of you being on your own in the cottage over Christmas!'

'I'll say 'Yes' and thank you, Iris. I'll bring Peter, too, if I may, as I have promised Daisy leave to be with her family, and she is due for a holiday. What can I bring?'

'Nothing, or maybe some wine. Just come and have fun. Claudia will be thrilled to hear you're coming. She'll phone you this evening. She's playing tennis with friends this morning.'

Cathy thought it was good of the Deans to invite her. She was pleased she would be with friends over the festive time. Her aunt Lucy, in Durban, her father's sister, phoned a few days later to ask her to come for Christmas Day. She liked Aunt Lucy. She and Uncle Sam had often visited them when her father was alive. She had been thankful to say she'd be with the Deans. Aunt Lucy and Uncle Sam had no children and the party would consist of their elderly friends and she knew she would be 'de trop.'

The art course was most interesting and stimulating. There were people of all ages, including three young people on the course and they quickly became friends. Cathy loved to draw and paint. She usually worked with water colours and was eager to try a new medium and to learn more about the art of oil painting. She loved the course and couldn't wait to do more painting. Marissa, the art teacher, praised her efforts, especially her study of still life.

She had chosen to paint a low wooden basket of fruit, using oranges, a large paw-paw, lemons and strawberries. The colours were vibrant and exciting. She knew it was good.

'You should study further, Cathy,' said Marissa, 'I'd like to help you. Could you join my studio classes in the afternoons next year?'

'I'd like very much to do so, but I'm not sure what my afternoon duties will be. I'm teaching at the Waverley Primary School and we do sport duties and coaching in the afternoons. I'll contact you once the schools have opened and I have my time-table.'

She packed away her art things and asked Daisy to fetch her suitcase from the small box-room at the back of the cottage where all her mother's excess furniture, crockery and linen had been stored after they had moved from Chelmsford House. December was a lovely warm sunny month, so shorts, skirts, T shirts and blouses, and her swimsuit would be all she would need, with something smart to wear over the Christmas festive days, something for evening wear and a light jacket.

Next she cleaned out Peter's cage and packed his birdseed. She bought some wine, party snacks, nuts, dried fruit and chocolates to give to Iris, and a smart handbag for Claudia. Shopping wasn't easy. All the shops were particularly busy with people searching for last minute groceries and gifts. Christmas Day happened to fall on a Sunday and most business houses were closing on Friday for the long weekend.

She gave hampers of groceries to Daisy and Elijah to take home, said Goodbye to the Simpsons at the Big House over a glass of sherry and visited Garth and Julia to give them their Christmas presents and wish them a happy holiday.

She packed the car, put Peter in his cage next to her in Pixie and on Thursday after lunch, she drove up to Estcourt on the highway.

She felt wonderfully free and happy!

Three


Christmas with Claudia's family


The Dean's house in the suburbs of Estcourt, was a large rambling family home which had been built by her great-grandfather, Charles Dean, for his young bride, Margaret Jane, when she arrived from England in 1890. The town was named after Thomas Estcourt, an English parliamentarian who did much to promote immigration to Natal. Earlier a small village had grown up round the fording place over the Bushman's River on the road to the north. Here blacksmiths and inn-keepers had first settled beside the shopkeepers and traders.

The extensive garden had been well laid-out with shady trees and lawns. A swimming pool and tennis court had been added over the years. Cathy drove through the gate and up the drive as Claudia ran out to meet her at the front porch.

'Hi! You're just in time for tea. How are you?'

Cathy stepped out to hug her. 'I'm fine. I'm getting used to living in the cottage without Mum. I miss her voice and doing things for her. I try to keep busy and not dissolve into tears every five minutes.'

David appeared and ran down the steps to meet them. He was her middle brother, a second year student at the Natal University College at Pietermaritzburg. He was studying to be an accountant.

'Hi, Cathy! I'll take your case for you.' He looked into the car and saw the packages and Christmas presents on the back seat, and Peter looking most important in his cage on the front passenger seat.

'Hello....hello!' said Peter moving over on his perch towards the window when he saw David looking at him.

'Hello, Peter. What a clever bird you are!' He saw all the presents on the back seat. 'I hope one of those is for me! I'll put them on your bed, Cathy. We're pleased you could come to us for Christmas.'

'Thanks, David. Good to see you again.'

'Mum has put a small table in the dining-room near the window for Peter's cage, so that he'll be part of the family and enjoy Christmas with us.'

Claudia took her arm. 'Come for tea. David will bring Peter inside to join us.'

They walked into the dining-room and Iris came to meet her.

'Welcome, my dear. We're so pleased you could come to us.' She kissed her cheek. 'Edward will be here any minute. They're closing early today. Guy and Terry will be coming later. Sit down and I'll start pouring the tea. You must be famished!'

David joined them and they sat around the table laden with all sorts of good things. Iris enjoyed baking for her family, especially for the three boys who could soon demolish a plateful of cookies. Cathy was hungry and tucked into the fruit cake and milk tart. Claudia's father, Edward, arrived from the office. He was a tall man with dark hair which had begun to turn grey at the temples. He went to greet Cathy.

'Hello....hello!' said Peter when he saw Edward coming.

'Hello! I've heard about you. You must be Peter.'

'Clever boy! Clever boy!'

'He's a clever little bird! I'm sure he misses your Mum. I'm glad you brought him with you for us to enjoy.'

He sat down next to Iris and she handed him his tea.

'Daisy, our maid, has gone home on leave so I asked Iris if I could bring him. I couldn't leave him alone in the cottage for Elijah, our gardener, to look after and feed.'

'Do you let him out of the cage to fly around?' asked David.

'Yes, but I make sure all the windows and doors are closed.'

'Fortunately we haven't a cat or a dog. Our terrier died last year.'

Edward asked about her mother's funeral and she gave them an account of it. 'Her death was a great shock for Garth, Julia and me.'

'How was the art course?' asked Claudia wishing to change the subject, and helping herself to another of her favourite sausage rolls.

'I thoroughly enjoyed every minute and learnt such a lot. I brought my art book with me. I want to draw a few landscapes while I'm here so near to the mountains. This is such beautiful scenic country.'

'You must do just as you like, my dear. You have stayed with us before and you know our routine. Your bedroom is ready for you. I'll leave you to get unpacked as I have a  phone-call to make. Claudia has a few outings lined up for you. Special events have been arranged over the Christmas period. You're in for a good time, by all accounts!' She excused herself and left them.

'I'll tell you all about it while you unpack.'

'It all sounds very mysterious. Oh, Claudia, it's so good to be here again with your family!'


It didn't take long and while she emptied her case and disposed of the packages Claudia told her what would be happening over the weekend. Life in a country town is so more friendly than the rather impersonal atmosphere of a bustling city. Cathy had met some of their friends on previous visits and enjoyed their relaxed life-style. Although they led busy lives they found time to meet their friends and enjoy their company.

While Cathy completed her unpacking Claudia launched into the holiday programme.

'There's a 'Carols by Candlelight' evening arranged for tomorrow night in Wagon-Wheels Park followed by a braai. We take rugs, a picnic basket and buy candles there. Dad will organise steak, chops, sausages and drinks, and Mom will pack the rest – all very informal, a lovely family evening. The Council provide the braai fires and the security police will be present. We're all going. Two of the children in my class have leading roles, so I must be there to watch them. Andrea is the Angel Gabriel and Thomas is one of the Kings. Our Estcourt choir will lead the singing. We all went last year and it was so special – a lovely way to herald in Christmas.'

'That sounds wonderful. Count me in!'


'Next day on Saturday a picnic has been arranged at the White Water Falls ten km away. The children ride there in pony-carts which is such fun, or we go on farmers' trucks or ride on horseback. We follow along the ancient route the Dutch Voortrekkers took when they came long ago from the Cape. They trekked over the Drakensberg Mountains looking for land where they could settle to farm and be free without jurisdiction from the Dutch government who ruled the Cape at that time. It must have taken courage to undertake such a tough, hazardous journey. To get their ox-wagons over those peaks was just amazing! Would you like to join us?'

'Yes, please. I've never ridden in a pony-cart, or maybe I could ride if there's a spare horse for me. I brought my riding gear in case there's a chance of a ride.'

'The children love the pony-cart rides. I'll ask Dad to find out if anyone has a spare horse for you. The 'oldies' go by car and take the food. On Sunday which is Christmas Day we'll all be going to St. Matthew's for the lovely Christmas service to sing the carols again. We usually open our presents after a late breakfast-brunch and then we're free to do anything we like.'

'It has been well planned. I can see I'm in for a good time.'

'It will be hot during the day. I hope you've brought your swim-suit. How's your tennis? The boys would like a game with us.'

'I'm not up to your high standard, but I'd like a game.'

'Terry's not as good as David but he's improving. We'll challenge them to a game tomorrow before the carols if there's time. Guy should be home soon. He's often kept late at the news office.'

'I remember he plays a good, hard game. I'd rather play as his partner than against him. He hits those tennis balls quite viciously!'

'The boys have bought a fair-sized pine tree at a nursery in town and after the picnic Guy will set up the fairy lights and we'll all help to decorate it with baubles, bells, ornaments and tinsel while Mum serves warm mince pies and port. It's an old Dean family custom. Dad likes to play us Christmas music which he has recorded. This is a family ritual and is always done on Christmas Eve. It's a magical evening of fun and laughter.'

'I'm sure it's a wonderful family evening.'

They chatted about their year's teaching. Claudia had taught a class of eleven year-olds in one of the local schools. She admitted that at first she thought it would be difficult as she preferred the younger children, but discovered that she had changed her mind. The older ones were far more interesting, more creative, and inquisitive to learn more. She found it was far more challenging for her to feed their eager minds with information of all kinds.

'At the end of November I am astounded at the amount of knowledge they have learnt in their year with me. For me it's a wonderful reward. Teaching is so satisfying, isn't it?'

'Yes, it certainly is,' agreed Cathy.

Friday dawned sunny and warm with a light breeze.

'It will be hot later on,' said Edward at breakfast-time, 'but it should cool down for the Carols. Fortunately no rain is forecast.'

They packed their picnic basket and left early to find a good spot near the front where a stage had been set up for the performers, narrators and choir. On a huge canvas backdrop a scene of the hills outside the town of Bethlehem had been painted. At the back in the centre stood the wooden stable with a manger and bales of hay. There were also two very real-looking cardboard cows and a donkey. Large trees in tubs and branches of various bushes adorned sides of the stage. A small group of musicians were tuning their instruments nearby while electricians placed microphones in position. The shepherds were there, ready dressed, waiting to the right of the stage with their sheep which were grazing in a small pen nearby. Cathy wondered how they would be moved onto the stage at the appropriate moment! Guy and Terry had disappeared to help with the costumes and props backstage.

The grassed seating area soon was crowded with rugs, families and picnic baskets. Children of all ages clutched their candles, waiting for the magic moment when they could light them. As the sun went down, one by one the candles were lit, illuminating the park and shedding light so that people were able to read the words of the carols from their programmes. A priest appeared smiling on the stage to welcome them and the service began.

Cathy found it was good to sing the old carols again and hear the words from the Bible as the scenes of the Christmas story unfolded before their eyes. The Angel Gabriel appeared to Mary with upraised arms to reveal enormous golden wings that shimmered in the candle-light. Andrea was a tall child with long, fair hair and looked every inch an angel. She spoke well in a good clear voice, fluttering away after telling Mary the good news – 'Unto you will be born a Son and you shall call his name Jesus. He will be great and of his kingdom there will be no end.'

The shepherds carrying their crooks made their entrance to the stable bearing their simple little gifts to the Christ Child. One of the shepherds opened the sheep pen and the sheep scattered all over the stage, chased by the shepherds to the other side where Guy was ready to herd then into another pen. One escaped the shepherd's crook and headed off to the manger. Mary took fright, screamed, and grabbing Baby Jesus from the manger she ran behind the stable with him, while Joseph chased the bewildered animal around the stage with his crook! It was all very spontaneous and had everyone laughing. One small voice in the audience shouted, 'Mom, they were *real* sheep!'

.Thomas as the first King, wearing an ornate embroidered cloak and golden crown, entered importantly bearing his box of gold, holding it high for all to see, before bowing and giving it to Mary. The second King had trouble keeping his crown from slipping down on his nose! The third King was late for his cue and was hustled onto the stage by a worried-looking producer. He did remember, however, to bow to Mary.

'I'm sorry I'm late, Mary,' he said to her. 'My camel lost its way in the desert and we couldn't find the star.'

That certainly was not in the script! Ripples of laughter ran through the audience. Claudia shook her head and smiled.

The evening concluded with the carol 'Oh, come all ye faithful.'

'What a wonderful presentation!' Cathy remarked. 'It's the first time I have attended a carol evening out in the open in a park and the story became so much more alive and more meaningful for me. I loved it all, even the mistakes, which gave it the human touch.'

The fires from the braai braziers had been burning some while and now glowed in the darkened sky showing that the red-hot coals were ready for the meat to be placed on the grids. Picnic baskets opened and the cooking began, mostly watched over by the fathers, who stood with long forks in their hands ready to turn the meat over while they chatted to their friends and drank a beer. Children, no longer confined to their places on the rugs, ran to find their school-friends, munching snacks and hamburgers. Claudia and Cathy stood up to stretch their legs.

'Those scenes were very beautiful and moving. Your pupils did well,' said Cathy as they walked to join Edward and David at the fires. Two little girls were standing near them watching the steaks, boerewors (spicy beef sausages) and chops being turned over. They seemed to be on their own and looked rather lost.

'Where are your sausages?' David asked. 'Would you like me to cook them for you?'

'My Dad has gone to fetch our meat in the truck. He told us to stay here and wait for him,' said the elder girl, holding the younger one's hand.

A man appeared out of the darkness carrying a brown paper parcel. Edward recognised him as Neil Middleton, a dairy farmer in the district.

'Hello, Neil. There's plenty of room here for your meat. Ours is practically done. The fire is still giving off a lot of heat. Come and join us round the fire.'

Neil undid the paper and began placing the boerewors and chops on the grid. He looked up at Edward, not seeming to notice the girls.

'Good evening, Edward. It's a perfect night for a braai.' He placed his meat on the grid. 'Here's a fork, Helen. You watch the chops while I go back for the rest of our supper and drinks.' He turned away and walked quickly back in the darkness to the truck before Edward had time to introduce Claudia and Cathy.

Helen battled with the long fork to turn the meat. Cathy could see she was frightened to get too close to the fire. She looked about six or seven years old, too young really to be left on her own to braai.

'Would you like me to turn them for you? Give me the fork, Helen. It's too hot here in the middle for them.'

She nodded and gave it to her, watching Cathy as she turned the meat over and moved them to the side where the fire was not as fierce. The chops were already burning on the one side.

As she did so, Neil returned carrying a basket. He looked annoyed when he saw a stranger handling his fork and turning the chops.

'Who are you? Those are my chops! Give me that fork!' He pulled the fork roughly from her hand.

'Steady on, Neil! She's our guest. She offered to help Helen. It's too much for her to do alone.'

'Hold the fork Helen and watch the chops and sausages, and don't let them burn! She has to learn sooner or later.' He disregarded Cathy and pushed the fork towards Helen to hold and took two orange drinks from the basket. 'Here are your drinks and a sandwich, girls. I can't wait any longer for a beer.' He had already opened the tin and was drinking it down in large gulps.

By this time Edward and David had removed the family's meat.

'Come for supper, girls. Our meat is ready to eat.' He walked off back to the rug and David and the girls followed him without a word. He put the hot platter on the rug. 'Dinner is served, Madam! Help yourselves, and there's plenty of it.'

Iris had the buttered rolls and salads ready on plates.

'It looks absolutely delicious! Thanks, guys. I love it when the men do the cooking. Take a plate, Cathy. I hope you're hungry.'

Guy and Terry found them after they had helped with the clearing-up and the meal soon disappeared.

It *was* good, too. It was a long time since Cathy had enjoyed a braai and she went back for another piece of boerewors and a chop. They all commented on the antics of the one sheep.

'It could have caused havoc. Fortunately Joseph chased it to me,' said Guy. 'Anthony Blake was the third King. He's quite a character. You're never too sure what children will do in a show. Their impromptu actions and comments always give it the unrehearsed, unforgettable moments. I love it!'

## Four

## The picnic at the White Water Falls

Next day was the picnic. Iris packed up the picnic basket once more with good things for the cold lunch beside the waterfall.

'The Turners have a horse for you, Cathy, if you'd like to ride. Claudia and the boys are riding on one of the trucks. We'll go by car and take old Mr and Mrs Wilson,' said Edward at breakfast-time. 'What would you like to do?'

'I'd rather like a ride in a pony-cart if it's possible and if there's a space for me, Edward. I've never ridden in one before.'

'Good. I'll get on the phone and let Tom know. He's arranging the pony-cart riders. There has to be an adult to ride with the children to see that they stay sitting down and are strapped in securely as the road is rough and can be quite bumpy.'

He came back to say there was room for her as Tom needed another adult. 'He would be glad of your offer, Cathy. He said you should wear a sunhat.'

'Thanks, Edward.' She was pleased to be with the children.

Edward and Iris dropped her off at an open area outside the town where the pony-carts and drivers were assembled. Five of the carts were already full of happy children. Edward introduced her to Tom Cathcart, a young farmer in the district.

'Hullo, Cathy. We're waiting for you. Come with me. As soon as you're settled we'll all be off. I'm riding in the last cart behind you. Please see that the children stay sitting down and strapped in all the way. It should take us about forty minutes.'

He took her to the cart and saw that she was comfortably seated between three young children. She recognised two of them to be the girls who were watching the meat cooking at the braai fires.

'Hello, Helen! We meet again. What is your sister's name?'

'I'm Louise,' piped up the little one, 'and this is my friend Susan. She lives on the next farm. We're having our picnic lunch with her Mommy and Dad and baby. They're going by car.'

'And I'm Cathy. This is such fun! I've never ridden in a pony-cart before – have you?'

'Yes, my Dad has one on the farm and sometimes we are allowed rides if there's a driver and he has the time to take us. Louise fell out the last time and hurt her leg, but it wasn't broken! Since then we're not allowed pony rides.'

'That's a pity. What else do you do on the farm?'

'We watch the cows being milked and ride our bikes and play in the doll's house.'

All at once there was a shout from Tom.

'Let's go, Johannes!' he shouted to the driver of the first cart which was leading the way. 'We're all ready.' There was no time for further conversation as they watched the ponies begin to walk and then trot, one behind the other, along the gravel road leading to the waterfall.

'Hooray! We're off on our picnic!' cried the girls waving to the young people as they rode past the two trucks.

The road gradually deteriorated into a mere track across the veld, the ride becoming bumpier and bumpier as the cart rode over stones and small pieces of rock, and the track twisted and turned to avoid trees and rocky outcrops.

'Hold tightly onto the strap, girls; you mustn't fall out!'

The scenery became more and more impressive as they travelled westwards towards the majestic Drakensberg Mountains, those ancient sentinels whose lofty peaks stretched high into the sky, guarding the entrance to Natal. The landscape was an exciting gift for any artist to capture. The thorn trees spread their leafy umbrella branches to provide shade for the many wild animals that roamed over the grasslands. Years before great herds migrated during the winter months from the Transvaal and the Orange Free State to feed on the sweet grass that grew on the hills and in the valleys. Water from the headwaters in the mountains was plentiful. Small streams eventually joined to create the great rivers of Natal, the uMngeni, uMnzimkulu and Tugela. Many species of antelope inhabited this area – eland, gnu, springbok and zebra. Very few still remain.

It was a fascinating ride.

Happily the drivers led their ponies through the small streams that ran down from the mountains and then climbed the hill slopes to the top. Louise began singing a nursery rhyme she knew.......

'Jack and Jill went up the hill to fetch a pail of water.......' and they all joined in the singing of the next two verses. Other songs followed.

'Who taught you all your nursery rhymes, Louise?' Cathy asked.

'We learnt them at Nursery School.'

'Doesn't you Mommy sing to you?'

'No, she's always sick and Daddy is too busy.'

'There's the waterfall! Can you hear it?' called their driver.

They caught a glimpse of it through some large trees and after rounding a corner they saw the picnic trucks and motor-cars. People had taken out fold-up chairs, rugs and baskets, setting up a shady picnic spot under some huge acacia trees. Cathy undid the straps and the children stepped down from the pony-carts. She watched as they ran to a young couple who were obviously Susan's parents. Her mother was carrying a baby in her arms. The drivers were leading the ponies away for a well-earned rest and drink. Cathy found the Deans in the midst of the Estcourt families.

'Come for a drink. How was the pony ride?' asked Iris.

'Bumpy but good fun! I sat with Helen and Louise, and their friend Susan. Her mother brought them into town. We sang all the way.'

'We did too – and some rather bawdy songs! Let's take a walk to the waterfall before lunch and stretch our legs.'

The children and adults were already there, throwing leaves and sticks into the pool at the bottom and splashing water about. The waterfall wasn't a very high or impressive one, but it was quite wide.

It was lovely to watch the water cascading over the rocks at the top and falling against the rocky walls into the pool below. Suddenly they heard a bell ringing in the distance.

'It's lunch time!' shouted the children and back they raced.

Everyone was hungry and the cold feast followed by fruit and cool drinks soon disappeared. Afterwards Tom organised games – an egg and spoon race, a sack race, a tug-of-war for the older boys. In an open space a cricket game was in progress, the Dads versus the Sons It was great fun, especially when the Sons won by ten runs.

There was time for another short walk, this time down to the Little Bushman's River. The children had fun stepping from rock to rock in the water – until one adventurous boy slipped and fell in. 'It's so cold!' he cried, shivering as he was fished out and taken back to the picnic spot to be dried. Some of the boys found tiny crabs in the river banks. On the walk back they collected wild flowers, ferns and different leaf shapes to take home.

Tom rang the bell once more. 'Time to pack up,' he called. The drivers harnessed the ponies and off they happily trotted back to town. Helen and Louise were still clutching the flowers and wild grasses they had collected. As Cathy undid the straps and she helped the girls down, she felt a hand on her shoulder.

'So you've been interfering with my girls again! Why can't you leave them alone? If I see you with them again I shall notify the police that you persist in interfering with them.' Cathy turned around to see Neil Middleton standing next to her, his hand still on her shoulder. He looked very angry.

She felt her temper rising and was about to reply and remove his hand, but Tom had heard him and came to see what it was all about.

'What's the trouble, Neil? Your girls have had a wonderful time. They have been well looked after in the pony cart and at the picnic. You should be thanking her.'

'Who is she? I've never seen her here before.'

'She's a guest of the Deans and came with Claudia. She has watched over your girls very well, Neil.'

He took hold of Louise's hand and looked at Cathy.

'It seems I owe you an apology.' He turned to the girls. 'Helen and Susan, get in the truck. It's late and I have to see to the milking.'

With that he turned away and walked with Louise to his truck.

'I'm sorry Neil was so rude, Cathy. He has a hard time at home and has become withdrawn and moody.'

'It doesn't matter. The waterfall is a special spot for a picnic and we've had a lovely day. Thank you for organising the games. The children loved them.'

'I hope to see you again, Cathy. Perhaps we can arrange a horse-ride for you. Edward says you're a rider. I'll be in touch.'

'That would be great. I'll look forward to it.'

Iris and Edward arrived in the car for her. She thanked her driver and said Goodbye to them all.

The family agreed that the day had been one of high activity and enjoyment, full of fun and laughter.

'It's Christmas Day tomorrow and we have the tree to decorate,' said Claudia after their light supper. They had all helped to dress the Christmas tree which looked beautiful when the lights were switched on. The family brought their presents and placed then under the tree ready for the present-giving after brunch in the morning.

Cathy thought it was a good time to let Peter out of his cage to fly around. It had not been a ritual with her mother to take him out every day, but the evenings seemed the best time when she was having her gin and tonic. He would sit on her shoulder and watch her. Each time she took a sip he would say 'Cheers!'

'I'm letting Peter out. Are all the windows and doors closed?'

Cathy sat with a glass of water in her hand and they watched him circling the room before he flew down and sat on the arm of her chair. As soon as she picked up the glass to take a sip he said 'Cheers! Clever boy!' It was quite uncanny

It had been a happy day and everyone was tired.

'I'm ready for a hot bath and bed. Goodnight all!' said Cathy as she put Peter to bed.

It was sunny and warm when they left early for the service at St Matthew's. The church was crowded with families eager to rejoice and sing their praises at the birth of the Christ Child. Everywhere there were large bowls of flowers lovingly arranged by the ladies of the parish. The young priest, Walter Langley, greeted them in the garden afterwards where he gave small Christmas presents to the children. 'Have a happy day with all your new presents.' he said.

After changing into cooler comfortable clothes, the family sat down to a late breakfast-brunch cooked by the boys.

'I see you have trained them well, Iris.'

'Oh yes, they were taught from an early age. They all like to cook a meal and try something new and I've always encouraged them. Sometimes there are flops, but we put that down to lack of practice!'

The Christmas brunch was so tasty with the addition of grilled sausages and mushrooms. They lingered over their coffee, toast and marmalade before Claudia declared she couldn't wait any longer to open her presents and please could they adjourn to the sitting-room. Cathy was surprised to find they had given her small gifts as well.

'Thank you all so much, but I haven't brought gifts for you!'

'Yes, you have,' said Iris 'You brought bottles of wine and a large box of chocolates and toffees. We shall all enjoy them.'

Claudia's parents had given her a new camera to replace her rather old one, and she tried it out immediately, happily clicking away, and proudly showed them the pictures. 'Thanks, Mum and Dad, it's a beauty and so easy to use. It gives the date on every picture – an additional bonus. The pictures are so clear and colourful. I'm thrilled with it.' She took it round for them to see the pictures. She was delighted with her new handbag Claudia had given her. Cathy had received a silken scarf and a book on famous artists with pictures showing some of their paintings.

Guy's journalist friend, Stephen Mitchell, arrived after lunch. He was a friendly young man and entertained them with many stories when he joined them under a shady tree in the garden. After tea when it had cooled down a game of tennis was suggested.

'Anyone for tennis? I've brought my racket,' he asked with a smile. 'I think Guy should partner Cathy and Claudia and I will attempt to beat them. It's cooling down at last and there's a welcome breeze. Get your shoes on and bring your rackets. The winners will be given a second helping of Christmas pudding and custard.'

'I'll be a hopeless partner! I haven't played for ages, Guy.'

'No excuses. We're due on the court in ten minutes.'

They all hastened to obey him!

Cathy found she wasn't so bad after all and with Guy's help they were announced the winners. The girls played with Terry and David as well, and then Iris and Edward partnered Stephen and Guy.

'You boys were too strong for us,' declared Edward.

'Considering you don't play as often as we do, I think you play an exceptional game, Dad.'

They changed and adjourned to the sitting-room before Iris served the Christmas Dinner. Cathy thought it was a good time to let Peter out of his cage. He flew around for a while and then settled on the arm of her chair, cocking his head at her and saying 'Hello....hello!'

'Hello, Peter. You're a clever bird.'

'Clever bird. Pretty bird. Cheers!'

He enjoyed being the centre of attraction.


That evening Iris produced a superb Christmas dinner. The turkey and gammon were beautifully cooked and presented.

'It's been a wonderful Christmas, one I shall never forget. Being with a family makes all the difference,' said Cathy when they eventually went to bed.

'It's been our pleasure having you with us. Sometimes I feel completely swamped being the only girl when the boys bring their friends here. I've loved having you with me, Cath. I wish I had you for a sister.'

Five

Exploring the country-side

Boxing Day, the day after Christmas, was always a public holiday in Natal and a great family day for outings. The beaches were always gay with coloured umbrellas and crowded with people of all ages enjoying the hot sunshine on the sand or the refreshing salty water in the waves. Up-country folk are denied these coastal pleasures but they have other enjoyments such as fishing or canoeing in the rivers, sailing on the large dams or visiting the many craft boutiques that abound in the Midlands. And there are many small restaurants that offer a choice of appetising meals in delightful surroundings.

'What shall we do today?' asked Claudia after breakfast. 'Mum and Dad have arranged a bowls game and the boys are out sailing with friends. We should go out somewhere. It's too beautiful a day to stay relaxing in the garden.'

'I'd love to sit in a quiet spot and do some sketching in preparation for a landscape picture to paint, but what would you do?'

'I'd take a rug, a cushion and a book. It would be good just to relax, look up at the sky and read. Our teaching days are really hectic. I had a difficult class this year with too many weak children and not enough time to give them the help they needed. I would like a quiet lazy day.'

'Good, let's do that. I'd love to explore and see more of this beautiful mountainous area. Do you have a particular spot in mind?'

'Yes. I'll get some sandwiches and drinks made for our lunch and you can pack Pixie with your stool and drawing stuff. How about taking Peter with us?'

'He'd like that. I'll put his cage on the back seat.'

They left a note for Iris and set off westwards towards the lofty Drakensberg peaks driving on a gravel road that Cathy had never travelled on before. Cattle grazed peacefully on the undulating hillsides or in the valleys where streams and rivers meandered leisurely through the natural grasslands. The summer rains had provided a rich verdant carpet covering the grasslands and there were all kinds of thorn bushes amongst the rocky outcrops. Clumps of tall, leafy indigenous trees, mostly acacias, swayed in the breeze. An eagle with something in its beak, glided above them heading for its nest in its mountain hide-out home. It was probably a small fish to feed her hungry babies. Here and there they came across clusters of circular beehive Zulu huts and small boys herding a few cattle. They passed the ruins of an old fort, a relic of the Anglo-Boer War. Many battles were fought here over those turbulent years.

They came at last to a crossroad.
'Turn left here, Cathy, and drive another five or six km until you come to an old deserted farmhouse. You can stop there and look for a good view, or you might like to drive further on.'
She drove on another six km to the farmhouse and liked what she saw. The old farmhouse had such character. It looked a sad and neglected old home, but it still had some beautiful trees framing it against the backdrop of the mountain. It might look lonely and dilapidated now, but some-one long ago had lived in it and loved it.
'I like this particular view of the mountains and I could use the old farmhouse in the foreground of my picture. Let's stop here and take a look around. There may be a grassy patch for you to lie on.'

They left Peter in the car while they inspected a spot under an acacia tree nearby. It seemed ideal for both of them. There was shade for Claudia under the tree.
'This would be fine for me. Can you still see the old farmhouse?'
Cathy was about to answer when they heard Peter's voice.
'Hello....Hello!' he called. 'Hello.....Hello!'

They turned around to see three Zulu umfaans (youths) with long sticks standing at the open doors of the car while a fourth was inside handing out their handbags and Cathy's drawing equipment and canvas stool. They rushed to the car and shouted at them.

'Put that down and get away from the car!'

They dropped Cathy's sketching stuff, but ran off with their handbags and the bag containing their lunch, with Claudia chasing hell for leather after them.

'Come back, Claudia!' Cathy screamed. 'You'll never catch up with them. It's too dangerous! They'll attack you!' but by then they had all disappeared between the trees.

Cathy wasn't sure what she should do. How foolish of Claudia to run after them! She had a few anxious moments before she came running back.

'Those young devils! I'm so mad! My new camera and my cell phone were in my handbag!' She was crying now, the tears rolling down her cheeks. 'What will Mum and Dad say?'

'They'll be pleased you weren't severely hurt! How foolish you were to go after them! You could never have stood up to four of them. They could have stabbed you with a knife or dagger. Your camera can be replaced but your life is precious.'

'Oh Cathy, I didn't think of that. I just wanted to get my camera back. I'm sorry this has happened. What was in your bag?'

'Very little, a few Rand. I never carry a lot of money with me and my cell phone was in my pocket.'

'What shall we do now? Do you think they'll come back?'

'No, I don't think so, but you never know. We'd better move away and find a spot nearer the town. It's very isolated here. We could go to the park in town. I have a good idea of what to paint now that I've seen the area. Let's do that. Get back in the car.'

It was the safest thing to do. They spent the rest of the morning in the Wagon Wheel Park, returning home in time for lunch to relate their story to the family.

Edward went to hug his daughter.

'Never mind, my dear. I did insure it for you, but the theft must be reported to the police. They may be able to find you handbags. I'll take you to the station after lunch and you can write out a statement. I'm happy Cathy's art things were left behind. I think by calling out, Peter alerted you that he had seen some-one and possibly he saved you both from a hurtful experience. Did you leave your keys hanging in the car, Cathy?' She pulled a face and nodded her head. 'That was also thoughtless. They could have driven off with your car and you might never have seen it again. These days we leave nothing to chance. Be aware of every possibility. Make yourself as secure as you possibly can in your home with locks, double locks, bolts and strong burglar bars. Let this be a lesson to us all.'

Edward offered a reward if the camera was returned, but it was most likely quickly sold. It was money they were looking for. The paper and paint brushes didn't interest them. From memory Cathy had made preliminary sketches of her picture and the farmhouse, and she was pleased with her morning's work.

After lunch Tom Cathcart phoned saying the Turners had a horse for her and would she like to join a small group for a ride later the next afternoon?

'I'm riding as well and will be there to help you. Please say you'll come. We'll leave at four o'clock when it has cooled down.'

It was weeks since she'd had a ride, so she agreed and he gave her directions to the Turner's home which she discovered was quite near to the Dean's house on the edge of the town. Tom told her they had a large plot and kept several horses.

'I'm leaving you tomorrow afternoon for a ride with Tom. He's asked me to join a small group. Do you mind?'

'You must go, Cathy. I know you love to ride. They will show you more of the country-side.'

She was looking forward to the ride as she put on her jodhpurs, shirt and boots next day and set off in Pixie. She easily found the Harrisdale Stables. Tom was waiting for her. He introduced her to the other three riders, Jane, Emily and Ben, three friendly young people about her own age. They walked to the stalls to meet their mounts. Hers was a golden brown mare called 'Honeybunch.'

'What a little beauty! She looks a gentle creature,' she said, looking her over, and patting her nose. Honeybunch nudged her as if to say 'I like you, too.'

'Yes, she has a gentle nature. Put on your hat and I'll help you up. I'm riding Trojan today. I often ride her over the weekends.'

'What work do you do, Tom? Are you also a farmer?'

'Not really, although I do help Dad and Mum on the small-holding. I work at a local bank in town.'

Soon they were all ready and walking the horses through the gates. They cantered for a while and Tom was satisfied that Claudia was handling Honeybunch well.

'We've decided to visit a farm called 'Mooiplaas' (Beautiful Farm) in the eastern district today. It belongs to a friend of mine, Richard Yates. It's an easy ride and you'll see something of our farmlands.'

'This area is new to me, although I have visited the Deans on other short occasions. Claudia and I trained together as teachers.'

Cathy found she and Honeybunch worked well together. As they rode into more open countryside Estcourt soon was left behind and the houses and farm-plots fell behind them.

'Long ago this area for miles and miles was once a great battlefield during the war between the Dutch Trekkers and the Zulus. The Battle of Blood River was fought slightly north from here near where the town of Weenen (Weeping) stands today. Later the Anglo-Boer War between the English and the Boers was also fought here. It's hard to believe that so much fighting and blood was shed on these peaceful hills and plains.'

Further on they stopped to examine some old grave-stones possibly left to mark the place where some soldier had died during the Anglo-Boer War. 'The British regiments were so conspicuous in their very hot red jackets – they were sitting ducks. Look, Cathy, you can see Mooiplaas to the left of those trees.'

Richard was there to meet them. He was a pleasant young man in his late thirties. He had inherited the farm from his father who four years previously had died suddenly of a severe heart attack.

'Welcome, Tom and your riding friends! Dismount and come inside. Tea is ready for you. Jacob and Aaron will take care of your horses, water and rest them.'

Half an hour was spent chatting over tea and biscuits before Tom announced that it was time to leave. They thanked him and mounted their horses for the homeward ride.

'It's been good to meet you all. Please come again.'

The ride home following a different route was equally interesting. She chatted to Jane and Emily and discovered that they were nurses and worked at the local hospital. Ben was Jane's boyfriend.

'It's been lovely meeting you,' said Jane. 'I know Claudia. I met her at a friend's party. How long will you be here?'

'I'm driving back to 'Maritzburg after New Year.'

'In that case there's time for more rides,' said Tom. 'We can ride to Mooiplaas again.'

The sun was sinking behind the mountains as they rode through the Harrisdale gates. Tom came to help her dismount.

'Thank you, Tom. I've enjoyed the ride so much.'

He took off her hat and handed it to her. They said Goodbye to the others and he walked with her to her car.

'I've enjoyed it too, Cathy, we must ride again. It's back to work for me tomorrow but I'll be in touch. Take care.'

He saw her settled in Pixie and waved as she drove off.

At dinner- time the family wanted to hear all about her afternoon's ride with Tom.

'I liked it very much. I rode a lovely mare called Honeybunch and Tom rode Trojan. Tom's a good rider. Three others joined us, two girls, Emily and Jane and Jane's boy-friend, Ben. Do you happen to know them? Tom's very knowledgeable. He told me a lot of the story of the old battlefields as we rode over the area. It made history come alive for me. Mooiplaas has a lovely old farmhouse. Richard has modernised and refurnished it since he inherited it when his father died four years ago. He lives alone there. He's such a nice guy. It's a pity he hasn't married. Tom wants me to ride again with them all before I return home.'

'Don't talk of going home yet, Cathy!' said Iris. 'Please stay with us as long as you like. We have all enjoyed your company – and Peter's. He's been no trouble at all.'

'Thank you, Iris. You have all been so kind. I have a home to look after, and Garth and I have papers to deal with in connection with Mum's estate. I should leave by the 3$^{rd}$. of January.'

'Until then please do whatever you wish. I see there's a good movie showing this week. Perhaps you and Claudia would like to see it. I know she likes a Nicole Kidman movie!

Six


The New Year's Eve party


Tom called her two days later to arrange another ride. The girls were on duty at the hospital and Ben couldn't make it, so they went alone later in the afternoon to visit Richard who was delighted to see them again. They managed a faster ride this time. Trojan and Honeybunch responded well, enjoying the faster pace over the hills and grasslands.

After discussing various subjects Richard asked what their plans were for New Year. Neither Tom nor Cathy had made arrangements.

'I'm not sure what the Deans have planned. Nothing has been said so far. I shall have to ask them if anything has been arranged.

'I haven't made any plans either. I hear there's a party and dance in the Town Hall and I was going to ask you, Cathy, if you'd go with me, and whether Richard was free to take Claudia. It's possible Jane and Emily would be able to join us. We could make up a table. What do you think? Are you free, Richard? You could sleep over with me.'

'It sounds a good idea. I'd be happy to take Claudia if she hasn't already made arrangements.'

'Let me discuss it with her and I'll let you know. It's deadly sitting at home on Old Year's Night when you could be out at a party having fun! As far as I know she hasn't a regular boy-friend.'

'Good, we'll leave it there. Talk to Claudia and I'll phone you. We mustn't leave it too late to get tickets.'

Claudia was a bit apprehensive about partnering Richard who she didn't know at all and had never met.

'What's he like? Supposing I don't like him and he can't dance? It will be a disaster! I'm no good at blind dates.....'

'I don't know if Tom can dance either, but at least I can tell you that Richard is a very nice person and I think you'd like him. Let's go, Claudia! It would be far better than staying at home and being miserable. Do you know what your brothers are doing?'

'They usually go to house parties with their friends, and Mum and Dad make up a party with their bowling friends. When I was friendly with Nigel we'd be invited to a party at one of his friend's homes. We broke up earlier this year so I'm at a loose end.' She hesitated, thinking it over, and said at last 'All right, let's chance it and go.'

When Tom called the next evening he was delighted to hear that they both had accepted.

'Richard will come to me and we'll call for you at seven-thirty and have dinner at a restaurant in town first. It's a long evening! How does that sound?'

'Perfect! We're looking forward to it. See you then.'


Next evening Claudia received a surprised call from Richard.

'Hullo, Claudia. I've phoned to thank you for coming to the party with me. I hope I won't disappoint you! Did Cathy tell you that I have a cleft palate, sticky-out ears and a ginger moustache?'

'No, she's too polite to tell me. If you can dance I'll forgive you all the rest.' They both laughed.

'My dancing is passable – I'll leave you to be the judge. I'm looking forward to meeting you. See you on the 31st.'

She put down the phone and came back grinning.

'What's so amusing?'

'He sounds very nice, Cathy. At least he has a sense of humour! Has he got sticky-out ears?' she added as an after-thought.

'I'll leave you to find out!'


The pool was the coolest place and the family spent many an odd hour cooling down there. Tennis games with the boys were played in the late afternoon. Two of Claudia's teacher friends came around for tennis one morning. Julia phoned to ask about her holiday and how she had spent Christmas Day. Cathy briefly filled her in on all their doings and asked what they had been doing.

'Very much the same as you, lazy days, but no pony-cart riding or horse rides! The baby is so active and the hot weather tires me, but otherwise we're having a good time and have met some new friends. Thanks for your presents. I love the necklace. Garth wants to know when are you coming home? We'll be home next week on Tuesday as Garth stats work again on Wednesday.'

'I'm also thinking of leaving after New Year on Tuesday the 2nd. Daisy will be back by then and I may be able to have a few more art lessons in January before the schools open.'

'We'll see you then. 'Bye.'


Plans to herald in 2012 went ahead. Iris intended to have a New Year's dinner at home in the evening of New Year's Day.

'It will also be a farewell for Cathy who will leave us the following day. I wish you'd stay longer, my dear, but I know you have to see to things at home. We've loved having you.'

Dressing up for a party is always fun. The family had all left for their parties and the girls were ready when the boys called for them. Cathy was wearing a pretty pink short dress and Claudia had chosen pale floral lavender one. Cathy brought them inside and Tom introduced Richard to Claudia who looked him up and down, and liked what she saw. She smiled at him.

'Hullo, Richard. I'm *so* glad to see you haven't sticky-out ears and a ginger moustache!'

'So am I and I've got on my dancing shoes for you. I thought if I came in my farm boots you'd take fright and send me packing!'

'In that case the sooner we get going the better. I'll lock up for you, Claudia. We're going in Richard's car.'


The restaurant was a small Italian one with a reputation for fine pastas and good wine. The helpings were generous and the meal was delicious. It was after nine when they arrived at the Town Hall where the music was loud and the floor crowded with dancers. They were shown to their table where Jane and Ben were sitting.

'Hullo! Emily's dancing with Leon. We're in for a good party. The hall is packed. So glad you could all come.'

They sat down and chatted while Tom ordered drinks. The music played by a small band, was good, and they were soon on the dance floor. Claudia found that Richard's dancing was much better than just 'passable,' in fact, he danced very well. She also danced with Tom. Yes, it would be a happy party.

Cathy was jiving with Tom when she saw a familiar figure near them and she recognised Neil Middleton. He was actually smiling! What a difference it made to his whole appearance! He looked so happy and quite a different person. His partner was a beautiful girl, a brunette with long hair. She wore a gold dress that shimmered as she jived. Cathy wondered if it was his wife. He was saying something to her that made her laugh, and at that moment he looked up and saw Cathy. He recognised her! Immediately he stopped smiling and turning his head away, he moved their dance steps in another direction. What was it that made him so stressful and rude when he had seen me previously?

When they returned to the table she quietly questioned Tom about his home life. He had seen Neil turn and dance away from them.

'Why is it that he's so distressed and angry at times? Do you know what is worrying him? There's got to be a reason.'

'They say he has a fine dairy herd on Hartleyvale Farm just outside the town. There's some mystery about the place. There's talk of locked–up rooms and strange noises that sometimes are heard during the night. No-one goes to visit him. The children have been brought up by Zulu nannies who tell of his moodiness and that he beats them. It's difficult to know the truth. Mum hears from the maids that he has a most dreadful time with his wife, Cathy. They say she's perpetually drunk and disappears for days on end. I hear he spends endless hours looking for her - in the bars and downtown dives. When he does find her he has to put her into the Rehab Centre to sober her up. The children are suffering, looked after by Zulu nannies, who also run the house. Some are good and some are not. He has a hard, worried life at the moment and we all feel for him. His large herd of dairy cattle needs constant supervision if his milk quota is to be maintained.'

'No wonder he's a worried man! It's understandable. Did you know the girl he was dancing with?'

'No, I've never seen her here before. She certainly is a lovely girl.'

'Has he any other children besides the two girls?'

'Yes, he has a son about nine years old who is at boarding school in the Midlands. He goes to fetch him home for the holidays.'

It was a worrying story and she kept thinking of him.

Later a light finger supper with dessert was served.

She looked for him at the refreshment tables but she didn't see Neil Middleton again.

Before they knew it, it was twelve o'clock. Bells from the Town Hall tower boomed out the midnight hours and mayhem broke loose. Sirens wailed, car hooters blasted non-stop, noisy bells rang and shouting shattered the air as the revellers and dancers wished each other a happy New Year. Tom shook Cathy's hands vigorously and kissed her cheeks before they went to each one in their party with good wishes. The band played 'Auld Lang Syne' and everyone made a large circle around the dance floor to join in singing and dancing the traditional song.

'May we all have good health and happiness in the coming year!' shouted the band leader. 'Let's dance the hours away!'

Coloured streamers were thrown around the hall and whistles blew. In grand style the New Year 2010 had been ushered in!

They danced for another hour. By then everyone was exhausted, but still the band played on.

'My poor feet! I think it's time we went home, Tom. Let's find Richard and Claudia, and say Goodnight to the others. It's been a great evening.'

They found them on the dance floor and waved Goodbye to the others who were still full of energy and jiving to a popular number.

They expected to creep into the house in the dark, but they arrived to find all the lights on and music coming through the open windows.

The boys and their friends were enjoying coffee, liqueurs and beers in the sitting-room. Everyone was all in high spirits.

'Come and join us! Happy New Year,' Guy shouted and the well wishing began all over again. The noise woke up Peter in his covered-over cage and when Cathy pulled off the cover and he saw the glasses raised, he joined in with many 'Cheers!.....Cheers!'

The girls eventually fell into bed at four o'clock.

What a lovely night it had been!

Cathy awoke at her usual time, but Claudia was still fast asleep. It was very quiet in the house. She padded along to the kitchen in her gown and slippers hoping for a welcome cup of coffee. Iris was there, also in her gown, sipping tea. She waved to Cathy.

'Come and join me. Help yourself to coffee or tea, and a rusk. There's hot water in the kettle. I'm not cooking breakfast for the family today. They must suit themselves this morning – whenever they wake up! How was the party?'

Cathy told her a little about it. 'I hope we didn't disturb you when we came in last night. We found another party in progress and joined in. The noise woke up Peter and he started cheering, too!'

'We'll miss you, Cathy. Come whenever you like. What time are you thinking of leaving tomorrow?'

'Sometime after breakfast. It's a short drive and won't take long. Daisy should be back from her holiday. She went to spend Christmas with her family in Zululand. Garth and Julia will be coming to talk about Mum's will. There's quite a lot to attend to.

'Yes, it will be a busy time for you. Fortunately you will have the rest of this month before the schools open.'

The kitchen door opened and Edward appeared, fully dressed.

'I knew I'd find you girls gossiping here! I'm due on the bowling green for a friendly game in half an hour. What's for breakfast?'

Cathy wisely disappeared to the bathroom for a shower.

The temperature rose steadily to become a very hot day. The inland Natal towns did not experience the addition of high humidity that Durban and the coastal resorts were subject to, but never-the-less it was unpleasant to be continually perspiring and best to take a siesta or stay indoors until mid-afternoon when the sun's rays were not as fierce. By far the coolest place was in the pool. Cathy and Claudia, David and Terry spent most of the day there, and only when the sun had started to set did they attempt a few tennis games.

Next morning Cathy packed her case, put Peter's cage next to her in Pixie and after breakfast said Goodbye to the family. Claudia was sad to see her go.

'You must come more often this year. I shall miss you.'

'I will,' she promised as she drove off down the drive, through the town and onto the highway. It didn't take long to reach the busy capital of Natal and Hibiscus Cottage. Elijah saw her car arriving as he raked up the leaves on the lawn. He lifted his garden hat to her.

'Hello, Miss Cathy! Daisy's in the kitchen.'

'Hello, Elijah.' He dropped his rake and came running to carry her case and Peter's cage inside for her.

'Did you have a good Christmas?' he asked.

'It was very good. Is everything well at your home?'

'Yes, I saw my mother and sisters. They say I must thank you for the food you sent them. The Christmas cake was very good.'

'I'm glad. My car is so dirty and needs a good wash. Can you do it today please?'

Daisy had heard the car and came to see her, clapping her hands.

'Now we are all home! How is Peter?'

'He liked being with the family. They made such a fuss of him and he was so spoilt. Claudia's brother, Terry, taught him to say 'Kiss, kiss.' Now he say's 'Kiss, kiss, pretty boy, kiss, kiss.' Very naughty!'

Seven

Neil Middleton

Things soon settled down into the normal daily routine. One evening that week she was invited to dinner at Garth and Julia's apartment. He was reading 'The Witness' when she arrived, but put it down, stood up and went to kiss her when he came into the sitting-room. He was very fond of his only sister.

'Hullo, Cath, you're looking rosy and well. You must have had a good time with Claudia's family. Happy New Year! It has to be a better one this year, especially with our new arrival expected at the beginning of April.'

'It will be, I'm sure.'

He poured her a drink while Julia put the finishing touches to her meal and he told her more about their holiday. He glanced at the newspaper on the coffee table as he put down her glass.

'I see there's an advertisement in the 'Jobs available' column of today's 'Witness' for a house-keeper/governess for an Estcourt family, some-one called Middleton. The word 'Estcourt' caught my eye and I wondered if by any chance they were friends of the Deans. Did you hear the name mentioned at all?'

Cathy was surprised. 'They aren't friends of the Deans but I rode with two little girls in the pony-cart to the picnic spot at White Water Falls and discovered they were Helen and Louise Middleton. Show me the advertisement please, Garth.'

He found the page and handed her the paper to read. It was an appeal for some-one to take over the running of a home with three children aged nine, six and four, to do the shopping, to see to the meals and to supervise the children. Applicants should apply to N. Middleton and be willing to start immediately. It gave a telephone contact number for after seven in the evening.

She read it twice.

Poor Neil, he was desperately in need of help!

'Yes, it's the girls' family,' she said at last. 'We helped them braai their chops on our brazier after the Carol Evening. Their father has a farm in the district and keeps a large dairy herd. He came later and was very brusque. He seemed most upset about something. It sounds as if he's having a difficult time, doesn't it?'

'Has he been recently widowed? Where is his wife?'

'I'm not sure about his wife. The Deans never mentioned her so she couldn't have been a friend of theirs. Little Louise did say during the ride that her Mommy was always sick. That could mean anything. I feel sorry for the children.'

To change the conversation she asked about their holiday. Julia joined them and she heard about new friends they had met. Later they moved to the dining-room to sample her delicious chicken casserole. They wanted to hear more about her Christmas holiday with the Deans and while they enjoyed her meal she filled them in on all their outings and festivities. Garth looked extremely worried when she told them how the umfaans had stolen their handbags and lunch-bag, and how upset Claudia was to lose her new camera.

'You're far too trusting, Cath. These are difficult times. You must be more careful. Never leave your car keys hanging in your car!'

'Yes, that was stupid of me. We were both very foolish.'

Nothing more was said about the Middletons but it worried Cathy all that night. She hardly slept. Was there no-one in his family who could help them? Neil Middleton must be an extremely worried man to reach this state.

She bought a 'Witness' every day to see if there was anything further about them, and after three days there was a repeat of the original advertisement in the 'Jobs available' column.

That means either no-one has answered it or there have been no suitable applicants, she thought. She felt like applying to see what his reaction would be. At least he would know that some-one cared about his children and was willing to help him.

'You have a good teaching position and a career to think of,' said a small voice inside her. 'You can't just give it up and walk out to help three children belonging to a man you know nothing about. Heaven knows what you would be letting yourself in for!'

'Don't worry,' she replied to the small voice. 'Neil doesn't like me. He won't even consider me. I intend to phone him and find out.'

She waited another day and then took the bull by the horns and dialled his number.

'Neil Middleton speaking,' he said.

'I'm phoning in reply to your advertisement in 'The Witness' for a house-keeper/governess for your children. Has the position been filled?'

'No, not yet. I have one applicant, an elderly lady, who would be suitable, but I think she's too old to handle my three children. How old are you?'

'I'm twenty-five and single. I have a teaching qualification and I've taught at a local school for three years. I like children. My home is in Pietermaritzburg and I live on my own now as my mother died two months ago. I have my own car and would be able to start immediately.'

He paused, taking in all this information. 'You sound most suitable. Could you come to meet me tomorrow? I'll give you directions to my farm outside Estcourt. It's not too far from your home. What is your name?'

'I'm Catherine Crawford. You can reach me on this number.'

'Come at ten tomorrow. The worst of the morning rush will be over by then. I would like to discuss the position more fully.'

He gave her directions and said Goodbye.

'Well, you've committed yourself now, my girl!' whispered the small voice inside her. 'Be it on your own head!'


Next morning she told Daisy she'd be away for the day and to take care of Peter. She put his cage in the kitchen by the window so that he would see Elijah working in the garden.

'I'll be back for lunch, Daisy. Just make me a salad. Cook the chicken breasts for dinner tonight.' When her mother was alive she had preferred a midday hot tasty meal with vegetables, especially in the winter months. In summer Cathy found this meal too much to enjoy in the hottest part of the day and instead Daisy made her a lighter meal, usually a refreshing salad. There was a variety of salad vegetables growing in Elijah's garden and what better than home-grown herbs to use? He was only too delighted to select them for her.

It was warming up for another hot day as she entered the highway. Already there was a never-ending stream of huge trucks, heavy vehicles and tankers carrying goods of all descriptions either up to the South African interior or down to Durban, probably to the docks to be shipped to ports all over the world. She reached Estcourt and following Neil's accurate directions she drove through the town. She found her way to his farmlands, turning into the open gate when she saw the signpost on which was painted 'HARTLEYVALE FARM' and underneath in smaller printing 'Neil Middleton.'

Her first glimpse of his farmhouse came as a surprise, so different from an old farmhouse which was what she expected. Ahead of her she saw a lovely home which had obviously been lovingly cared for. It had been newly painted a pale grey and white in keeping with the grey roof which she thought would be slate. There was a veranda running along the front of the house, enclosed with a low railing, and supported with white colonnade pillars. A few steps lead up from the drive to the front door. The house was surrounded by shady old trees and green lawns. There were many different flowering shrubs and indigenous plants in the well-kept garden.

Later she learnt that his parents had modernised, altered and rebuilt the house, adding two upstairs dormer window bedrooms, and the attractive front porch.

She pulled up at the steps leading to the porch and got out of Pixie to see Neil waiting on a porch chair for her to arrive. He took one look and saw who it was.

'My God! ...... It's you again! What on earth are you doing here? Have you come to find my girls and take them away from me?'
'No. I was the one who phoned you and offered my help.'

He turned away and strode into the house. Cathy ran up the steps after him, following him into the sitting-room, tugging at his sleeve, pulling it hard and not letting go.
'Don't run away from me! I've come to help you. I think you have two lovely little girls and I'm worried that they are being left to nannies. Please give me a week with them before you send me away.'
At that moment they heard a loud cry and some-one was sobbing and crying. It was coming from the another part of the house.
'It's Louise! What has she done now?' He sounded fed-up and thoroughly exasperated.
He ran through the house to the back door leading onto a large enclosed veranda with Cathy following after him. The Zulu nanny was walking inside carrying Louise, whose leg was bleeding from a bad gash below the knee. Helen was also crying.
'What happened, Helen? Stop crying and tell me.' He sounded cross and unsympathetic.
'I was pushing her on her trike and she hit a big stone and cut her leg on the rocks. She didn't look where she was going, Daddy.'
'I think you were pushing her too fast! Go to your room! I'll deal with you later.' He spoke roughly to her. She looked so frightened, but obeyed him and ran to their bedroom. 'Rachel, put her down on a chair and fetch the disinfectant cream, some cotton wool and a bandage. I'll show you how to clean her up. Louise, stop crying!'
'It's.... so ......sore.... Daddy.' She looked up and saw who was with him as she wiped a dirty hand across her eyes. 'Cathy..... I fell off my trike.... into the rockery...... Please make me...... better.'
Cathy went to kneel down beside her and took her hand in hers.
'Don't cry any more. First Rachel must clean your leg to wash away the sand and blood, and then put on the medicine and bandage.

You'll soon feel better.'

'I want you to do it, Cathy,' she whimpered.

Neil brushed past Cathy. 'No, I'm doing it. Stop whining, Louise. I'm so tired of hearing you always moaning. Rachel, please bring me some warm water in a bowl. And hurry up, I'm very late with everything today and there's so much still to do.'

Cathy stood up next to the chair. Louise looked at her with frightened eyes, her cheeks still wet from crying.

'I'll stay with you. It has to be cleaned first, Louise. Your Daddy will wash all the dirt and blood away....'. she looked at Neil.... 'and he will be gentle.'

Neil scowled and gave her a defiant look, but said nothing and when the water arrived he cleaned the wound carefully and patted it dry before gently smearing on the antiseptic cream.

'Now Cathy will bandage it up for you.' He looked sternly at her. 'Come to the sitting-room when you are finished. Rachel will make us all a cup of tea. I'm going to talk to Miss Helen.'

'Don't smack her, Daddy!' Louise looked worried, pleading with him. 'It wasn't her fault. I didn't look where I was going and I hit a big rock.'

'I wasn't going to smack her, just to talk to her. She has to look after you more carefully in future.'

He strode off angrily down a passage to the bedroom.

Did he always smack them and what did he use? His hand, his belt or the wooden spoon?


Cathy bandaged the leg up lightly and took her hand.

'See if you can walk to the sitting-room and have some tea. Does your leg feel better?' Louise nodded her head. They sat together on the sofa to wait for Rachel to bring the tea-tray. Cathy took a tissue from her pocket and wiped her tear-stained, dirty face.

'Now you look like the happy Louise I knew at the picnic.'

Louise smiled. Neil returned with Helen following meekly behind him. Cathy saw that she had been crying. They sat down without saying a word. Rachel arrived carrying the tea-tray. She put it down on the coffee table and looked at Neil.

'Shall I pour it now, sir?'

'No. Miss Crawford will do it today. Please bring the biscuits.'

'We finished them two days ago, sir. There's nothing left.'

'What about the rusks? Surely there's something in the cake tins.'

'No, the tins are all empty. I have put them on the shopping list for you to buy tomorrow. We also need bread, milk, sugar, ......' He pulled a face and cut her short.

'That's enough. I'll go shopping after Miss Crawford has left. You may leave us now, Rachel.' He watched as she left the room.

'Pour the tea, Miss Crawford!' It was an order, not a request.

She did so and handed him his cup and the girls their mugs after putting in a little sugar and milk. All was quiet in the room as they drank their tea. The girls finished first and put down their mugs.

'Now go and play with your dolls in the play-room upstairs. I want to talk to Miss Crawford.'

When they had left the room Neil glared at her for a long time. He looked so worried, running his fingers through his hair. He seemed to be thinking of what to do, what to say. Cathy kept quiet and waited.

At last he made up his mind.

'I would like to give you a trial week. Can you start tomorrow?'

'Yes, I'll go home, pack some clothes and be back in the morning.'

'Good. I've written up a daily schedule for whoever takes over. Study it and we'll discuss tomorrow any problems you may have. Excuse me now. I'm way behind with my work because of these constant interruptions with the children. I haven't the time to deal with them. Be here at nine.'

He left her still finishing her tea and came back with a long piece of paper which he pushed into her hand.

'Goodbye, Miss Crawford.' He marched out as she put down her teacup, not giving her time to reply. She heard him running down the porch steps, a car door slamming, the engine starting up and the farm truck roaring down the dusty drive. He was in a filthy temper. Heaven help his work staff!

Why had she agreed to help this horrible man?

What on earth had she let herself in for?

Cathy got into the Renault and drove home. She found Daisy in the kitchen preparing the vegetables. Peter saw her and called 'Hello!'

'Hello, Peter! Clever boy! Did you have a good holiday, Daisy?'

'Miss Cathy, we had such a good Christmas! My father killed a beast and we ate very well. All my family was home. My sister has another baby. A girl this time.' She gave Cathy all her news.

'I'm going back to Estcourt for another week, Daisy. Please get my suitcase down. I'll be leaving early in the morning.'

'Hauw, Miss Cathy, you've only just come back!'

'I know, but there are people there who need me. I'm going back to look after two little girls. Their mother is sick and she can't help them. I'll take Peter with me. The girls will like him. I'll only be away a week and I'll be seeing Claudia as well.'

'You must go to help them, Miss Cathy. I'll be here and will look after the house. It will be a good time to take down all your bedroom curtains and wash them.'

It wouldn't be as easy breaking the news to Garth and Julia! She decided it would be better to do so in the evening when Garth was home from the office. She waited until seven and them called them. Her brother answered the phone.

'Hello, Garth. I'm phoning to let you know that I'm going back tomorrow to help the Middleton family for a week.'

'You don't mean the family of the man whose advertisement we saw in 'The Witness' for a house-keeper/governess, do you?'

'Yes, I do. They're badly in need of help. I have nearly a month before the schools open and I want to help them. I'm going back, Garth.'

'Cath, are you crazy? You don't know these people from Adam! You may be letting yourself in for all sorts of trouble! It would be senseless to go. Please don't go. Julia and I will be terribly worried for your safety. I've never known you to be so headstrong.'

He sounded worried and quite cross.

'I don't think I'll be in any danger. From what Claudia has told me those children have been so neglected and left to nannies. I want to help them. They are lovely little girls. I've promised to go, Garth, just for a week. I'm starting tomorrow at nine o'clock. I'll keep you informed and phone often. Neil Middleton has a farm outside Estcourt and keeps a large dairy herd. Claudia's family know a little about them. They have had a very bad time and as I'm free this month until the schools start up again at the beginning of February, I feel I can do a lot for the children. After all, I'll only be away a week; there's no need worry.'

'I hope he'll pay you well. Don't commit yourself to any further time there. I'm not at all happy about this arrangement! I would like to meet Mr Middleton first. You shouldn't even have considered helping them.'

'I've said I'd be there, Garth. I'll be fine. Don't worry. Claudia and the family are there close by if I find I need help. I'll phone you when I get there and if anything goes wrong.'

He reluctantly gave in. 'Promise you'll keep me informed and phone me immediately if there is any trouble.'

'I promise. Say Goodbye to Julia.'

The conversation had gone better than she expected. He hadn't forbidden her to go, but he had been extremely worried for her safety. Cathy cleaned out Peter's cage and after dinner packed her case ready for the morning.

She phoned Claudia to tell she was coming back to help Neil. She guessed she'd be pretty surprised.

And she was! Cathy briefly told her what had happened and that she would be returning in the morning.

'Well, good luck to you! I think it's very noble of you to help the family. I'll be here if you need me, and I have three brothers who might come in useful if Neil gets difficult! Please keep in touch and call if you are worried about anything - anything.'

She had no idea what was in store for her, but it was reassuring to know she had friends there close by.

Eight

Hartleyvale Farm

She left early next morning hoping there would be less traffic on the highway, but it was just as busy as ever. She took the off-ramp into the town as the Town Hall clock struck half-past eight to see the stores opening their doors for another day's business. It wasn't far now to Hartleyvale Farm. When she entered the drive-way she saw Neil sitting on one of the chairs on the front porch. She drew up to the steps and as she turned off the engine she found him opening the door for her. She stepped out. He looked tired and extremely worried. She could tell something was wrong.

'Miss Crawford, thank God you've come! I've been up most of the night with Helen. I didn't know what to do! She's fallen asleep at last. I've phoned my friend Doctor Wood and he'll be here any minute now.' She hurried up the steps after him. 'I'll take you to the girls' bedroom.'

The door was almost closed; he opened it for her; the curtains were still drawn. Clothes and toys were strewn over the armchair and on the floor. On the bed Helen lay curled up between the sheets and a light blanket, her one arm flung over the pillow. She was very flushed and still asleep. Cathy went to put her hand lightly across her forehead. It was very hot. An empty glass surrounded by small toys stood on the bedside table. She glanced at Louise's bed which was a crumpled mess. She moved back to the door. He followed her to the sitting-room and sat down opposite her.

'What do you think?'

'She's a very sick child with a high fever. When did she say she was feeling sick?'

'Yesterday morning. I didn't take much notice. They had been playing in the doll's house in the garden most of the day. She wouldn't eat her dinner last night, started crying and said her throat was sore. I put her to bed with half an aspirin. I had just got to sleep when she called me and I've been up with her every hour or so.'

'I think she's quite ill.'

There was a knock on the front door and a middle-aged man walked into the room. He smiled at them as Neil stood up.

'Hello, Kevin. This is Miss Crawford, She has come to help us.'

He looked at Cathy. 'Good morning. Where is Helen? You said you were up all night with her.'

'She fell asleep an hour ago. Miss Crawford has just arrived and we've been to look at her.'

Cathy stood up. 'She's very hot and I think she has a high fever.'

As they made their way to the bedroom they heard her calling Neil in a weak little voice. 'Dad - dy! Dad - dy! I want some wa - ter.'

Neil opened the curtains and Kevin went straight to her side.

'Do you remember me, Helen? I'm Doctor Kevin. You came to see me when you were sick with chicken-pox and I made you better.' He smiled at her and sat down on the bed, his hand feeling her head. Then he lifted her up to sit on his knee. 'Open your mouth for me, Helen.' He looked down her throat and into her ears and laid her back on her pillow. He took her temperature.

Cathy smiled at her and went to the other side of her bed to hold her hand while Kevin was writing down a prescription for her.

'Hello, Helen. I've come to stay with you for a little while. Doctor Kevin will give you some medicine to take and we'll soon have you feeling better.'

Helen gave her a little smile. 'Stay with me, Cathy.'

'I see she has no water. Give her lots of liquids, Miss Crawford and soft foods when she feels like eating. Ice-cream will help. Her tonsils are very inflamed. I'll come to see her tomorrow. Get her started on this as soon as possible.' He gave Neil the slip of paper as they walked out of the room. 'Goodbye, Miss Crawford. I'm pleased you're here to look after her.'

Neil saw him to his car. 'She's picked up a virus, Neil – there's a new one going the rounds this year. This mixture should kill it. Keep her in bed a day or two. Call me if you need me – anytime. I'll see her tomorrow. I'm pleased you have some help at last. She looks a capable, sensible girl. You really need a woman to help you with the children and run the house. This has gone on far too long, Neil. Where's Mark?'

'He's gone to a school-friend for two weeks. Thanks, Kevin, for coming. I'll go into town and we'll start dosing her straight away.'

Cathy left her to call Rachel to bring her a basin of warm water while she fetched soap, towels and a face-cloth from the bathroom. When Neil came back he was surprised to see she had started to cool her down to make her more comfortable and Rachel had found clean pyjamas and clean sheets for her bed. Rachel was making Louise's bed and tidying up the room. She asked Rachel for a jug of water for Helen and helped her sit up and drink half of it. Then she put her head back on her pillow and covered her lightly. Neil was still there sitting in the armchair watching them.

'I'm going to bring my case inside, Helen. I won't be long.' She looked at Neil. 'Where's Louise? Is her leg better?'

'Yes, she's gone to spend the day with Susan. Joy Watson, our neighbour, fetched her after breakfast. I hope she doesn't pick up this germ as well. I'll bring in your case and things from the car.'

He followed her outside and saw Peter's cage on the front seat.

'What is this creature doing in your car? Is it yours? You didn't ask my permission to bring animals!'

'I intended to do so but you were in such a filthy temper you hardly gave me a chance! This is Peter, my mother's pet budgie. I thought the girls would like him and I knew he would miss me and be lonely. He's no trouble at all, but if you won't let him stay with me, then I'll go back home.' She opened the driver's door and sat down, looking in her handbag for the car keys.

At that moment Peter joined in with 'Hello!.......Hello, clever boy!'

Neil just glared at him. 'Oh, very well. I suppose I'll have to put up with him. Open the boot and I'll take your case inside and come back for the cage. Where shall I put it?'

'I think in the dining-room. I'll ask Rachel for a small table to stand it on. He likes to be part of the family.'

Neil marched inside with her case without a word.

But Cathy knew she had won that round!

'Your things are in the guest room. I'm off to the chemist for the medicine. Ask Rachel to make you some tea. I'll show you where to garage your car when I come back. I won't be long.'

He strode to the truck and whizzed off down the drive.

Further down the passage Cathy found the guest room and en suite bathroom. Helen was fast asleep so she quickly unpacked and went to find Rachel who had found a table suitable for Peter's cage.

'I like birds,' she said, looking at Peter as he sidled up to her on his perch, cocking his head on one side and looking at her. 'This one is a lovely blue colour, so pretty.'

'Hello.......hello! Pretty boy!'

She stepped back, shocked and amazed.

'Hauw! This one can talk! What a clever bird! What's his name?'

'He is a budgie called Peter. He was my mother's pet bird. She was an invalid in a wheelchair and he was good company for her. She died suddenly two months ago, so I must look after him now.'

'You must miss your mother. Would you like some tea or coffee or a cool drink?'

'I'd love tea, please. You must call me Cathy and show me where to find things in the house. I'm staying for a week to help you all.'

'The walk-in pantry is off the kitchen. Look around and use anything you need. I'm glad you have come to help us. Mr Middleton is very worried about his wife. He put her in a home a month ago where she can get better. He needs help with the children.'

She left Cathy to make the tea.
No wonder Neil was so stressed!


Cathy looked over the pantry shelves and found two jelly packets. She quickly made them up to set in the fridge while she waited for Neil to return. He stayed and watched as she got Helen to sit up and gave her a dose. Cathy found her very feverish and fretful.

'Cathy, my throat's so sore,' she whimpered.

'I know. I'll stay with you, Helen. Close your eyes and try to sleep. You'll feel better when you wake up.'

She made her comfortable and held her hand as she closed her eyes. It didn't take long before she fell back asleep. Cathy drew the curtains and she partially closed the door as they silently walked out.

'The garages are at the back of the house. Drive your car round and I'll show you where you can park it.'

She did as he said and he was there to guide her into an empty parking space next to a small sports car and a large family car. She got out and locked it.

'This is an empty spot so please use it whilst you're here. The garage is locked at night and I have two guards on duty. The farm vehicles have another garage at the main sheds.' He looked at his watch. 'I might as well stay for lunch. Ask Rachel to put it on the table and call me as soon as it's ready. I'll show you around the farm and dairy later when we have more time.'


Rachel was finishing off the green salad when Cathy delivered the message. She went to the dining-room where she found him already seated at the table.

'Please join me. Help yourself to whatever you'd like. In this summer weather we have a midday cold meal.'

'I do, too. It's refreshing and is quite sufficient.'

She sat down It was a simple lunch of cold meat, salads, pickles, cheese and brown bread. He ate well and left soon afterwards, hardly speaking to her. She gave Helen two more doses and fruit juices during the afternoon before Joy brought Louise home. Cathy went to the car to meet her and tell her about Helen. She was a pleasant young girl. The baby, Nicholas, was sitting in a seat in the back with Susan who waved at her. Louise got out and went to hold her hand. Cathy peeped into the car.

'Hello, Susan. Have you and Louise had a lovely day together?'

'We had a tea-party in the garden and washed all the dolls' clothes.'

'I'm glad you're here to help Neil,' said Joy. 'The girls get on well together. How is Helen?'

'Dr Wood has been and Mr Middleton fetched medicine for her. She has a high fever and sore throat. It's probably an infection of some kind. Thanks for having Louise. The girls would like to have Susan here one day when Helen is better. They like to be together.'

'Louise is no trouble at all. I'll be in touch and phone you.'

Joy said Goodbye and drove off with Susan waving to them. They passed Neil's truck as he turned in at the gate. He drove right up to them and climbed out.

'How's your sore leg, Louise? Is it better?' he asked. She nodded her head. 'Is Helen's temperature down?' he asked Cathy.

'She's still in bed but she says she is better. I made jelly to have with her ice-cream to-night. There's enough for both of them. Rachel has made us a cottage pie and vegetables.'

'Good, I'm hungry. Can we eat early? I have to go out for a while.'


He disappeared to shower and Cathy took Louise to meet Peter. She was so excited to see him and fascinated with the way he talked to her. Cathy closed the door and took him out of the cage and let him fly around. He landed on Louise's arm.

'He's tickling my arm!' she cried.

'Naughty Peter! Kiss-kiss!' he said to her quite plainly. He flew around the room landing on Cathy's head.

'He's on your head! He's on your head!' laughed Louise.

The door opened suddenly. 'What's all this noise about?'

'Please close the door. I let Peter out for Louise to hold.'

'Is that wise?' He looked at her sternly as he closed the door.

'It's perfectly safe if the windows and doors are kept closed. His wings have been clipped slightly. My mother took him out every day.

He would sit on the arm of her chair when she had her gin and tonic each evening and say 'Cheers!' She loved him.'

'I do, too! Can I help you feed him? What does he eat?'

'I'll show you tomorrow. Go and wash your hands. We must have dinner now.' Peter was put back in his cage and watched them while they enjoyed their dinner. Rachel sat with Helen while she ate her plate of supper. Neil left them soon afterwards

'Let's see if Helen has finished her ice-cream and jelly, and then I'll read you a story before bed-time. Where are your story-books?'

'I only have two books, but Helen has one more. They're at the bottom of my toy-box. We hardly ever look at them.'

Cathy was shocked. Most children love their books and having stories read to them, especially at bed-time.

'Doesn't your Mommy read to you?'

'No, she's too busy or she's away working.'

'Do you watch the TV children's Story-Time programme?'

'No, Mommy doesn't let us watch TV. Only sometimes. She doesn't like any noise when she's working. We have to play outside.'

Cathy was amazed but tried not to look too appalled by this news.

'Does Daddy ever read to you?'

'Sometimes, but he knows lots of nursery rhymes to sing.'

'Do you know the story of Cinderella or the Three Little Pigs or Goldilocks and the three bears?'

'Daddy read us the pig one. I only know that story about the three little pigs and the wolf that came down the chimney, but he didn't catch them!' She laughed. 'He fell in the stew-pot and died. Ha-ha!'

'Which little pig do you think was the cleverest?'

'The one that built his house with bricks so that the wolf couldn't blow it down.'

'Good girl! I'd do the same.'

'And what do you think the story tells us, Louise?'

'That if you get too clever and climb down the chimney to get inside the house, you'll fall into the stew-pot and die.'

Out of the mouths of babes!....... She was four and a half.

'Louise, you have made my day!' She gave her a big hug.

'Can you find me one of your books to read now?'

'I think so.'

Cathy followed her and after digging into the box she found one. At least she had something to read to them! She would buy a few more as soon as she could go into town. She put Helen's gown on and propped her up on the pillows with the bedclothes round her so that the girls sat on either side of her. Cathy read from the book and they could look at the pictures and follow the story.

'Helen, you choose the first one.' She chose Snow White and the seven dwarfs. 'Have you heard this story, Helen?'

'Yes, at nursery school a long time ago but I've forgotten it.'

'What are dwarfs?' asked Louise.

'Here's one. He's a funny little man with a long beard and this is the grumpy one, so his name is Grumpy,' said Cathy pointing to him.

'Start reading, Cathy.'

They sat beside her totally engrossed in the story, asking questions as they went along. Then it was Louise's turn and she chose The Little Red Hen. Cathy was reading Goldilocks and the three bears when she heard Neil unlocking the front door.

'Please finish the story, Cathy,' begged Louise.

She continued reading as he came into the room. The girls were listening to the ending and didn't look up.

'Why are the girls still awake? Get into your bed, Louise.'

'I promised to finish the story and then I would put out the light. They have brushed their teeth and there's only one page to read. Please let us hear the ending.'

'Very well, but no more stories to-night. Goodnight, girls.'

They said Goodnight and he walked out. Cathy read the story to the end and closed the book.

'I'm glad she ran away from the bears! I liked the hen story the best. Will you read again to us tomorrow, Cathy?'

'Of course. Into bed now.'


She gave Helen another dose of her medicine, replaced the bandage on Louise's leg, tucked them up and switched off the light.

'Goodnight, Cathy. Thank you for reading to us. I'm feeling much better. The jelly and ice-cream was so nice and cool for my throat.'

'I'm glad you're better. Goodnight, girls. Sweet dreams.'

She left the door slightly open to give them a little light and went to the sitting-room where Neil was sitting reading the newspaper.

'I'm making myself a mug of coffee. Would you like to join me?'

He looked over the top of the paper. 'Yes, that would be good.'

She brought in the tray and made her own mug with a little milk and sugar. 'Help yourself, as I'm not sure how you like it.'

He threw down the paper. 'Black and no sugar.....' Then as an after-thought he added........'please.' She put in the coffee and hot water and gave him the mug.

'Thank you.' He looked at her for a while. It grew embarrassing and she dropped her eyes down. She sipped her hot coffee, waiting for him to say something. There was a long spell of silence.

At last he ran his hand across his eyes.

'I can't keep awake. I'm so tired.'

He looked worn out and in need of a good night's sleep.

'I can see you are. Get to bed as soon as you've had your coffee.'

She didn't attempt to question him for further details. He would tell her in his own time. 'I'll see to Helen to-night.'

'Thank you. Help yourself to whatever you need.'

He drank the coffee, said Goodnight and disappeared to his room.

As soon as she had drained her mug she switched off the lights and went to her bedroom. She showered and got into bed.

It had been an eventful first day. She tried to read her book for a while, but she found the story slow-moving and the plot too complicated. Her eyes kept closing and she found she was reading the same paragraph twice. She  put down her book, switched off the lamp on her bedside table and soon fell asleep.

## Nine

## Settling down on Hartleyvale Farm

Neither of the girls called her during the night. Helen's medication probably had something in it to make her sleep. Cathy woke early and looked at her bedside clock. It was six o'clock. She could hear noises coming from the kitchen – <u>some-one</u> was awake! She put on her gown and slippers and went to investigate, to find Rachel washing up the dinner dishes and the kettle on the boil.

'Good morning, Cathy! Tea won't be long. Mr Middleton left half an hour ago to see to the milking. How is Helen?'

'The girls are still asleep and Helen only called me once. I think she's over the worst and another day in bed will see her practically better. She must try some soft foods today. Can you make scrambled eggs for breakfast for me and the girls? Do they have porridge?'

'Yes, they all enjoy their porridge whatever kind I make. Today it's mealie meal. I'll make scrambled eggs and toast for everyone.'

'I'll have some porridge too, please. What time is breakfast?'

'At seven o'clock. When the school's open Mr Middleton will take Helen to the local school at half-past as she finished nursery school last year and this year she starts in the pre-school grade at the local school until twelve-thirty. Louise will still go to the nursery school nearby and I walk with her there as she starts later at nine, and I fetch her at twelve.'

'I'd like to take a quick run into town this morning. Will you watch the girls for me? What is the best time to go and where will I find a good book shop?' She was making her tea while Rachel stirred the porridge.

'I usually have my breakfast when I come back after I've taken Louise to school. Then I start on the housework, but the children are on holiday this month. I think you should go early, about nine, before it gets too hot. I'll look after the girls.'

'Thanks, Rachel. I'll be away about an hour. Helen needs to stay in bed today. Louise can stay with her and they can dress their dolls.'

They all enjoyed their breakfast, especially Helen who was hungry, which was a good sign. She ate a few spoonfuls of soft porridge and the scrambled egg and finished off with a little weak tea.

'My throat is better today, Daddy. Can I have some more jelly and ice-cream?'

'Yes, you've been very good and taken all your medicine.'

I must buy jelly packets, ice-cream and custard! thought Cathy.

She left the girls playing happily together on Helen's bed and drove into Estcourt. The town was quiet at that early morning hour and the bookshop was easy to find. She chose two simpler storybooks for Louise, and for Helen two others which she thought she'd like. The supermarket was close by. In addition to the soft pudding items she bought a fruit cake, a box of crunchies, some fresh bread rolls for lunch and a cooked chicken which could be sliced up to have with a salad. It would be a change from the cold meats. She drove to the farm, pleased with her purchases.

'Hullo, Rachel. I'm back. Is everything all right?'

'The girls have played quietly together. They are fine.'

As she was unpacking her shopping bags on the kitchen table Neil arrived and walked into the kitchen. He saw the parcels of groceries and the chicken.

'Where have you been? Spending too much money around the town by the look of it. I didn't ask for a chicken and bread rolls!'

He sounded quite angry.

Louise came running in to interrupt them..

'We were very good and played quietly while you were in town, Cathy. Helen's asleep now. Did you buy us more ice-ream and jelly?'

'Yes, and some custard and a chicken for lunch.'

'There was no need for you to go buying food for us. Why didn't you tell me and I would have done it?' He didn't look too pleased.

'I knew you were busy and besides, I really went to buy something for the girls.' She fished in another bag. 'This is for you, Louise. I bought you a present.'

'But it's not my birthday.'

'This is a *late* birthday present and you may open it now.'

Louise opened the bag and saw the books.

'*Two* story books! Wow! Now we can have more stories to-night! There's another present,' she pulled out something else – 'a paint box, two brushes and a painting book! We've never had paint boxes. Oh, thank you, thank you!' She was feeling the different colours. 'This is red and that one is green. There are so many colours.'

'I'll show you how to mix the paints with water to make a pretty picture and teach you the names of the other colours. This one is called turquoise. So often the sea is this colour.'

'You have spoilt them. There was no need for presents.'

He looked very displeased, frowned and turned away from her.

'They are well-behaved girls and it's my pleasure.'

'Rachel, make the tea, please,' he shouted as he abruptly left them.

He was more annoyed than ever when the tea-tray arrived with a plate of crunchies, but he said nothing. Cathy noticed that he helped himself to a second one. Helen woke up and called Cathy. She dressed her in her gown and slippers and she came to join them.

'Look what Cathy's given me, Helen, books and a paint box!'

'There's a present here for you, too. Helen.' She looked excited as she took the bag from Cathy. Out came the books and painting set.

'I've got two as well, a book of fairy tales and Winnie the Pooh! My teacher at nursery school told us a story about this teddy-bear and now I have my own book. Oh Cathy, thank you!' She put her arms around her waist and kissed her. 'There's something else in the bag,' she said, fishing inside. 'I've got a paint-box and brushes, too, Louise. Now we can both paint. We've done finger-painting at school, Cathy. How lovely it will be to paint with a brush!'

Neil watched all that was happening. Cathy wondered what he was thinking of it all.

'You have both been very spoilt. Helen should get back to bed.' He looked at Cathy. 'I must get back to the milking shed. The tanker will be coming soon to collect this morning's milk. I'll be home for lunch at twelve-thirty.' He seemed reluctant to leave them.

'I'll see she has a quiet day. Painting lessons will begin tomorrow.'
He said Goodbye and left them.
For the first time he didn't slam the truck door.


Helen continued to improve and Dr Wood was pleased with her progress when he called during the morning and examined her. She still had a slight temperature.

'Is she drinking plenty of fluids?' he asked.

'Yes and she has begun to enjoy her meals again.'

'I had jelly and ice-cream *and* custard for lunch, Doctor Kevin, and my throat wasn't so sore when I swallowed them down.'

'That's good news. Do you like yoghurt, Helen? You should try the strawberry flavoured one. I'm sure you'd love it.


In the afternoon she sat and watched Cathy and Louise cleaning out Peter's cage.

'Close the doors, Louise. I'll let him out. Keep still, Helen, and he'll fly to you.'

He flew around the room several times, finally landing on Helen's arm and sat looking at her. He was most talkative. 'Cheers! Clever bird! Kiss-kiss, naughty boy!' he said over and over.

'We must teach him something new to say,' said Helen as the cage was being cleaned. 'I'll teach him to say 'Rachel put the kettle on for tea' and see what he says.'

'That's too long. Try just 'It's tea time!' Say it over and over.'

He managed 'Tea time,' adding Cheers! which was quite cleverly appropriate.

'He'll get it eventually,' said Cathy. 'We've finished the cleaning. Louise is filling the feeders with seed and water. I'll put him back now, Helen.'

As she closed the cage door her cell-phone rang. It was Claudia.

'I had to ask how you were managing. Are you OK?'

'Yes, it's going well. Helen's been quite ill though, with a strange virus and sore throat, but a Doctor friend came and fixed her. She's on the mend and is now able to swallow soft food.'

'That would be Kevin Wood. He's our doctor, too. Tom has asked after you. Is there any chance of seeing you?'

'I doubt it. I'm only here a week. If Neil agrees I could bring the girls over for a swim once Helen is well again. I'll call you. 'Bye.'

That evening after the girls had been put to bed and she and Neil were alone in the sitting-room, she felt it was a good time to ask after Mark. The girls hadn't mentioned him – in fact nothing had been said about him at all. She felt it strange that there were no photographs of the children or family members anywhere in the house. Most people had a few framed photos hanging on the walls or in frames standing on bookcases or on pieces of furniture somewhere in their houses to mark an important birthday or family celebration occasion, but Hartleyvale was devoid of any family likenesses. She was hoping to see a photograph of his wedding or of his wife with the children, but there was not a photograph anywhere to be seen. Perhaps he kept one of her in their bedroom. During ten years of his marriage surely some photographs must have been taken?

Why weren't there any photographs in the house?

What had she done to hurt him so much that he could no longer bear to see her with the children?

She also wanted his permission to take the girls swimming at the Dean's home. It seemed a good time to question him about it.

'Mr Middleton.....' she began. He looked up from the newspaper.

'I think it's time you called me Neil. I find I'm already thinking of you as Cathy and calling you Cathy. Please let's not be so formal.'

'It would be easier!' She smiled. 'I'll begin again. Neil, please tell me about Mark. Where is he and when is he returning? What should I know about him?'

'Mark is nine years old, a very normal nine year-old, full of energy and loves sport. He misses not having a brother to tease, or anyone nearby that he could be friends with or play with. The girls are too young for him. I was happy that he was asked to go to the Mackenzie family for Christmas and spend a holidays with them so that he would have companionship and fun. Ian and Fiona have three boys, and Donald is the middle one. He's in Mark's class and they are great friends. Ian runs a cattle farm nearer to the mountains. Fiona has a small chicken farm. She sells her eggs and poultry at their farm-stall on the main road and to the 'Berg resorts. They're bringing him home on Saturday.'

'Good. I'll be able to meet him then.'

At that moment the phone rang in the hall and Neil got up to answer it. She heard him say 'Neil Middleton speaking,' and after a pause he said, 'Yes, I'll call her.' He came back to the sitting-room.

'It's for you – a man's voice.'

'Thank you.' She got up, thinking it would be Garth. Neil settled himself again in his armchair and sat half watching the TV news.

'Hello........ Why, hello, Tom! This is a nice surprise!'

'I phoned Claudia hoping you were still there to ask if you'd ride again with me and she said you had gone home, but had come back to help the Middletons in their hour of need. I must say I was most surprised – very noble of you.'

'I happened to be free in January before the schools open and I'm working here to care for the children. Now that my Mum has gone, I'm at a bit of a loose end, and it's better to keep occupied otherwise I find myself dissolving into tears! Not like me at all!'

'Is there any hope of a ride? I'll come and fetch you. We can dine somewhere afterwards.'

'Unfortunately I don't think it's possible, Tom, as much as I'd like a ride. It's sweet of you to ask me. How's Richard?' She felt she needed to change the subject.

'I haven't seen him since the dance. My number's in the book if you find there's a possibility of a ride. Please call me, Cathy.'

'I will. Goodnight, Tom.'

She walked back and sat down. She certainly hadn't expected to hear Tom's voice! He was a nice guy and a good rider.

'I imagine that was an admirer of yours. Did he want you to go out with him?'

'Yes, he lives in Estcourt and my friend Claudia Dean told him I was here. He wanted to take me riding.'

'I think you should go.' She was amazed to hear him agree. 'You must have some time off. Rachel can watch the girls and it can be arranged for that day. Call him back and say you have my permission.'

She thought quickly. It would make a break  Why not go and enjoy a ride with Tom? He was good company, and an hour's ride in the country would be refreshing.

'I'll need to look up his number.'

'I can do that for you. I'll get the directory. What's his name?'

'Tom Cathcart.'

He came back with the book.

'I found it. Here it is. Call him now.'

She took the book to the hall and dialled Tom's number.

'Tom, it's me again. Neil says I must have some free time. I'd like to go riding. Late afternoon would be a good time when it's cool.'

'That's great! What about Friday? I finish early and I can pick you up about three o'clock. I know how to find the Hartleyvale Farm although I have never been there. How would that suit you?'

'I'll be ready for you. Thanks, Tom. See you then.'

She came back with the directory. Neil looked up. 'All fixed up?'

She nodded. 'Yes, Friday at three. He'll come for me.'

'Good, I'll ask Rachel to look after the girls in the afternoon. If it's a warm day they play with their dolls under the trees.'

'I also wanted to ask if I could take them to my friend Claudia Dean's home to swim in their pool as there's a shallow end for them and I would swim with them. Have they water-wings?'

'Yes, they always wear the wings. If you are with them it would be quite in order. Helen should be over her illness by then. Watch Louise – she's as slippery as an eel and quite fearless.'

'Thank you, Neil. I'll look after them.'

He seemed to be in such a good mood! He was quite a different person, especially when he smiled. Cathy made their coffees and in one of the plastic cake boxes she found some shortbread biscuits which he must have bought. She brought those with the coffee.

'Have some coffee and a shortbread biscuit. They are one of my favourites. Susan's coming tomorrow. I thought of giving them a cooking lesson. Helen should stay quiet and not run around. This is a good way of keeping them quietly occupied and they love it.'

'Sounds a very good idea. I'll be the chief taster.'

Well, thought Cathy, wonders will never cease!

It didn't last long, unfortunately.

It was eight-thirty and Cathy was about to say Goodnight when the phone rang again. Neil looked worried as he went to answer it. The message was very brief.

'Damn! Sorry, I've got to go out. Don't wait up. You get to bed. I may be very late.' He mumbled something to himself and Cathy caught the words.......'another damn crisis.' He put on his jacket, grabbed the truck keys and slammed the front door as he went out. She heard the truck roaring down the drive.

She showered and got into bed, but sleep evaded her. She tried to read her book. It was no use. She lay awake in the dark, wondering what his wife had done. Finally she dosed off, to be awakened by the front door being unlocked. Neil had returned! She heard his footsteps passing her door on his way to the office where he slept. She had noticed that he used the shower in the children's bathroom.

Why didn't he sleep in the main bedroom in the wing on the other side of the house? Why was the door leading to this wing always kept locked? I'll ask Rachel when I have the opportunity. Surely some-one must open the wing to clean the rooms there.

Her bedside clock said two-thirty. No lights were switched on and all was quiet again.

She did sleep then, but six o'clock came all too soon.

He could only have had, at the most, three hours' sleep.

She got out of bed and wearily made her way to the kitchen.

Rachel was at the stove making the porridge.

Another day had begun!


They had started their breakfast when Neil arrived. He sat down and noticed that Helen had come to join them and was enjoying her Mabela porridge. (porridge made from the coarsely ground seeds from sorghum, an East Indian grass plant similar to sugar-cane. Children called it 'chocolate porridge.')

'Good morning, girls. It's nice to see you back at the table, Helen. How is your throat today?'

'It's nearly better, Daddy.'

'I had a call from Joy. She's bringing Susan over to spend the day today, and Cathy has something exciting for you to do. Bring my porridge, please Rachel.'

'What is it? Learning to paint?'

'Aha, it's a secret! You'll have to wait and see.'


Susan was taken to their bedroom as soon as she arrived to see their new presents.

'I wish I had a paint box.' She sounded so envious.

'I'll let you use my paints because you are my friend, and I have another brush you can paint with,' said Louise graciously with her arm around her friend.

'That's very kind of you, Louise, but today is a cooking day,' said Cathy. 'We're making cup cakes for tea!'

'Oh, yay! We've never made them before. Can we put icing on?'

'Yes, first wash hands and come to the kitchen.'

Cathy had told Rachel what they would be doing and she had helped her find the ingredients, scale, cake mixer and patty tins she needed. She taught Helen how to use the scale and weigh out what they needed, Louise was in charge of switching the mixer on and off, and Susan buttered the patty tins. Soon all three were busy little bees. Each had a spoon to spoon the mixture into the patty tins and Cathy put them in the oven. The best part was scraping the mixing bowl clean! While the cup cakes were baking they were each given a small bowl of icing to mix. Susan chose to make pink icing for her cup cakes, Louise chose chocolate and Helen green colouring. Cathy had found the food colour bottles in the pantry and also an icing set.

There was much excitement when they peeped through the glass oven door and saw the cakes rising high up in the tins.

'We must wait for them to cool once they are taken out of the oven,' said Cathy. 'Come and sit on the sofa with me and I'll read you a story from Louise's book while we wait. Susan is our visitor so she must choose one.'

Susan flipped through the pages. 'I'd like this duck one.' They hadn't heard the story of the ugly duckling and were happy to know she grew up to become a beautiful swan. 'What a lovely story!'

The girls managed to lift out the cakes onto drying racks and then came the fun of icing them. Cathy showed them how to use the icing tube to make little stars all over the tops of the cup cakes. When they had finished there was more icing on their fingers and faces and on the floor than on the cakes! Neil arrived and popped his head around the kitchen door. Cathy wondered what he would say when he saw the mess in the kitchen, but to her astonishment he smiled at the girls and said 'You *have* had fun! I'm having one of each colour. Make the tea, please Rachel, and juice for the girls. I can't wait to taste them! Which one should I taste first?'

'Mine!' they all shouted.

They sat around the dining-room table enjoying them. Neil was most diplomatic and ate one of each colour, pronouncing them to be the best he'd ever tasted.

'Please can we cook again tomorrow, Cathy?'

'We'll do more cooking lessons another day. Tomorrow I want to teach you how to use your new paints.'

'Can I come, too, Cathy? I'll ask Mommy to bring me.'

'I'll ask her and see what she says. We would like you to join us.'

Ten


Painting and riding


Joy brought an excited Susan over bright and early next morning.

'I've shopping to do and then I'm visiting a friend for morning tea,' she told Cathy. 'I'll come for her at twelve if that's OK.'

'That will be fine. We're having an early lunch before I take the girls to my friend Claudia Dean's house for a swim. Enjoy your morning tea party.'

She waved Goodbye to young Nick in his car-seat and went to find the girls who were in their bedroom finding their paint-boxes, brushes and colouring-in books.

'Are we painting in the kitchen, Cathy?' asked Helen.

'No, Rachel will be busy there. We'll work on the outside veranda where it won't matter if you spill water and paint on the tiles.'

There was a wooden table on the veranda and Cathy had put down sheets of old newspaper and three small empty jam bottles.

'Put down your things and fill your jam bottle half full of cold water at the sink. Come and sit down with it and then we'll begin.'

They got settled and then chose a new page in the colouring-in book to paint.

She started by handing them each a plain piece of white paper on which she had drawn three large circles one on top of each other inside a long box standing on a pole.

'What's this for, Cathy?' they asked.

'Have you ever seen three circles one on top of each other like this before? Perhaps when you were riding through the town in the car?'

'Yes,' said Helen after she had thought for a while. 'It's like the traffic lights, but there are no colours in the circles.'

'Clever girl! You're quite right. We're going to paint in the three colours and learn their names and where they go. What colour is at the top of the box?"

'Red!' said Susan. 'Mommy stops at the red light, and green is at the bottom when we can go.'

'Good girl! Now find the red and green paint colours in your paint-boxes.'

'Which is the red colour, Louise, and which is the green?'

They all found the correct colours and Cathy showed them how to wet the brush and rub it over the red colour several times to produce a good red colour.

'Don't have too much water on your brush; wipe some off on the side of the bottle, like this, otherwise your colour will be too pale and the paint will run all over the page. Now let's test your colour; make me some strokes on the newspaper, like this.' She had given them small pieces of newspaper to practise on and they had fun trying out their paint brushes.

'Look at my strokes. I've made lots of marching soldiers!' said Susan, 'and Helen has made a line of sausages!'

'Now clean off your brush and do the same with the green colour.'

After that they coloured in the red and green circles and while they were drying Cathy taught them to say the traffic light rhyme:-

*'Stop!' says the red light; 'Go!' says the green;*
*'Changing!' says the yellow light, winking in between.'*

They did the same with the yellow colour and when their papers were dry they painted in the yellow colour and Cathy took them away to dry.

'Now find a picture in your colouring-in book that you would like to paint, and choose something near the top of the page to paint a red colour, so that as you paint down the page you won't smudge your picture. Try to paint inside the lines.'

'This doll's house should have a red roof,' said Helen as she painted the roof red, mixing more paint when she needed it. She quickly filled in the roof.

'That's very good, Helen.'

'I'll paint the walls yellow and the trees and bushes green.'

Cathy helped the younger ones to get started and soon they had learnt the names of the three colours. Louise chose a page with big balloons floating in the air, and Susan painted tall trees. Helen being older was careful to mix the colour well and was more accurate in her painting. The younger ones were quite happy to fill in the paint in their own way and Cathy left them to produce their own pictures. They stopped for cool drinks and a cup-cake as Neil arrived for morning tea.

'Daddy, come and see what I've painted for you! Don't touch it – it's still a bit wet,' said Louise proudly pointing to her splodgy page. He inspected their efforts, commenting on their work, surprised at what they had achieved.

'You have made me lovely pictures. We'll hang them up in your bedroom when they are dry. I think they have earned an extra cup-cake, don't you, Cathy?' he said, winking at her. 'Can I have two as well? You have iced them so beautifully.'

The younger two played on the jungle gym and rode their bikes, and Helen sat with Cathy while she read a fairy tale to her. Joy came to fetch Susan and she was taken to the veranda to see what they had painted. She praised their work.

'What lovely pictures! You have all done so well. I bought a present for you in town this morning, Susan. You can open it now.'

There were squeals of joy when she saw the paint-box, brushes and painting book.

'Now I have my own paint-box and brushes! I won't need to use your paints, Louise. When you come to play at my house, you can play with my tea-set and be the Mommy and pour out the tea.'

'What are we doing this afternoon? Can we paint again?' They were playing with Peter while Cathy was cleaning his cage. Helen was teaching him to say 'It's tea time' while he sat on her arm, but he hadn't said it yet, much to her annoyance. 'He'll never say it,

Cathy!'

'Yes, he will. Keep on repeating it and he'll surprise you. We're going swimming this afternoon. It's such a lovely day and my friend, Claudia has invited you to swim in their pool. Put on your costumes under your shorts and tops, and wear your sandals. I'll rub you with sunburn cream when we get there. Bring your water-wings and a towel to my car.'

'Is Daddy coming, too?'

'No, he's busy on the farm. I'm putting on my swim-suit and Claudia and I will swim with you.'

They were very excited. It was a hot day, ideal for swimming. Claudia met them as the car drew up at the veranda steps.

'Hello, girls! Come to the pool. My brother Terry is here with a friend but you will have the shallow end to yourselves. There's a big rubber ball there to play with and a little canoe to ride in.'

They were soon all having fun in the pool. Cathy and Claudia were able to give the girls a swimming lesson in the big pool.

'You'll soon be swimming without water-wings, Helen.'

After fifteen minutes Cathy called her out to get dried and dressed.

'You haven't been well this week and you're not quite better. Let's go slowly today. Helen. The little ones can stay in a bit longer.'

Iris brought out a tray with cool drinks and cake, and met the girls.

'Thank you, Mrs Dean, for letting us swim in your pool,' said Helen, very politely. 'and for the chocolate cake.'

'Come whenever you like, Helen, but Cathy or your Mum must be with you in the pool. That's one of our rules.'

'My Mommy is sick so Cathy will have to bring us,' said Louise. 'She's always sick in hospital.'

'She'll get better soon and then she'll bring you.'

'No, she won't. She'll be too busy working.'

'Well, we'll have to make a plan.' Iris looked knowingly at Cathy.

Neil was sitting on the porch as Cathy drew up. The girls climbed out and ran to tell him what they had done.

'You have had a wonderful day, first painting and now swimming.

Say Thank-you to Cathy.'

'They have been so good and both will be swimming after a few more lessons.'

She went to shower and change into her riding clothes to be ready for Tom who was arriving for her at three o'clock. Neil was there to meet him as he walked up the steps.

'Hello, Neil. This is my first visit to Hartleyvale. You have a well-run farm here in a beautiful scenic part of the Midlands.'

'Yes, I took over the farm when my father died two years ago. He left me a good herd of Jerseys. Previously I had farmed in northern Natal. I prefer the climate here and ......' at that moment Cathy came through the hall and they both turned to meet her. She had dried her fair hair, wet from her swim, and brushed it so that it waved slightly and the curly ends twirled charmingly into tiny ringlets. She looked lovely in her jodhpurs, tailored shirt and riding boots. Over her arm she carried her jacket, riding hat and purse.

'Hello, Tom,' she smiled as he came to meet her, and to her surprise he took hold of her arm and kissed her lightly.

'Cathy, farm life must suit you – you're positively blooming!'

She laughed. 'I have enjoyed being with the girls this week. It's so much easier than controlling and teaching a class of thirty-five children. Some are eager to learn and they are a delight to teach, while others are undisciplined, bad-mannered and rude. But enough of that! Are we riding to see Richard at Mooiplaas today?'

'No, we're taking another route and the sooner we get started the better. 'Bye, Neil. I'll bring her back after we have dined out.'

'Goodnight, Neil.' She looked at him for a moment before taking Tom's arm as they walked down the steps to his car. She didn't look back. Tom started up the car and they drove away.

Trojan and Honeybunch were saddled up and ready for them at the Harrisdale Stables when they arrived. They left their jackets in the office and put on their hats. Tom thanked the grooms as they were handed the reins. He helped her mount, adjusted the girth and saw that she was comfortably settled on Honeybunch. He swung up on Trojan and they were on their way, walking over the fields to the open land beyond the town where the Zulu people had been given homes to rent, or had made their own 'shack' homes using any kind of material they could buy cheaply or could find on the town's rubbish heaps. It developed into a township that became their home.

'This is so peaceful, quite perfect. I think we're heading south.'

'Yes. I thought I'd take you to Willowmore, a stud farm belonging to a client of mine. There are several of these special farms in this area on the way to Pietermaritzburg. Hundreds and hundreds of horses were used by both the British and the Boers in the Anglo-Boer War in this part of Natal. We sometimes forget the huge part they played in the war and most of them were killed. I think it's good to think that today they are remembered. Without them transport would have been a major problem for the British – for them all. Many horses were brought over from England. I suspect that they were buried in these hills that we are riding over right now.'

It was a sobering thought.

They came to a beautiful valley where they could see a farmhouse, barns, stables and outbuildings. There were several large paddocks where a few horses were lazily grazing. Large willow trees bordered a stream that flowed leisurely through the pasture. Around the perimeters were lovely old indigenous trees affording abundant shade for the horses. Cathy followed Tom along a side road to the farmhouse where a slim middle-aged man stood at the side entrance.

'Hello, Tom!' he called. 'I've been looking out for you. Welcome to Willowmore, Cathy! Dismount and come inside for tea. The stable hands will look after the horses. Olivia has tea ready for you on the side patio where it's cool.'

They swung down and Tom introduced Roger Summerfield to her.

'What a beautiful farm and paddocks you have! The horses we have seen are in excellent condition.'

'The climate here is most suitable for them. Here's Olivia!'

She came forward to meet them, a charming woman with long brown hair tied back in a pony-tail. She was dressed in navy jeans and a check shirt and wore sensible brogues.

'Hello, Cathy! It's lovely to meet you. We often visit Tom's parents for a game of bridge. Come and sit down. The tea's made.'

They spent an enjoyable half-hour with them. They were interested to hear that she was helping to look after Neil Middleton's children.

'He needs a full-time housekeeper and governess for the children, not one for a week! They have been horribly neglected. Celeste was too busy with her designing business to give them any attention and she was often overseas arranging fashion shows in France, London and New York. Poor Neil has had a difficult time for years.'

So that was why she was always too busy to attend to her children!

'The girls are delightful. I haven't seen Mark yet. He's been spending Christmas with a friend, but will be returning tomorrow.'

'Come, Cathy, we must ride back. It' s getting late.'

'Please come again, Cathy,' they said as they waved Goodbye.

It was dusk and quite late when they returned to Harrisdale. Tom paid the grooms and they drove to the little Italian restaurant where they had eaten their meal on Old Year's Eve. The room was full but Tom had reserved a table and they were ushered inside. Tom ordered a bottle of light white wine which they enjoyed while they waited for their starter and plate of lasagne.

'It's been great having you to myself today, Cathy.' He took her hand in his over the table. 'You know, I've got awfully fond of you!'

'Please, Tom, let's remain good friends. I have no wish to become entangled and tied down just yet. I've looked after my mother for several years, more or less tied to her apron strings and now that she has gone, I'm enjoying this time of freedom to do what *I* would like to do. I'm sure you will appreciate that and understand.'

She quietly drew her hand away.

They arrived back at Hartleyvale a little after nine. Tom came with her up the steps to the front door.

'Thank you, Tom.' She kissed his cheek. 'The ride to Willowmore and meeting the Summerfields was most interesting, and our dinner was delicious.'

'I'll take you there again someday. They are a delightful couple and often come to visit Dad and Mum. Goodnight, Cathy.'

He stood looking at her for a while, then turned and walked back to his car, got inside and drove away. Cathy opened the front door. A light shone in the hall and voices came from the sitting-room. She went quietly and cautiously inside, not knowing what to expect, wondering who was with Neil, and peeped around the door. He was the only one there, fast asleep in his chair and the TV still switched on. She crept across the room to switch it off, but he stirred, opened his eyes and saw her..

'I'm sorry I fell asleep. The programme didn't interest me.'

'There was no need to stay up for me, Neil. You should be asleep in bed. You are up very early and it's a long day for you.'

'I wanted to be sure Tom brought you home safely. Did you enjoy the ride?'

'Yes, it was a new route for me. We rode to the Willowmore Stud Farm and I met Roger and Olivia Summerfield, the owners. Do you know them?'

He stood up and yawned.

'I've heard of the farm but I haven't met them. You must get to bed now, Cathy. It's late. Goodnight.'

'Goodnight, Neil. Thank you for waiting up for me.'

She walked to the guest-room as he switched off the lights.

## Eleven

### Meeting young Mark Middleton

The sound of her alarm clock woke her. Six o'clock! It was Saturday, but there was no chance of a lie-in and a later breakfast when there were animals to care for! And Neil had been up and seeing to the milking for over an hour. There was no sound coming from the girls' bedroom. She got out of bed and took a quick shower which finally had her wide-awake.

Mark's coming home today! I must ask Rachel about preparing his room which the girls had told her was next to their room and Neil's office. She had looked inside when she arrived and found it to be a typical nine year-old boy's room with pictures of sport personalities, posters of racing cars and old-fashioned steam trains on the walls. There were two beds in the room, probably so that a friend could sleep-over. A small globe of the earth stood on top of a bookcase which housed very few books, but instead there were nine or ten fascinating Lego models which he had made. This obviously was what interested him. There was a huge tractor, a racing car, a model of a London bus, a harvesting machine, an old wartime Spitfire, as well as many others. There was also a small table on which was a half unfinished jigsaw puzzle of the Sydney Harbour Bridge.

She had opened his built-in cupboard and had found his shirts and jackets neatly hanging on coat-hangers and the rest arranged in orderly piles on the shelves. His shoes were placed in pairs along the floor. There were running shoes, soccer boots and a soccer ball. She saw a cricket bat, wickets and cricket balls. Cathy wondered if Rachel kept it tidy or if he did so himself.

She hurried to the kitchen where she found a new maid, an older Zulu woman, busy at the stove.

'Good morning! I haven't seen you here before. I'm Miss Crawford and I've come for a week to help Mr Middleton with the children and house-keeping.'

'Good morning, Madam.' She stopped stirring the porridge and gave her a small curtsey. 'Mr Middleton has told me about you. My name's Betty. I've been working here for the family for four years. These last two weeks I've been home on holiday and now Rachel will be on leave for the next two weeks. We work together. I'm glad you're here to help us, Miss Crawford.'

'Please call me Cathy. I'll be happy to help you. What porridge are we having this morning?'

'It's oats today, Mr Middleton's favourite, and then I'm making a large bacon and cheese omelette, and toast for the family.'

'That sounds delicious. Do you know that Mark comes home this morning? Have we to get his room ready?'

'Yes, Mr Middleton has told me. Rachel has made up his bed and tidied the room. The girls will be so excited to see him! Mr Middleton says the Mackenzies are bringing him in time for lunch. His friend, Donald, has often been here to spend a weekend with him. We all call him Don. You have to watch those two! They get into all kinds of trouble.'

'I'm looking forward to meeting him. Is the family staying for lunch? I can make a salad or two to help you.'

'That would be a big help. They'll all be here for lunch. I'll cook the potatoes for you. They all like a potato salad. Mr Middleton has bought two cooked chickens for lunch, and I'm making a fruit salad for a pudding.'

So Neil had approved of the cooked chicken she had bought and had decided to buy more for today's lunch!

'I'll make the fruit salad as well, Betty, and help you carve up the chickens.' She did a quick calculation. 'There'll be ten of us for lunch and that's a lot for you to do. I'll get the girls up and dressed.'

Neil came inside for breakfast as Cathy and the girls sat down at the table. 'Good morning, Daddy,' they said.

'Good morning! Cathy, I'm sorry I hadn't told you that Betty will be here this morning. Rachel goes on leave from today. I intended to tell you yesterday but there were other things on my mind.'

Betty came in with a tray of porridge plates to interrupt him.

'Hello, Betty!' The girls were happy to see her. 'You've come back from your kraal! Did you kill the beast?' asked Helen.

Neil and Cathy smiled. This was usually done at Christmas-time when most of the family was at home.

'We've already met and I'm sure we'll get on well together.'

The girls asked to do more painting after breakfast, so that they could finish their pictures to show Mark She taught them the blue, turquoise and brown colours, and while they were occupied she prepared the vegetables for her green salad as well as making a fruit salad which they would serve with cream from their cows. The girls helped her set the table and all was ready when the Mackenzie's white station wagon arrived at the veranda porch.

First out of the car was Mark. He came bounding up the steps

'Hi guys! Where's everybody? I've come home!'

The girls came running out of their room, all smiles, and Cathy was there, too, to meet him.

'Hullo, Mark! I'm Cathy.'

'I know. Dad told me about you.' He saw Neil emerging from his office to meet his guests, and waved to him. 'Hi, Dad! We're all here! I've had a super holiday!'

There was a great deal of noise and chatter amongst the children. Somehow in between it all, Neil managed to greet the family and introduce Cathy to them.

'What did you get for Christmas?' Helen asked the boys.

'I got a bow and some arrows, and a golf club, and an electronic man,' said Thomas, the youngest Mackenzie.

'I got some computer games,' said Colin the eldest boy, waving them around for everyone to see.

'My new bicycle is *my* best present,' said Donald. 'Mark and I have had lots of fun riding it all over the farm. We had to take turns and we washed it every day to get all the mud off the wheels. Mark can ride very fast, but I think I go faster!'

'What did you get, Mark?' asked Louise.

'I got a new Lego model to make. It's one I've been saving up for. It's the Jedi warship.'

'I've kept your real Christmas present until you came home, Mark. Stay here and I'll bring it to you,' said Neil.

They all waited expectantly, wondering what it could be, while Neil went to his office and wheeled out a new, shiny red bicycle! There were shrieks of delight as Mark and Don ran to take it from him and there were smiles on everyone's faces.

'Oh, Dad, thank you, thank you! This is *my* best present! Next time you come to stay with me, Don, you must bring your bike, too, then we can ride all over the farm.' He inspected it all over, opened the little bag at the end of the seat and rang the bell. They were all so excited.

'What did you get, Helen?'

'A new doll's tea-set and Louise got a Barbie doll and a necklace and a puzzle and I got a skipping rope and lots of other things.'

They ran to fetch them from their room to show everyone. Mark couldn't wait to try out his bicycle. He wheeled it to the steps and the boys followed after him, hoping they'd get a turn.

'Get your bikes, girls, and we'll have races!' he called.

The children all disappeared and Betty brought a tea-tray to the front porch. Neil asked Cathy to pour out the tea while he passed around a plate of crunchies and some biscuits. Fiona, a friendly vivacious brunette, was slightly older than Cathy. She asked Cathy about herself, while Neil and Ian discussed the current farming problems.

'I've brought you three dozen eggs and two of my chickens, Neil,' she said, handing him a basket she had been carrying. 'Thanks for the milk and cream you sent with Mark.'

'These are most acceptable, Fee. Food disappears here like grease lightning. The children are always hungry. I seem to spend every second day at the supermarket! I'll be happy if Cathy will soon take over the shopping. I have so much else to worry about.'

He's taken it for granted that I'll be staying on, thought Cathy, but I haven't been asked! Besides, I have a permanent teaching post to go back to and that's what I intend to do. I'm only here for a week.

Neil, Fiona and Ian walked over to one of the large barns.

'I want to inspect a sick cow with Sam, my assistant, and tell him the Vet. will be here soon. Would you like to come with me and look at the latest milking machinery I've bought? It arrived last week.'

Cathy went to the kitchen to finish her salads and carve the chickens. She had hard-boiled four eggs and used them and some small cherry tomatoes which she knew the children liked, to decorate her green salad. Sprigs of parsley gave the large potato salad a festive look. She had seen a bottle of olives in the pantry and for the grown-ups she made a small salad with them to add to the lettuce, cucumber slices and feta cheese she had seen in the fridge..

'Your salads look lovely, Cathy,' said Betty, when she had finished.

Betty called everyone to the dining-room table for lunch. On the table she had placed all the salads and two platters of chicken together with two plates of buttered rolls. There were also cool drinks. They all took their places. Neil's eyes travelled over the table. It all looked so good! He knew it was not Betty's work. He looked at Cathy and actually smiled at her!

Mark instantly noticed the budgie cage and went to examine it.

'Oh, look, we've got a budgie! Did he come for Christmas?'

'He belongs to Cathy, Mark. You can examine him later. Come and sit down for lunch. Fee and Cathy, please serve the children first and when Mark has said the Grace they may begin. Then we'll serve ourselves. Thank you for giving Mark a wonderful holiday. We'll hear all about it in due course. It's good to have you here with us today.'

Mark said a short Grace he had learnt at boarding-school and they all tucked in.

He's a younger edition of his father! thought Cathy. He has the same features, the same brown eyes and hair. This is what Neil had looked like as a young boy.

It was a happy meal with lots of laughter. The children came back for 'seconds' and then enjoyed the fruit salad and cream. There wasn't much left on the chicken platters or in the salad bowls!

'That was an excellent lunch,' said Fiona. 'Full marks to the cooks!'

'Cathy did most of it and we thank her for helping Betty. It was a good home-coming meal for you, Mark,' said Neil. 'You children can now get down from the table and can play outside while we have our coffee in the sitting-room.'

The six filed out to play on the jungle-gym and bikes. Cathy felt she should leave them to discuss their farming conditions but Neil called her to join them.

'You must stay with us, Cathy. We need you to be here with us.'

It was the first time he had said he needed her. Did he really mean it? He had become quite human during the past two days! Would it last or was it just said because the Mackenzies were present?

Later Mark and all the children trooped inside. He went up to Cathy's chair and whispered to her.

'Can you show us your budgie now, please Cathy? Does he talk?'

'Yes, he says a few words. Come to the dining-room and I'll close the door and windows and take him out. He needs to fly around and have some exercise. His name is Peter. You must all sit still.'

They sat down and watched as she opened the cage. She called his name and he came hopping along to the door to perch on her finger. 'Hello.....hello!' he said, to their delight, cocking his head.

'Hello, Peter. Clever boy!' she said.

'Hello...... hello. Clever boy, Peter. Kiss-kiss! Kiss-Kiss!' he answered quite plainly.

'I'll bring him to you, Mark, to sit on your arm. Keep quite still so as not to frighten him.'

He perched on Mark's arm for a while looking at him and saying 'Hello.....Hello!' before flying off to land on Helen's head and all the children laughed but she didn't panic and remained still. He flew around the room several times before flying back to Cathy's hand.

'He must go back in his cage now. Say Goodbye to him.'

As he sat back on his perch he said quite clearly, 'It's tea-time!'

'He said it!' cried Helen. 'I taught him to say that!' She was so excited. 'It's tea-time!' she answered back to him and he said it again.

The sky grew darker and lightning was seen over the Drakensberg mountain peaks. It looked as if a summer storm was brewing and at half-past three Ian called the boys to say Goodbye.

'We should get home, Neil, before the storm breaks. We have had a most enjoyable day, especially meeting you, Cathy. Thank you so much. It has been a pleasure having Mark. He must come again.'

'We'd like to have Don with us first, perhaps during the Easter break? I'll have to see what happens in the next few weeks. I'll be in touch, Ian.'

The boys climbed into the station-wagon and Ian drove off home. Neil and Cathy stood watching them disappearing as more lightning flashed across the sky and the first raindrops fell. The children brought their bicycles onto the veranda,

'Tomorrow we'll find a place for it in the garage, Mark. It can stay in the office to-night. Helen's fairy-cycle and Louise's trike can also live in the garage now, and be locked up at night with the cars.'

That night after Cathy had read the girls their bedtime story, and Mark had bathed, he came to her in his pyjamas and asked her if he could hear the stories too. She was surprised. She didn't think he'd be interested in their fairy stories.

'I'd love to read to you as well, but some of them are rather babyish for you, Mark. I'll have to buy some story-books with stories that boys will like.'

'It doesn't matter, Cathy. I was listening when you were reading to the girls and I want to hear them, too. I don't know those stories you were reading to the girls. Mommy never read to us and I only know the ones in our school readers and in the books I read from the school library. I don't want to be left out.'

She put her arm around his shoulder.

'You can come with pleasure, Mark. We certainly won't ever leave you out. I'd love you to join us. Perhaps later on you can help me when I get tired by reading a story to all of us. We could make some of the stories into little plays. Do you like play-acting?'

'Yes. Our class acted in a 'Robin Hood' play last year and I was one of his Merry Men. We tricked the Sheriff of Nottingham into riding to Sherwood Forest and while he was away we rescued Maid Marian from the castle. It was good fun.'

She saw him into bed and switched off the light. He was a very nice well-mannered child. 'Goodnight, Mark. We're glad to have you safely back home.' He must have fallen asleep as soon as his eyes closed. They had never stopped riding bikes the whole day!

She joined Neil for coffee in the sitting-room and they watched the news bulletin and the weekend sports results. Neil obviously liked the rugby games, commenting on the players and criticising their play. He also switched over to see the overseas tennis games which they enjoyed watching. Then he turned to her.

'Cathy, thank you for making today so enjoyable. The lunch table looked so attractive and appetising. I appreciate what you did to help Betty. It reminded me of our meals when I was a boy at home. We weren't a large family but when other members of the family came for special birthdays and Christmas, meal-times were great family fun times, when we discussed all sorts of things and got to know each other better. This, I believe, is so very important and is what keeps a family together.'

'I enjoyed the day, too. You have a delightful son. He's so full of life and energy, and has that mischievous grin. The way he controls his peers shows he has leadership qualities. I'll be interested to see his school reports.'

'He can be headstrong and needs guidance. The others follow him regardless of the risks involved. Unfortunately I'm not always around to check him, but never-the-less he's a good kid.'

She said Goodnight and left him. She found she was quite tired and after a hot shower she was happy to climb into bed. She had picked up her book to read a few pages when the phone rang. He spoke very briefly and then she heard the front door closing and the truck door slamming. He started up the engine and the truck whizzed down the drive.

Had he been called out once more to find his wife in some awful pub or low-class dive, to help rescue her from whatever sinister trouble she had landed in? She wished he would tell her something about Celeste, but obviously it was too embarrassing for him to disclose, and he chose to keep it to himself.

She found she couldn't concentrate on the story – the plot was too complicated anyway, and there were too many long descriptive passages. She switched off her lamp-light, closed her eyes and it wasn't long before she fell asleep.

It had been an enjoyable, eventful day.

Twelve

Decisions

'What are we doing today, Dad?' asked Mark after Betty had cleared their Sunday breakfast plates away. 'Can we go fishing?'

'What would the girls do? They aren't keen on fishing.'

'I could take them to swim in Claudia's pool. The Deans have said we can come as often as we like. I'll take them in my car and you and Mark can enjoy the fishing. How would that do?'

'Yes, let's go to Claudia's house to swim! I like it there. Helen can climb in the canoe and I'll push her,' said Louise.

'In that case it's decided. You'd better start hunting for worms.'

'I'll go to 'Muddy Pool' on my new bike. There are lots there.'

'Put on your costumes, girls. We must swim before it gets too hot.'

They left together, Neil turning off to drive down to the Bushman's River, while Cathy drove to the Dean's house. Some friends with children had also arrived for a swim and before long there was much noise and splashing in the shallow pool.

'How are you managing with the children?' Claudia asked when they were alone, sitting on the poolside with their legs dangling in the water, and watching the girls playing with a large rubber ball. 'And more specifically, how are things going with Neil?'

'The girls are easy, lovely little girls, but they have missed such a lot not having a mother to be with them and teach them all the things mothers teach their children. They have missed out on so much love and caring, too. I met Mark yesterday for the first time as he's been with the Mackenzie family for Christmas. They have three boys. The middle one, Donald, is his best pal. Mark is a fun-loving, harum-scarum mischievous boy, always active and the centre of what's happening. He's a boarder at Mount Eagle, the prep school about twenty km away. I think he's better off there than the girls are here, left in the care of Zulu nannies all day.

'As for Neil, well, I don't think he enjoys life. He's an unhappy, mixed-up man. He works long hours and comes home exhausted. His wife is a perpetual worry for him. I presume she's in a rehab home, but she seems to be able to escape somehow from it and Neil is forever being contacted to help bring her back. The phone calls usually come late at night. I feel very sorry for him. The poor man doesn't get enough sleep.'

'Did you go riding again with Tom? Did he call you?'

'Yes, Neil insisted I go as he said I needed some free time. We rode to Willowmore, the large stud farm and met the owners, Roger and Olivia Summerfield, a lovely middle-aged couple, who are friends of Tom's family. Afterwards we ate at the Italian restaurant in Estcourt. I enjoyed the ride and the meal very much. Tom is so knowledgeable about the history of this area. I liked listening to his war stories. He also told me more about Celeste, Neil's wife. Did you know she was a top dress designer, arranging fashion shows in New York, London and Paris, and that's why she was never at home.' She paused for a minute. 'I was surprised that Neil waited up for me. He's been quite human at times!'

Iris arrived with tea and cookies and news of the Middletons came to an end. They arrived back at the farm before the boys in good time for lunch. Louise heard the truck arriving and ran to the porch.

'Did you catch anything, Mark?' Louise shouted to him as he stepped out of the truck.

He held up three small fishes hooked on a line for them to see.

'Yes! Three small yellowtails, but they are big enough to eat and we can each have one for supper. I'll ask Betty to cook some chips as well. We haven't had fish and chips for ages.'

After lunch Neil took the truck to the sheds to check on the sick cow. She had been no better that morning and Neil had called the

Vet. who had visited her and given her a shot of some medication. Cathy could see Neil was worried about her.

It grew very hot and humid and Cathy told the children to stay and play indoors. The girls were happy to play with their dolls in their playroom, dressing them in the new clothes they had received for Christmas, while Cathy sat with them working on a tapestry picture she was making. She had left Mark in his room engrossed in studying the instructions of his new Lego model, the warship of the Jedi.

'I want to get started on this model, Cathy. It's not going to be an easy one, but Dad will help me if I get stuck.'

He went to his room to read the instructions again.

The afternoon was very quiet, hot and sultry. The hot sunshine and their swim in the pool had made Cathy feel drowsy. She felt her eyes closing and she dropped her needlework down on her lap. If only she could get on her bed and have a quick nap!

All at once the stillness was shattered. There was a loud shout and an agonised cry from the front garden. Cathy recognised Mark's voice! What was he doing outside? She had left him in his room studying his new Lego model instructions. Instantly she was wide awake. She dropped her tapestry, jumped up and ran to the front porch door to meet an almost hysterical Mark running inside. He was crying and sobbing.

'Cathy, Peter's flown away! I'm so sorry! I took him out of the cage to play with him and he flew out of the window. I thought it was closed.' He ran into her arms and hid his face in her T shirt. 'I've been trying to catch him......but he keeps flying in the trees.... and it's too high up......for me to get him.' He clung to her and sobbed, tears running down his cheeks. By this time the girls had come to see what had happened, concerned for him. It had to be something bad. Mark didn't often cry.

Cathy managed to extricate herself from his clutches.

'Don't cry anymore, Mark. We'll find him,' she said, patting his head, trying to calm him down.

'What's the matter, Mark? Did you fall down?'

He was too distraught to answer Louise.

'Mark took Peter out of his cage and he flew away through the window. We must all try to catch him. I don't want to lose him. Start looking in all the trees near the house. I'll phone your Dad to come. He'll know what is the best thing to do.' She took out her cell phone.

'Neil, Mark has let Peter out of his cage and he's flown into the front garden. Please come quickly. We must try to catch him.'

He didn't waste time answering. He ran to the truck, and drove up to the farmhouse where he found them gazing up into the trees near the house, looking for the blue budgie.

'Hello....hello, Peter,' called Cathy. 'Pretty boy, come to me, Peter. Cheers!' called Cathy several times. She turned to Neil. 'We saw him in these shrubs and in the tall indigenous trees, and he was here in this hibiscus shrub a few minutes ago. He can't be far away.'

Suddenly they saw him emerge from the leaves of a high tree.

'There he is!' shouted Mark.

He flew back and forth between the trees, cleverly perching on high branches where he knew they couldn't reach him. Then he flew down to them and Cathy heard a flurry of wings above her.

'Hello.....Hello, Peter! Cheers!' again and again she said softly.

Eventually Helen softly called. 'He's landed on your head, Cathy.'

'Keep still. I'm getting something to cover him to try to trap him.'

Neil took two steps at a time onto the porch and into the house. He saw that the lunch plates had all been removed but the table-cloth was still on the table. Pushing the remaining pieces of cutlery and condiment sets aside, he whipped off the cloth and quietly ran with it to Cathy. Standing behind her so that Peter didn't see him, he carefully threw it over her so that she was completely enveloped in it. Neil held the sides down with his arms around her to prevent Peter from escaping.

'Don't squash him, Neil. He's so little,' came her anguished cry.

There was no time to reply. He lifted her up, gathering her in his arms and carried her into the dining-room, with the children anxiously following behind him.

'Close the door, Helen. Mark, close the window.' He held the table-cloth tightly around her body while they obeyed his instructions. Cathy heard the door and window closing. She could feel Peter flying about inside the cloth and scratching her head.

'I hope it won't take much longer. I'm suffocating in here.'

'Is everything closed up?'

'Yes, Dad,' said Mark, very meekly.

Slowly the cloth was pulled off and Peter escaped to fly happily around the room several times. He seemed non the worse for his flight for freedom, landing at last on top of his cage.

'It's tea-time. Cheers!' said Peter. 'It's tea-time!'

Nobody spoke.

'I feel more like a brandy!' Neil looked at Cathy. 'I'm sorry I grabbed you so roughly. I had to act quickly.' He tried to smooth down her hair which had become all ruffled up.

'I'm so relieved that you caught him and that he's not hurt. Thank you, Neil. He wouldn't have survived on the farmland amongst the wild birds. It was lucky that he landed on my head.'

Neil looked at Mark.

'I need to talk to you in my office, young man. Get going!'

Cathy looked at Neil long and hard. Mark didn't need a hiding, her eyes pleaded  There were other ways of punishing children instead of beating them. Mark knew what trouble his disobedience had caused. She prayed Neil would find a better punishment.

Cathy took the girls to their room and shut the door.

'What will happen to Mark? Will Daddy give him a hiding?' Helen was terribly concerned for him. Cathy knew then, that this child at some time previously had been punished with a beating from Neil.

'I don't know. He's been disobedient and has given us a lot of trouble. Peter might have flown away forever and I would never have seen him again.'

'Daddy would buy you another one.' Louise was sure that would be the best solution. 'You'd still have a budgie.'

'But it wouldn't be my Peter, would it?'

A bell rang and they all gathered on the porch for tea. Mark's eyes were red from crying; he looked very sheepish and subdued. Betty brought a plate of scones topped with apricot jam and cream.

'Thank you, Betty. Cathy will pour the tea for us. I have forbidden Mark to ride his bicycle for one week. It will stay locked up in my office. That's his punishment for disobeying Cathy. Let it be a lesson to you all. '

Cathy had handed round the tea when they saw a car driving through the farm gate and up to the house. Who could be arriving on a Sunday afternoon? The car stopped and a tall fair-haired man got out. Cathy had recognised the car at once. It was her brother's BMW! Had he come to check up on her? Or was something seriously wrong at home? Had anything happened to Julia? He got out without saying anything while the family wondered who he could be. Cathy jumped up and ran to the car to meet him.

'Garth, what are you doing here?'

'Thank God, I've found you!' He bent down, put his arms around her and couldn't seem to stop kissing her. 'I've been so worried! Why haven't you phoned me? A whole week has gone by without a word from you! I had no idea what Mr Middleton would be like.' He looked up at Neil and called up to him. 'I've come to take her home. She should never have come to you. Go and pack your case, Cath.'

'No, don't take her away!' cried a little voice as Louise ran to Neil and clutched his hand. 'I don't want her to go!'

The children looked completely stunned. Cathy felt it was time to introduce her brother.

'Garth, come and meet the Middletons.' She took his arm, pulling him towards the steps as Neil stood up, ready to go to her assistance if it would be necessary. 'I'm perfectly well and I've spent a happy week here.' They reached the family. 'Garth, this is Neil Middleton and these are his children – Mark, Helen and Louise.' Mark stood up. 'I'm Mark,' he said politely. 'Neil, this is my one and only brother, Garth, who looks after me.'

Neil stepped forward and put out his hand.

'I'm very pleased to meet you. Please sit down and join us for tea. Mark, tell Betty to bring more fresh tea.'

Garth looked rather bewildered, but he sat down next to Cathy on the settee. 'I have been entirely wrong and I apologise.'

'Garth, I sent you a message on my cell phone the day after I had arrived, but it seems you didn't receive it. I'm sorry, I probably should have spoken to you on the phone as well, and given you more news. It's all my fault.'

'I'm to blame as well,' said Neil. 'I should have asked her about her family and insisted she phone them. I've been too pre-occupied with my own affairs. Let's forget it and enjoy our tea. Here's Betty with another tea-pot and hot water.'

The girls settled down next to Cathy, happy now that the tension had eased and that she was staying with them. Garth recovered once he knew she had not been harmed in any way. After tea Neil asked Garth if he'd like to see more of the farm and took him in the truck on a quick tour. He was pleased with what he saw and admired his splendid herd of cattle and his new milking machinery.

'I must leave to get home before sunset. Are you coming back with me, Cath?'

'No, I've promised to stay a week and I'll keep my word.'

'When will you be leaving?'

'I'll drive back on Wednesday morning.'

'But you'll come back to us, won't you?' asked Helen.

'I don't think I can, Helen. I have to teach at the Waverley Junior School in 'Maritzburg this year. I've been teaching there for three years. I can't just leave all those children without a teacher, can I?'

'But the schools don't open until the end of this month. You could come back until then, couldn't you?'

'No, I have joined a painting group and I want to learn how to paint with oil paints. I only came for one week, Helen. I must go back on Wednesday.'

The girls looked so downcast and Louise was about to cry at any moment. She looked away from their sad faces and asked after Julia.

'How is Julia? Is everything going well?'

'She's very fit. Doctor Walters was pleased when he saw her on Thursday. There should be no problems.'

They said their Goodbyes. Cathy walked with him to his car and after kissing her Goodbye he drove away. 'Take care driving home!'

That evening while the girls were in the bath Cathy felt it was a good time to suggest they have their hair washed. It was looking very dull and bedraggled, and hadn't been washed while she was there. They both had fair hair, unlike Mark who had dark hair like his father, so she presumed Celeste was a blonde. She found a bottle of shampoo in the bathroom cupboard and showed it to Helen.

'Is this the shampoo Betty uses when you wash your hair?'

'Yes, but we haven't used it for a long time.'

'I think it's high time we had a shampoo bath to-night to make your hair soft and shiny again. Wet your head, Helen, with your sponge and keep your eyes closed. Louise can watch while I rub on the shampoo and wash your hair. I'll be very quick.'

She washed her head thoroughly and quickly.

'I don't like it when Betty does it,' complained Louise, as she watched Cathy. 'I always get soap in my eyes. It burns and I cry.'

'You'll like it when Cathy does it,' answered Helen.

'Lie back in the water while I hold your head and rinse the soap off. Don't open your eyes, Helen, until I tell you.'

It was all over in a few seconds and Cathy had a towel ready to dry her face and hair.

'Now open your eyes. That wasn't too bad, was it?'

'No, it was lovely. It's your turn now Louise.'

She pulled a face, but Cathy took no notice and wet her hair.

'Be a good girl and close your eyes. It will all be over in no time and when you're in your pyjamas I'll read you stories.'

The promise of stories kept her from complaining any further as Cathy kept talking to them.

'Mark's coming to listen as well to-night. It's a story about a great big giant who lived in a castle up in the sky. He had a magic hen that laid golden eggs......'

'What is a giant? Can you eat a golden egg? We haven't heard that story yet.'

The hair-washing was accomplished without any tears. Cathy found some blue ribbons in a drawer and after a good brushing she tied up their hair with them and took the girls to the mirror to see their soft shiny hair.

'I like my hair in this style. Daddy will be surprised. Call Mark, Louise, and let's start the story.'

They settled themselves on either side of her on Helen's bed and Mark sat behind her so that he could look over her shoulder to see the pictures and follow the story. Cathy began reading 'Jack and the Beanstalk.' She read well, dramatically, with great expression and they said the giant's lines with her, enjoying every minute –

*'Fee, fi, fo, fum! I smell the blood of an Englishman!*
*Be he alive, or be he dead, I'll grind his bones to make my bread!'*

Neil had left after dinner to attend a short meeting in town. It was very quiet when he arrived home, and no-one was about, but he heard Cathy's voice and followed it to the girls' bedroom. He popped his head around the door and was astonished at what he saw. They made a wonderful picture that remained with him forever. No-one had seen him, so engrossed were they in the story. He stood outside and listened to the end, and only then did he step inside. Louise spotted him first.

'Daddy, you missed a lovely story about a giant and a magic hen!'

'I've been standing outside the door, listening. It's a great story and Cathy read it so well. Now it's bedtime. First a visit to the bathroom and then into bed. Who'll be the first in bed tonight?'

They scampered away. Cathy sat on the bed facing him, smiling.

'You need children of your own, Cathy.'

'I have to find a man who will love me first. All the best ones have been snapped up or else I haven't met the right one yet.'

'I think you have yet to meet him. Come and have coffee with me. Betty has put the tray on the coffee table all ready for us.'

They sat watching the evening news and a sports programme for a short while. Cathy went to cover Peter's cage with the covering she had made for him and said Goodnight.

'I'm off to bed. It's been quite a day, hasn't it?'

'Yes. It has. Goodnight, Cathy.'

He watched her as she turned and walked down the passage to her bedroom.

Before she fell asleep she went over the events of the day.

Why had she said she had joined the art group and couldn't return for the rest of the month? Nothing had been finalised with Marissa. She could stay on another ten days. There was nothing to keep her at the cottage now that her mother had gone.

She was already so attached and fond of the children that she knew she had to go now before it became impossible for her to leave them.

Was it a decision she would forever regret?

Thirteen

An offer from Neil

It's Monday, the 15<sup>th</sup> January, thought Cathy as she lay awake waiting for her six o'clock alarm bell to ring, and it will be another hot day. The weather prediction on the TV news had said 'expect high temperatures of over 32 degrees' for northern Natal.

I have only two more days at Hartleyvale. What should I do with the children? They should stay indoors or play in the shade. Since there'll be no riding of bikes or fun on the jungle-gym or ball games on the lawns, it would be a good day to have another baking day. Mark can join in as well. After all, most chefs were men, weren't they? The more she thought about it, the better it sounded. Betty would be occupied with the Monday washing and the kitchen would be free after breakfast for them to use.

That got her out of bed and to the bathroom for a quick shower. It was very quiet. She popped her head into the children's rooms. They were still fast asleep. She went to the kitchen to find that Betty was there and had started the breakfast.

'Good morning, Betty! It's Monday, the start of another week. Are you washing today?'

'Hello, Cathy! Yes, I do a big wash in the machine on Mondays, Wednesdays and Fridays after breakfast. Bring anything you would like me to put into the machine.'

'Thanks, I have a few things. Betty, could we use the kitchen for a cooking lesson? It's much too hot for the children to play outside and I promised them we'd have another one. We'll work on the back porch as much as possible so as not to disturb you. Would that be

OK? I'll help them to clean up afterwards.'

'It would be fine. What will you be cooking?'

'I thought of making pastry and jam tartlets. Kids love rolling out the dough and cutting out shapes.'

'You'll find patty tins and cutters in the pantry. They haven't been used for months, or years, and will need a good clean! Help yourself to anything else you need. You should have enough flour.'

She went to investigate and found the patty tins and cutters were indeed dusty and needed as good wash. They obviously hadn't been used for years. She took out the scale and other ingredients which they would need, checking if there was sufficient flour as she intended doubling her mother's recipe. She saw a bottle of lemon curd which some kind neighbour must have given Neil, and a tin of pie apples which she could use for a large plate pie. The children would work on the wooden veranda table to measure and rub the butter into the flour, and the surface of the kitchen table when the time came to roll out the pastry. She washed the patty tins and cutters and was satisfied that, although old, they were still useable.

She woke up the children. The girls were very sleepy but Mark was awake, reading the Lego instructions again. She got them up and dressed. Neil was already seated at the table, reading the morning paper when they all trooped into the dining-room at seven o'clock. He put down the paper and stood up.

'Good morning everybody! How is my family this morning?'

'Very sleepy. They had a hectic weekend. They'll be awake by the time we start cooking, I hope.'

Cooking! A magic word!

'Please can I cook with the girls? I'll lick the basins clean!' Mark had a merry twinkle in his eyes.

'Yes, you may also cook, Mark, if you promise to behave and not tease the girls. We'll start after breakfast and when you have tidied your rooms. There are a lot of toys still lying around on the floor.'

'What are we making, Cathy?'

'We're making pastry for little jam tarts.'

They were all awake by then!

Betty arrived with the porridge plates and scrambled eggs followed with toast and a glass of milk. Neil disappeared as soon as he had eaten.

'Good luck with your cooking! I'm looking forward to those jam tarts for morning tea!'

After washing their hands the fun began. Cathy took them to the pantry and they carried out what they needed to the veranda table. She had written down the quantities for Mark to read out to Helen.

'Helen, will you weigh out the ingredients – the flour, castor sugar and butter? Mark will read out how much we need and I'll divide them into three basins, one for each of you. Mark, will you also help Louise grease the three patty tins?'

They set to work. Helen added the baking powder and a little salt and then 'rubbing-in-the-butter' began. Meanwhile Cathy whisked up two eggs and a very little milk to turn the mixture into dough. Mark decided to taste what he was mixing together. By now, inevitably, there was flour and crumbed mixture on the table, over the floor and decorating their faces.

'Oh, yuk!' he cried and spat out a mouthful of his mixture onto the floor. 'What yukkie stuff! This will never make tarts!'

'Carry on rubbing, Mark. It not fine enough yet, and when it is I'll pour in some egg and milk mixture which you will mix up with a knife to turn it into a dough that you can roll out. Watch Louise; she has kept up the rubbing and now it's like breadcrumbs. Good girl!'

At last the three doughs passed the final test and they moved into the kitchen for the next stage. Of course they needed another washing-of-hands before rolling out the dough. Cathy showed them how to switch on the oven to the correct temperature so that the oven would be ready for them. They were each given a space on the table.

'What do we do now? Why are there empty beer bottles on the table? Only Dad drinks beer.'

'You'll see. First I'll take Louise's ball of dough and I'll show you how to roll out your dough.'

Using a wooden rolling-pin she demonstrated how it was done, until she reached the required thickness. Then she handed Mark and Helen each a clean beer bottle rubbed over with flour.

'If you haven't a rolling-pin a beer bottle or any cool-drink bottle does just as well, but be careful with it. Roll out lightly. Louise will use the wooden rolling-pin. Now start rolling!'

Mark and Helen were quick and soon got the idea of what to do. Louise rolled hers so hard until the pastry became too thin to use, stuck to the table and had to be bunched together and rolled out again. Cathy helped to get it workable and she rolled out again.

They were now ready to cut the tart shapes and place them in the patty tins. This required careful handling and produced some rather peculiar tart shapes as they were pulled into position to fit the tins.

'I like this cutting-out part the best,' said Mark. 'I can make the best tarts.'

'And mine are the wonkiest!' said Louise, never-the-less very pleased with her funny shapes. Into the oven they went!

While they were baking the children watched Cathy make the pie. First she placed the bottom piece of dough on the greased pie-plate, rounding off the sides with a knife, then she spread the chopped-up apple pieces over the dough and finally covered it with the thinner top layer of dough. They all helped her decorate the edges with a fork and make apple 'leaves' from the few remaining bits of dough to place on the top. It looked very professional when they had finished. Into the oven it went when the tartlets came out.

They were delighted with their golden tartlets cooling on the wire cooling racks. It was even more fun filling them with jam. They had never seen or heard of lemon curd. Cathy explained how it was made and after sampling a lemon curd tartlet they declared it was 'cool' and 'yummy.'

'Dad will like these for sure,' was Mark's comment.

And so he did.

'Make the tea please, Betty,' he said as soon as he saw them and helped himself.

'He's eating all our tarts! He's had three already!'

'They are so delicious I can't stop.'

It was such a happy time. Morning tea turned into a jam and lemon curd feast.

'I'm saving some for Susan. We can eat them at the doll's tea-party in the doll's house when she comes to play this afternoon,' said Louise, putting them into a plastic box. Cathy packed the rest away for another tea-time.

'I'd like to take you to visit the sheds and dairy now, Cathy. It's a good time. Put on a sun-hat and meet me at the truck. The children will be fine with Betty. First I have a quick call to make.'

She had wondered if he'd forgotten the proposed tour of the farm, but evidently he hadn't. She saw that the girls were busy in the doll's house and Mark had begun his model.

First he took her to the dairy which was empty at this time.

It was a long narrow shed with milking machines down the side walls and a large passage-way in the middle. It was tiled with white tiles and it was spotless having been washed down and thoroughly cleaned after the early morning milking. He showed her the new milking machinery and explained how it was attached to the cow's udder and how it worked.

'The cows assemble here in this paddock at the one end of the shed where they are automatically washed by sprinklers and sprayers from the concrete floor, so that their udders are clean. They love this! They know the time for milking and walk to the gate, waiting to be washed and milked! Once they have been washed the shed door is opened. They know their own stall and go straight to it and wait for the machine to be attached. It gives us a chance to inspect the cows for any illness. Then the machine is started and the yield per cow is noted. Some fodder is placed in a feeding bin in front of them. After they have been milked the machines are then detached and they are led out of the door at the opposite end of the shed. The milk has been automatically noted as it is pumped into a cooling tank to await the arrival of the milk tanker.'

'How wonderful! With all this modern machinery it only needs a few workers to supervise the whole procedure.'

Cathy was most impressed.

'We keep a certain amount of milk for our own use and for all my staff. It is bottled here and distributed. The bottles are hygienically washed, disinfected and bottled by machine.'

'Are all your cows Jerseys?' she asked.

'I mix Friesland heifers with the Jerseys. Jerseys give better quality milk, but Frieslands give a higher production, so a mix is the best.'

'How many litres would each cow give per day?'

'Approximately twenty litres a day.'

'What is their normal feed, Neil?'

'I grow my own hay and mealies. They are fed twice a day depending on their individual yield of milk per day. They live outside in all weathers, except in the very cold winters, when they sleep in the sheds.'

They walked through the shed to the other end where the tanker would be waiting to pump up the milk from the cooling tank. Here Neil had an office. He pointed out more sheds where the fodder was stored and the farm machinery kept.

'What happens when the calves are born? Do they stay with their mothers?'

'No, to separate them later once they have bonded is too traumatic. They are taken away immediately and kept with other calves to be bottle-fed until they are old enough to join the herd.'

Cathy noticed there were stables for six horses.

'Do you ride?' she asked.

'Yes, when there is time. I've kept two horses, hoping Celeste would learn to ride, but she refused. I want the children to ride. Mark has made a start, but since he's been at boarding school there has only been the holidays for riding lessons and I haven't always had the time to teach him. Also I think it's more important that he spends time to mix with boys of his own age, so I encouraged him to play soccer and join a club where I take him to play every Saturday morning. He's a friendly, popular child and gets on well with his peers.'

This was a long, enlightening speech from Neil, and, for the first time, he had mentioned his wife's name!

If Celeste was a fashion designer, surely she must have some office and large room where she could work? Walking past the back of their bedroom wing she noticed two large rooms attached to their bedroom suite. Had Neil built on these rooms as a 'studio' and workshop for her? The one room had a separate entrance into the side garden. It was some distance from the sitting-room and the other bedrooms, away from the children's noise. Surely she wouldn't be disturbed if the TV was switched on for a short while for the children to enjoy their programmes?

They got back into the truck and he drove her around the farm, pointing out the perimeter fences.

'These boundary fences need to be checked every day so that no cattle stray or are stolen. Sam and my Zulu workers repair any sections that have been deliberately cut or damaged. I cannot afford to lose any of the fine herd I have built up over the years. Often Sam and I ride to do this inspection to exercise the horses. If I had known you were a rider, I would have invited you to join us. Perhaps there still may be time for a ride.'

He pointed out fields where the cattle grazed and small dams he had established under a few indigenous trees where they could drink and rest.

'I love these rolling hills and valleys covered with so many wild grasses. They must be preserved for our future generations. The violent summer storms we have over the years have created gaping dongas scarring the earth, washing away valuable topsoil to be forever lost. This is a problem that has been a perpetual worry for me. Gradually I have been able to fill up these unsightly holes, so that the rolling landscape can be restored to its natural contours covered with thick grass to hold the precious topsoil forever.'

He looked at his watch.

'I didn't think we'd be so long. We better get back for lunch.'

'I've enjoyed the tour so much. Thanks for taking me.'

When they reached the farm house and he had switched off the engine, he turned to look at her.

'Cathy, I would like you to stay on with us. Won't you reconsider your decision? The children like you and need you.'

'I don't think I can. I have very mixed feelings at the moment. I have my teaching career to consider, and there's the question of what to do with our cottage if I do come. I've grown very fond of the girls in this short time. I love children. I would like to marry one day when I meet the right man and have children of my own.'

'I'll make it worthwhile if you come. We all know that teachers in government schools are not paid attractive salaries. You fit in wonderfully well in this farm environment. Please say 'Yes.' I can give you a good home and life-style, as well as a salary far more than you are receiving at present.'

She gave this proposition a lot of thought before replying. Neil kept quiet watching her face.

The children needed her, that was so true, but did she want to be a governess/cum/housekeeper living on a farm with not much chance of meeting a man would love her for herself and not because she could teach and possessed an endearing way with children? Neil was a man with difficult marital problems which would possibly become even more stressful, and there was every likelihood that they would continue in the future. Did she need to become involved with this sort of situation?

'No, Neil. I can't stay on,' she said at last. 'I must go now before I become too attached to the children. The longer I stay the harder it will be for all of us. Believe me, it will be hard enough for me to say Goodbye on Wednesday as it is.'

He was thoughtful and quiet for a while.

'I'm sorry you won't stay. I see I can't persuade you.' He got out and opened the door for her.

'Come, we must go. Lunch will be ready.'

That afternoon when the girls had settled down to their painting and Mark had gone off to ride with Neil, she took out her sketchbook to make a few drawings. She wanted to take away with her some memories of the time she had spent at Hartleyvale, but she had been far too occupied with the children to sit quietly and sketch. She chose a view of the front of the house, set down her stool and started sketching. She could always complete it later at home and paint it with water colours. After a while Helen came out to find her and see what she was doing.

'Cathy, how clever you are! I wish I could draw like you do. The farmhouse looks lovely and there's my bicycle on the porch,' said Helen, peering over her shoulder. 'Won't you draw me and Louise?'

'I'd like to have a picture of you. Call Louise.'

She would draw them in charcoal as was usual for portraits. The lines could be rubbed lightly with your finger to give a softer effect, and they were easier to work with.

The girls sat together on the lawn, Louise with her Barbie doll and Helen with her old teddy-bear, Mr Teddy.

'You must sit still while I get started, and don't jump up. Good, stay like that. You can talk to each other but don't move about too much and try to keep your heads still.'

She quickly drew a few basic lines and soon the drawing took shape. When finished she knew it would make a delightful picture.

'Now you can get up and have a look.'

They were so surprised to see what she had drawn.

'Cathy, I didn't know you could draw so well! Now will you draw Mark and Daddy, please?'

'I can try. They aren't here for me to study, so I'll draw them from memory. Go back to your painting and I'll show you later.'

She decided to draw Neil as she saw him after dinner seated in his armchair with his coffee mug in his hand, and Mark standing next to him showing him Peter sitting on his arm. It took some time, but it would also look good. She knew she had captured their expressions well, particularly Mark's infectious grin. She called the girls.

'Gosh, Cathy, you *are* good! I can see that it's Daddy and Mark, and Peter! Why are you using this black stuff?'

'It's called charcoal and is especially used when you make drawings of people. I'll take them home to finish and have them framed. They will look lovely in my sitting-room at the cottage and I'll see you every day.'

'I wish you weren't going. We'll miss you so much.'

'I'll miss you, too. Let's pack up now and watch 'Dora' on the TV.'

Dinner that evening was special. Betty had roasted a chicken which they all loved, followed by Cathy's apple pie and whipped cream. Neil asked for a second helping.

'What a superb dinner!' declared Neil. 'No wonder you're all looking so well and healthy. Thanks, Cathy, for your delicious pie.'

'I watched her and I think I could make it, too,' said Mark. 'She's a good teacher.'

'It's good to learn how to cook. I hope you all will be good cooks when you grow up.'

Fourteen


A day with Mark


Cathy woke next morning when her alarm rang at six. It's Tuesday, my last day at Hartleyvale, she thought. What shall I do with the children today? It was decided for her when Neil announced at breakfast that Joy had phoned asking if she could fetch the girls to spend the day with Susan and he had agreed to the arrangement. Helen immediately said 'Yay! We like to go to Susan's farm.'

'She'll come for them at ten o'clock, Cathy. Mark isn't interested in spending a day with the girls and I can't take him with me today. Can you keep him occupied?'

'I'm sure we can do something together. It's another lovely day for swimming. I'll phone Claudia and ask if we can go and swim there. Would you like to do that, Mark?'

'Oh, yes please, Cathy. Are there any boys there to play with?'

'I'm afraid not. My friend Claudia has a young brother called Terry but he's finished high school. He may be there with friends.'

Neil left them to attend to the farm work and she called Claudia who was delighted that she would be seeing Cathy again.

'Come as soon as you like. Terry has friends coming later on but that's not a problem. The boys live in the pool in this weather. If Mark can swim he can join them in their water-polo games.'

'He does swim, but I'm not sure how good he is. We'll come as soon as the girls have left. Thanks, Claudia.'

Mark smiled and looked happy when she told him.

'That will be great,' he said. 'I'll put on my costume and be ready.'

Susan was in the car with Joy when she came for the girls.

'Hello, Joy. Thanks for having them. They're looking forward to being with Susan.'

'Get in, girls. I'll bring them back about five, Cathy, if that's OK.'

She waved them off and collected Mark who had made a good start on his model.

'We'll leave as soon you are ready. Bring your towel and come to my car in the garage.'

She told Betty they were going to swim at the Dean's house..

'This is the number if you need me. We'll be home for lunch and there'll just be the three of us. Do something easy today.'

Mark sat next to her, chatting all the way about his holiday.

'We had some good mud fights at the dam, Cathy. I hit Don with a big ball of mud in his back. He fell off the boat into the water. Then Colin got me on my neck and I fell in. Thomas laughed so much he didn't see the ball coming for him and he got hit on the head and he fell in. Colin jumped in and the splashing began. It was good fun.'

'I hope you'll behave yourself at the Dean's house, otherwise it will be the last time I'll take you there! No mudball-throwing!'

Claudia saw her car arriving and met them at the porch.

'Park in the shade under those trees, Cathy, and walk round to the pool. Mom's friend, Kate, is here with her twin boys. They're a little older than Mark but will be good friends for Mark to play with.'

The twins, Peter and Paul, were already in the pool, throwing a ball at each other. It didn't take Mark long to dive in and catch the ball when Peter threw it at him. He promptly hurled it back at him hitting him hard on his cheek. Cathy could see she needn't worry about Mark – he could hold his own. She and Claudia sat in deck chairs in their swimsuits at the poolside watching them.

'I must keep an eye on him. He's a bit of a dare-devil. Always getting into scrapes, I hear.'

She told her how he had let Peter out of the cage and how Neil had caught him in the garden. Neil had forbidden him to ride his new bicycle for a week. It was now locked it up in his office as his punishment. They chatted away. It was good to catch up on her news. Claudia told her she had met a new guy at a tennis party and been out to lunch with him twice.

'His name is Jeff Newman and he's come from Durban to open up a new textile factory. The boys liked him and he's a terrific tennis player. A pity you won't be here to meet him. How's it going with Neil? Any further information about his wife?'

She told her she was a fashion designer and of Neil's offer if she would stay on, but that she had refused. Claudia was impressed with the offer.

'I would have accepted! Imagine – no more lessons to prepare or mountains of books to mark, reports to write up and all the new .administration paper-work to do *and* a good salary increase! You're crazy not to accept. You can always go back to teaching if it doesn't work out. Think about it again. You can change your mind and tell Neil now.'

Cathy was quiet for a minute or two, watching the boys playing 'Tag' in the water.

'No, Claudia,' she said at last. 'I think it's best if I go. It's easy for you to say 'Accept.' You haven't lived with them as I have, to know all that goes on or what Neil is really like.' She paused, remembering the children's faces alight with happiness when they were cooking and painting, and how they loved it when she read stories to them. 'I've grown so fond of the children. I hate to leave them. It's a hard offer to refuse.'

'You must do what you think best. It's only my opinion.'

'I've told them I'm leaving on Wednesday morning when my week is up. The longer I leave it the harder it will be to leave them.'

Mark was happy to have made two new friends.

'They are good fun. I like Paul the best. Peter is a bully, but I gave him back what he gave me, and he will know what to expect in future!' Cathy smiled but didn't comment.

Neil breezed in for lunch and left as soon as he had finished.

'See you at tea-time. I have a meeting with Sam in my office at the sheds if you need me.'

Cathy wondered what she could do with Mark for the afternoon.

'I'd like to see your new model. Will you show me how you assemble it? I've never seen one being put together.'

'Come to my room and I'll show you,' he said, pleased that some-one had taken an interest in it. It looked like a massive jigsaw puzzle with pieces everywhere. He had put several parts into groups ready for the various stages.

'It looks very complicated!' said Cathy. 'I wouldn't know where to begin. Where's the instruction book?'

'You have to read the instructions carefully and do exactly as it says until you have put all those parts together. Then you go on to the next stage. I'm on stage eight.'

'You've done very well. I'm beginning to see what the Star Wars fighter plane will look like.'

'These are two of the little characters. They are lesser known Knights of the Jedi. This one is Plo Koon and that one has a number for a name, R7-D4. Aren't they cute?'

She sat with him working on her tapestry cushion cover while he worked on stage eight. After half an hour she could see he was tired of it and needed another diversion.

'I have an idea! Have you ever made crumpets? You're such a good cook, Mark. I think you'd enjoy making them and we'll have them for tea. My mother taught me when I was about ten years old. She came from Yorkshire in England where they love making crumpets. I often made them for her tea before she died.'

'Why did she die, Cathy?'

'She had a weak heart amongst other illnesses. I think she was very lonely after my father died two years ago. Peter was her pet and it cheered her up to have him with her. Then two months ago she had a bad heart attack and died.'

'I'm sorry, Cathy. Now you haven't anyone to look after you.'

'I have my brother, Garth, and my aunts and uncles, so I'm lucky. Shall we make crumpets and give your Dad a surprise?'

'This is the recipe. I've written it out quickly for you to keep. Always read your recipe first to see if you have all the ingredients you need, just as you read your Lego instructions to tell you what to do. I have checked and there are enough eggs and flour, and there's always plenty of milk in this house.'

He set to work, reading the recipe as he went along, and soon had the batter made. Cathy let him do it himself, and watched, giving advice here and there.

'It won't harm if you leave the batter to stand while you get your frying-pan ready. Choose the largest one with a flat bottom, and get it hot to a medium heat; not too hot or the crumpets will burn. Grease the bottom well.' He did all she said.

'I'll make the first three to show you what size they should be. They should sizzle softly as you pour out each crumpet onto the pan and you'll know that's the right temperature. Use a large tablespoon and reckon on one spoonful to make one crumpet.'

They watched as the crumpets rose up and small bubbles appeared on the top of the batter. Mark was shown how to turn them over with a knife. It looked easy, but if you weren't quick the crumpet would slip off the knife and probably fall into the others.

'Now it's your turn!'

He couldn't wait to try it. The first two he did too slowly and they were flops, but the third one was wonderful in the correct oval shape. They were taken out and left to cool on a cloth on a wire rack.

'Now grease the pan well and do another three.'

He improved with each round and soon there were twenty-four crumpets for tea. They were covered by the cloth and left to cool, except for the first four flops. These were buttered and topped with strawberry jam and cream for the cooks to taste, and they were pronounced ' absolutely yummy!'

'Thanks, Cathy! Now I can surprise Dad. Don't tell him.'

They washed up and tidied the kitchen. Then he helped her put jam and blobs of thick whipped–up cream on top before Neil arrived. They sat down for tea on the front porch where they usually sat for afternoon tea as it was a lovely cool spot.

'What have you two been up to this afternoon?'

'Cathy watched me work on stage eight and it's almost finished.'

Betty appeared at the porch door with the tea-tray.

'There's not much to eat for tea, I'm afraid. I should have gone shopping today. Did you find a few biscuits, Betty?'

She put down the tray and when he saw the plate of crumpets, his eyes popped with surprise.

'Where did these spring from?'

'I made them for tea, Dad.' Cathy winked at him.

'I don't believe you! You couldn't possibly have made them.'

'I did make them, didn't I, Cathy? She gave me the recipe and showed me how to turn them over in the frying-pan and they taste just yummy.'

'Pour the tea, Cathy. I'm tasting one right now.' He polished off four. 'I had better stop and save some for the girls. Mark, I have taught you how to braai chops, steak and boerewors (beef and spice sausages ) but with these crumpets I think you have the makings of a very good chef. I'm proud of you!' Mark beamed.

Joy brought the girls home and they were allowed to taste the crumpets too, provided they are their dinner as well! They had played with their dolls and teddies, and later made mud pies and splashed in a little pool Graham had built for Susan in the garden.

'We had a lovely day, Daddy, and I love Mark's crumpets!' Louise's mouth was ringed with cream.


After their baths and as soon as they were dressed in their pyjamas and gowns and had brushed their teeth, the children gathered around Cathy on Helen's bed for their stories.

'It's Helen's turn to-night to choose the first one,' said Louise.

'I'd like to hear a Winnie the Pooh story from my new book.' Mark and Louise hadn't ever heard of Winnie the Pooh at all, so Cathy began to read about the teddy-bear and his friends, Roo and Kanga. Mark chose 'The Frog Prince' from Helen's new fairy-tale book and then it was time for bed.

'You say the Grace very nicely for us before dinner at night, and I know everyone says Grace at boarding-school before meals. Do you say your prayers at boarding-school before you get into bed, Mark?'

'Some boys do, but I don't, because I don't know what to say.'

'What are prayers?' asked Louise.

'Prayers are words we say when we talk to God, our Father in heaven, who is the Father of us all, and we thank Him for what He gives us - the sunshine, the rain, our food and clothes, our parents and friends, the trees, the birds and animals, and for all sorts of things. You can talk to Him about anything you like.'

'Is heaven up in the sky?' asked Helen. 'Does God live in a castle up there at the top of a beanstalk like Jack's giant?'

'Does He live in Durban?' asked Louise.

'No, we don't know exactly where His home is, and I'm sure He doesn't live in a castle, or in Durban, but we do know He has an enormous house with lots of rooms.'

'Can I talk to God to-night?

'You can talk to Him whenever you want to. Sit up in bed, put your hands together like this, close your eyes, and say whatever you want to Him.'

'But I don't know Him and He doesn't know me, so how can I talk to Him and tell Him things?'

'He does know you, Helen. He loves you and He looks after you, and the more you talk to Him, the more you will get to know Him.'

'I'm going to try to-night,' said Louise. 'I want to thank Him for my Barbie doll which Father Christmas brought me. I've wanted one for *such* a long time. Will He really hear me, Cathy?'

'I'm sure He will.'

'And I'll thank Him for my story-books and my paint-box,' said Helen. 'What will you thank Him for, Mark?'

'I'll thank Him for my new bicycle and.....' he thought a bit longer 'and for Cathy for showing me how to make tarts and crumpets.'

'Those are all fine prayers. Now off to bed. I'm coming to tuck you up and switch off the lights.'

Neil's head suddenly appeared round the door.

'And I've come to say Goodnight to my children. Did you enjoy the stories?'

'Oh, yes, We love story-time, especially when Cathy reads to us. Goodnight, Daddy.'

She saw the girls into bed and switched off the light; then she went to Mark's room and said Goodnight to him.

'I've said my prayers, Cathy. It wasn't a bit hard to do. I like talking to God.'

'Good for you, Mark. Go to sleep now. We've had a lovely day together, haven't we?'

As she made her way to join Neil in the sitting-room she wondered how long he had stood outside the door before coming in, and how much he had heard. Would he approve of their prayers? She hadn't asked his permission first, but Louise's question came out of the blue and she had to answer it as she thought she should.

He had boiled the water and brought in the tray, setting it down on the coffee table in front of her armchair. She made his coffee and handed it to him. He took it from her and looked at her

'I don't know how to thank you, Cathy,' he began, 'for all you have taught my children in the short week that you have been here. I want you......' he was interrupted by the phone ringing. 'Damn!' he said, putting the mug down and getting up to answer it. I hope he doesn't have to go out to find Celeste, she thought.

She heard him say, 'I'll call her for you.' He came back and looked at her. 'It's Tom Cathcart. He'd like to speak to you.' He didn't look at all pleased.

She went to the hall and picked up the phone.

'Hello, Tom.'

'Cathy, hello! I wanted to say Goodbye to you. You said you were leaving on Wednesday for 'Maritzburg. I've been asked to work there for a week to sort out a problem and wondered if I could meet you some time and take you to dinner? We could also possibly manage a ride over the weekend.'

'That would be nice. You can either call me on the landline number which is in the directory or on my cell number which you have. The cottage is easy to find. I'll look forward to seeing you.'

He asked after the children and she answered briefly before saying Goodnight and returning to her armchair. She picked up her mug.

'I'm sorry the call interrupted what you were about to say. Please go on.'

'It doesn't matter now. I take it Tom will be in 'Maritzburg sometime soon and wants to see you. He's very persistent.'

'Yes, he is. He's coming for a week on business for the bank. We'll try to fit in a ride over the weekend.'

'Do you know he's in love with you?'

'Maybe he is. I'm not experienced enough to know whether it's the real thing or not. I haven't had many boy-friends. I always stayed at home to look after my mother, so I didn't have the opportunity to meet many boys. He's very nice and I think Garth would approve of him. I like him and enjoy being with him.'

'That's not enough, Cathy. When you really fall in love, it hits you so hard you can think of nothing else.'

'I'll have to wait for that moment, won't I? I'm off to bed. It's been a challenging day. I've loved  being with Mark – he's such a delightful child. I hope I have a son like him one day. You have three wonderful, lovable children.............. Goodnight, Neil.'

He looked at her and said, 'Goodnight, Cathy,' and watched her disappear down the passage. He looked miserable, poured himself a brandy, swallowed it down and went to bed.

She showered and climbed into bed.

She thought about her stay at the farm. It had been a tremendous week and to say Goodbye to them all in the morning would break her heart. Why did I throw away the chance of staying with them? I love the farm life and the children, yes, she had to admit, I even like Neil. With all his faults he has become to mean something to me.

Fifteen

Back home

Six o'clock came all too soon.

There was packing to complete and she wanted to have it done before breakfast. She had made a start the previous day and managed to complete it before she woke the children. They were sleepy-eyed, reluctant to get out of bed. She saw them dressed and at the table at seven when Neil walked through the back door.

'What a lot of sleepy-heads you are! Do you know what happened during the night? We have a new baby calf and Cathy will have the honour of naming her.'

'I really haven't a clue about names for cows!'

'Have you a second name?'

'Yes, it's rather unusual and I try not to use it. I was named after my great-grandmother in England, the one who taught us to make crumpets, Mark.' She paused, reluctant to tell them. Eventually she blurted out, 'It's Meredith.'

She waited for them to start laughing, but they didn't.

'Meredith,' repeated Neil. 'You know, I quite like it. It's nice to be different. I think we should shorten it and name the little heifer 'Merry' after you.'

'Yes, Dad, let's do that. I like it, too!' agreed Mark.

'And we do, too,' echoed the girls.

So Merry she became.

'What time do you intend leaving, Cathy? I'd like to be here to help you with your cases and put Peter in the car.'

What a difference, she thought, from the day when I arrived! What had made him change so much in ten short days?

'I thought about ten o'clock. I'd like to take a walk around the farm with the children before I go.'

'If you leave us today, Cathy, will you please come back soon?'

'I don't think I can, Helen, although I'd like to. It's difficult for me at the moment and I start teaching again next month.' She looked around at their sad faces. 'I'm going to miss you all so much, but don't worry, you'll all do fine without me. I'll come and visit you when I come again to see Claudia.'

'How many days will that be? I'll count the days on my fingers till you come back,' said Louise.

She had to end this sort of conversation before the tears started!

'Put on your sunhats and come for a walk with me around the farm so that I will remember you and your lovely home. '

As if she'd ever forget the happiness she had shared with them!

'You must see Merry before you leave. She's in the main shed with her mother. I'll be off, Cathy. See you at ten.'

She put the last bits and pieces into her cases and closed them down. The room looked empty and bare without her cosmetics and hair-brush on the dressing-table, her books, glasses, alarm clock, water carafe and torch on her bedside-table, dressing-gown and slippers beside her bed. Her personality had disappeared. She would be leaving Hartleyvale today, forever.

'I can't bear to leave them!'

No time now for regrets! She put on her hat and went to join the children on the porch. They were there waiting for her.

The girls walked on either side of her, holding her hand, and Mark ran on ahead.

'Look, Cathy, there's a fork-tailed drongo! He's flying to that high flame tree. Can you see him?'

'I can see a wagtail,' said Helen.

'I can see a big ant in the grass,' said Louise, not to be left out.

'I think it would be lovely if your Dad built a small fish-pond,

Mark, in the rockery, and put a bird-bath nearby. The birds like to splash in the water and take a bath every day.'

'That's a good idea! We could hang a bird-feeder in the tree near the rockery and we could watch them eating,' he said. 'I'll ask him to build a fish-pond when he has time.'

They walked past the flower-beds and flowering shrubs round to the back of the house, admiring the flowering shrubs, the perennials and the daisy bushes.

'This is where Mommy used to work,' said Helen, pointing to the extension rooms. 'We weren't allowed to go inside and see what she did there. Dad said it was her drawing- room. I wonder if she drew people, like you do, Cathy, or just trees and birds?'

What secrets did this farmhouse hide from the outside world? What was behind the locked doors? The windows were never opened and were fully curtained. No bright lights shone at night. The outside door was barred and padlocked. Why?

Some people swore the house was haunted and that they'd seen a ghost floating through the trees late at night. It was the ghost of a beautiful young woman dressed in white. She had long blonde hair and she carried something in her hand – was it a pencil or a stick?

The farm workers' quarters were far away, at the other side of the farm. If they heard any noise during the night they wouldn't worry to say anything – it was a white people's party and didn't concern them.

Neil arrived in the truck, parking it in the garage, and she was saved from answering Helen's question.

'I came back in time to go with you to see Merry. The children will love her. You lead the way to the main shed, Mark.'

He was so proud to do so. 'I'll be the first to see her.'

The girls took each of her hands and they made their way there.

'What colour is she, Daddy?' Louise wanted to know.

'You'll soon see for yourselves,' he replied.

And there she was, a black and white Jersey cow like her mother, standing next to her while she was being licked all over.

'Hello, Merry. You are so pretty,' said Helen. 'Now we still have a little bit of Cathy with us.'

Neil was looking at Cathy and smiling.

'I hope there's time for tea before you go. Run and tell Betty to make it now, Helen. Cathy, bring the Renault round to the front porch. Mark will help me carry your cases and put Peter's cage beside you.'

Was she hearing Neil correctly? Was he really sorry she was going or was he eager to get rid of her?

Louise still held her hand and looked up at her.

'I don't want you to go, Cathy.'

'I'll come back whenever I can to see you. You will see me again.'

'Promise?'

'Yes, I promise.' She knew she would have to come back and make sure that they were happy.

They finished their tea and she went to say Goodbye to Betty, giving her some Rand notes, a small 'bonsella' for all her help.

'Buy yourself something you are wanting. You have been a good friend. Thank you for what you do for the children.'

'I'll miss your help, Cathy. I hope you come back to us.'

She phoned Daisy to tell her she'd be home at lunch-time while her cases and Peter's cage were put inside her car. All was ready. It was time to leave them.

They stood around the door of the car ready to say Goodbye. She hugged and kissed them all, determined to keep a happy face and not cry. She turned to Neil and said, 'Goodbye, Neil,' but to her astonishment he pulled her towards him and bending down he kissed her tenderly on her open mouth. The children watched, smiling.

'Goodbye, Cathy. I wanted a kiss, too. Thanks for everything you have taught us.'

'Now we *all* have one of Cathy's kisses! Cathy kissed us all,' said Louise, clapping her hands.

There was a difference, though.

She had kissed the children.......... but Neil had kissed her.

He pressed an envelope into her hand. 'You've forgotten to ask for your pay cheque. Drive carefully and keep your car doors locked.'

She got into Pixie, turned on the ignition and drove down the drive. 'Goodbye,' she called. Glancing in her rear mirror she saw the children all waving and Louise clutching Neil's hand. Now the tears were gathering in her eyes, trickling down her cheeks and blurring her vision. She drove out of the gate and away from the farm.

It was no use. She pulled into the side of the road and stopped the car and had a good cry. After blowing her nose several times and wiping away the tears she felt better.

'I must pull myself together and get on with my life without them. They won't collapse without me. I know I have taught them how to do and make all sorts of new things. It will be a challenge for them.'

She started up again and continued her journey home.

It was lunch-time when she arrived at Hibiscus Cottage. Elijah saw her car, dropped the rake and was there to help her with her cases.

'Miss Cathy, it's good to have you home again! I have missed you.' He opened her door and shook hands with her. Peter recognised him and cocking his head at him, said 'Hello.....hello.'

'Hello, Peter. Have you been a good boy?'

'Clever boy. It's tea time! Cheers!'

'No, it's lunch time. Here's Daisy.'

She came bustling out to meet her, still holding a tea-cloth.

'Hello, Miss Cathy! I didn't hear the car. Did you have a good time with the children on the farm?' She took her hand in hers and shook it vigorously. 'How well you look!'

'Yes, Daisy, they are good kids. I feel I have known them all my life. It was hard to leave them and say Goodbye.'

They took her things and Peter's cage inside. Everything looked clean and polished. Daisy had picked a few flowers and arranged them in a vase on the coffee table and Elijah had put her post there as well. They were good people. They looked after her well.

'Thank you both for the welcome home. It's good to be here.'

'Lunch is ready, Miss Cathy.'

She found she was hungry and tucked into the ham and cheese omelette Daisy had made for her.

Life at the cottage would continue as before!

She phoned Garth to tell him she had arrived.

'I was pleased I had gone to find you and that I had met Neil. He has a well-run farm. I was impressed. How is his wife? I didn't like to ask.'

'She's in a rehab clinic to try to cure her drinking habits. She was once a very successful dress designer. She has no interest in the children. It's very sad and stressful for him.'

'I'm sure your stay would have helped them. I hope he paid you well.' She had quite forgotten to open the envelope! 'Come and have dinner with us soon. Julia will be phoning you.'

She had completely forgotten about it!

'I haven't opened the envelope yet, but he was very grateful for all I did. I shall miss the children.'

After enquiring after Julia she put down the phone.

In her handbag she found his envelope, opened it and inside was a cheque for double the amount she had agreed on. It was way beyond her normal month's salary! It was most generous of him. There was also a short note in his large legible hand-writing.

'*Cathy,*

*Please accept this from me. The care and love you have given us is worth far more than this meagre amount. I have come to expect you at the farm when I come home. It will be hard not to find you there. I'll miss you. I'm here if you ever need me. I'll come to you wherever you are.*

*Neil.'*

She sat down and read it again. It made her more homesick for the farm than ever!

That evening as she was watching the news the phone rang and she got up to answer it, expecting it to be Claudia, but she heard Neil's voice.

'Cathy, I'm phoning to see if you arrived home safely.'

'Yes, thank you. It was an easy run and I arrived in time for lunch. Elijah and Daisy were here to meet me. We got Peter settled and I phoned Garth to tell him I was home.'

'I was worried about you. There are so many hi-jackings these days, and you were on your own. The children are missing you. After their baths they begged me to read them a story which I did, hoping to read it comfortably in the sitting-room on the settee, but Helen said they were *bedtime* stories, and they had to sit on a *bed*! I didn't argue. Louise complained that you are a far better story-reader than I am! She said I must change my voice for the wolf's voice, like you do, and growl more! I'm afraid I need some story-reading lessons.'

'I'm sure they enjoyed every minute. Neil, thank you so much for your cheque – I was over-whelmed by your generosity.'

'Buy yourself a pretty blue dress to match your eyes. Goodnight, Cathy.'

She said Goodnight and put down the receiver.

She smiled as she pictured the three of them with him on Helen's bed while he read to them. There was one thing she knew for absolute certainty - Neil loved his children and he would never give them up to Celeste. He would fight tooth and nail to keep them.

Sixteen

Tom Cathcart

It took her a long time to fall asleep that night, and when she did, she awoke after two or three hours imagining that Helen or Louise was calling for her. When her alarm went off at six o'clock she felt like turning over and sleeping for another hour. She dragged herself out of bed and into a cool shower. That got her wide awake!

It would be another blistering day.

'Maritzburg was noted for its summer heat. Situated in a warm valley with water nearby, it was chosen to be the capital city by the Trekkers after they had defeated the Zulus in 1838. They had come from the Cape Colony in their ox-wagons, crossing the mighty Drakensburg Mountain peaks to find new land where they could settle and farm, thus escaping the restrictions at the Cape at that time. It was a hazardous journey, a marvellous feat of courage and endurance. Those who survived gazed with wonder at the undulating green pastures and flowing streams.

They chose farmland in this area and in northern Natal. Some Trekkers settled further south in a warm fertile valley which is where the capital city of Natal, Pietermaritzburg, stands today. Here the soil was rich and fertile; there was plenty of water for irrigation from the Msunduzi River and its tributary. They named it after two of their Trek leaders, Piet Retief and Gert Maritz. Above the town the Midlands of Natal rise rapidly four hundred metres.

The British took over the administration of Natal after the Dutch defeat in 1843. Martin West became the first Lieutenant- Governor of the new colony of Natal and made his home in Government House, a fine two-storey red-brick building built for its Lieut-Governors. The town of Pietermaritzburg was planned around a very large square and because of its position on the road to the north, the large central square was used as an outspan place for ox-wagons on their way from the coast to the hinterland beyond. Explorers and traders passed through the town, their wagons packed with animal skins, horns and tusks from their hunting excursions in the interior of Africa. Shops, houses and inns sprang up. In 1893 the huge red-bricked City Hall with its domes and fine clock tower was completed. Shady trees were planted on either side of the streets.

The gardens of the city are beautiful and colourful with many different flowering plants. Azaleas grow here in profusion, along with bougainvilleas, roses, arum lilies, fire lilies, red-hot pokers and many species of aloes. The people who made their homes here loved their gardens.

Cathy's great-grandfather and great-grandmother had emigrated from Yorkshire after the First World War in the early 1920s and their family had lived in Pietermaritzburg ever since then. Her grandfather had bought Chelmsford House and two adjoining plots in order to establish a fine garden. Now that her father and mother had died, in the terms of her mother's will Garth would inherit this valuable property.

While the two portrait pictures were still fresh in her mind Cathy decided she would try to finish them. She knew that once the schools opened there would be very little time for sketching. After breakfast she worked steadily and had practically completed the picture of the two girls. She placed it standing up on the mantel-piece and stood back to admire it. Yes, it made a charming picture.

After lunch she worked on the one of Mark and Neil. It took her longer to get Neil's features to her satisfaction but at last she was satisfied. She would take them to the art shop in the morning and choose frames for them. The landscape scene she would paint in oils later when she had learnt something more about painting in oils.

Julia phoned while she was watching a programme on TV to ask her to dinner the next evening.

'We want to hear more about your stay at Hartleyvale Farm. Garth has told me how impressed he was. Mum and Dad are coming as well. They haven't seen you since Mum's funeral and keep asking after you. Come at seven, Cathy.'

Next day she took the drawings to the art shop in town where she bought all her art requirements. The owner, Frans Fourie, knew her and came forward to greet her.

'I haven't seen you for some time, Miss Crawford. How are you?'

'I'm very well, thank you. The year-end at school is always hectic and I was on holiday over the Christmas holidays. I've brought you two portraits to frame.'

She undid the package and brought out the pictures. He studied them closely and smiled, obviously impressed with them.

'These are very good. What lovely girls! I don't recognise the children. Are they relations of yours?'

'No, just new friends. The children are delightful. I had to capture them on paper so that I can see them every day.'

He made suggestions about the framing and she decided finally on a simple narrow black frame.

'I'll have them ready for you on Monday. Come for them then.'

She thanked him and walked to where she had parked the Renault, passing several small shops on the way. In the window of a little boutique her eyes caught a vivid blue dress on a stand. She stopped to look at it more closely. It was made from a pretty floral silky material, the skirt falling in soft folds below the knee. The neckline was low, edged with a frilly loose collar and it had short, slightly puffed sleeves. I wonder if it would fit me? she thought. On impulse she went inside and asked the assistant if she could try it on.

'Certainly, madam. It looks your size.'

She came from the cubicle to study herself in a long cheval mirror in the boutique. It fitted perfectly. Being shorter than the model in the window the length was longer and suited her.

'It's your colour, madam. It could have been made for you!'

'I love it. I'll take it.'

It was expensive, a model from the 'House of Eve,' but she didn't hesitate and took out her credit card to pay for it. She drove triumphantly home and hung it up in her wardrobe cupboard.

'It's time I gave Daisy some of my clothes and bought myself some new things. I'll wear it to-night and watch the family's reactions.'

That night she dressed carefully. She chose a short string of pearls to wear with the dress, applied a light make-up and fluffed out her hair. Cool evening sandals were all that was necessary on her feet. In the wine-rack where her mother kept her wines she found a bottle of Cape Merlot red wine which she knew Garth and the family enjoyed and wrapped it up to take to them. The stars were out when she left the cottage.

It wasn't far to Garth and Julia's apartment in a nearby suburb. She hadn't seen Julia's parents for some time. She liked Rose and Ted Newbury. They had a gracious home in one of the newer residential suburbs. Julia was their only child, and they were inclined to dote on her. Their apartment was full of expensive gifts they had given her on her birthdays over the years - art treasures, valuable pieces of pottery, oil paintings, sculpture and glassware.

She knocked on the front door and Garth came to open it. He smiled when he saw her. He was very fond of his sister.

'Hello, Cath. Come inside. How pretty you look!' He kissed her.

'Hello, Garth. A small contribution for our meal,' she said, handing him the bottle.

'Thanks. Go through to the lounge and I'll get you a drink. Rose and Ted arrived ten minutes ago.'

She walked into the lounge and they watched her as she came smiling through the door. Ted stood up and went to kiss her.

'My dear, how well you look! Farm life must suit you. We want to hear all about your time there with the children.'

Rose got up from her chair and put an arm around her.

'Hello, Cathy, you look terrific! What a gorgeous dress! It must be a model from the 'House of Eve.' She was feeling the material and looked quite envious. 'How were your New Year celebrations?'

'We had a great party – finally got to bed around four o'clock.'

'Good gracious! You young people do live it up!'

Julia also commented on her dress. 'That blue is definitely your colour. You should wear more of it. It matches your eyes.'

They chatted for some while. She told them a little of her stay at the farm and related stories about the children. Then Julia announced that dinner was ready to be served. She had roasted a piece of sirloin which she knew was her father's favourite roast, and with it served Yorkshire pudding, roast potatoes, cauliflower au gratin, green beans and a rich gravy. It looked and smelt perfectly scrumptious! Garth carved the meat while Ted opened the wine. 'Please help yourselves and enjoy your meal.' There wasn't much left on their plates! Julia had attended a cookery course before she married Garth and delighted in cooking tasty meals. A creamy mousse followed.

It was nearly eleven o'clock when she got home and garaged the Renault. She hung up her blue dress carefully. It had been a success. She wished Neil had been there to see her wearing it. 'Perhaps there may come a time, but that possibility is very unlikely. Oh, well,' she thought, 'I'll keep it to wear for him.'

On Friday afternoon Tom called her.

'Hello, Cathy!' he sounded very happy. 'I arrived this afternoon so that I could be with you over the weekend. My work here starts on Monday. Are you free to have dinner with me to-night?'

'Yes, that sounds lovely.'

'I drove down this afternoon, so I have my car. Can I come for you at seven, or is that too early?'

'That's fine. I'll be ready.'

It would be good to see him again and hear the Estcourt news.

'I'm dining out again, Daisy. No cooking to-night! You may have the night off.'

'My, you are popular, Miss Cathy. You always stayed at home when your mother was alive. It's good that you are getting out more often. Go and enjoy yourself.'

She chose a strawberry pink floral dress with pin-straps to wear, and put on her pink sandals and gold jewellery. Tom thought she looked charming when she opened the door for him. He kissed her cheek.

'I've haven't seen you for seven whole days and I've forgotten how lovely you are!' He kissed her again 'Shall we go if you're ready?'

He took her to a small French restaurant that had a reputation for fine food. She had never eaten there before as it had been difficult leaving her mother in the evenings. Soft music was playing and most of the tables were already taken. After the hearty meal she had eaten the night before she chose something lighter - grilled hake in a delicious mushroom sauce served with a light salad. It was more than enough. Tom enjoyed a medium-rare steak which he said was 'perfectly grilled.'

She asked if he'd been riding during the past weekend, but he said he's been tied up at home as relations and friends had been to visit his parents. However, he did give her some news of Neil.

'I thought you'd be interested to hear that there has been a report in our local newspaper this week of the capture of an escaped alcoholic addict. No name was given but I'm sure it was Celeste. She had stolen money from the office and bribed the guard to let her out, escaping from the rehab clinic by taxi to the local night-club 'dive' where she had obtained alcohol and drugs. The police found her a day later lying on a dirty pavement a block away from an African downtown shebeen.' ( an African drinking house.) She was taken back to the rehab centre to sober up.'

'How dreadful! Poor Neil! It seems impossible to keep her in a home where she can be treated. It's been a perpetual worry for him for years. Apparently she has been cured from time to time, and released, returns home, only to run away some months later and start all over again. I wonder if she'll ever be able to lead a normal married life? She has no time for the children, which I think is so sad. I wonder what it was that started her off on this downhill road.'

'No-one knows and Neil is very secretive about her. A lot of what we hear is purely hear-say.'

'I tried to give the children a normal life. They have been so neglected. It's such a pity as they are bright, lovable kids. I miss them, Tom.'

He changed the subject to more pleasant news and spoke of a new show that was opening in February at the Estcourt Theatre Club.

'It's called 'Thank heaven for little girls!' It's one of those naughty laugh-a-minute shows which we all love. I think you should come up to see it. I hear it's very good. I'll book you in at a B&B and Mum will be only too happy to feed you. Would you come?'

'I'll think about it. We will have started the new school year with new pupils and it's a busy time, Tom. I'd love to see the show. It sounds great.'

'We'll put it on ice for the moment. I do want you to ride with me tomorrow. I've made enquiries and there's a school on the outskirts of the city called 'Come ride with me.' Sounds fun. The owner, Theresa Sampson, can let us have mounts so I booked them for nine o'clock. I hope that suits you.'

'I like that arrangement. We must go early before it gets too hot.'

'I'll call for you at eight. We have to find the riding school.'

They finished their coffee and he drove her home. She didn't invite him inside and after kissing her Goodnight he drove to his hotel.

'Goodnight, Tom. Thanks for a lovely evening. Until tomorrow.....'

She liked Tom very much as a friend, but she didn't want their relationship to develop any further than that. She had told him clearly so in Estcourt.


He was there at the cottage just after eight next morning and dressed for riding. Cathy invited him inside while she gave Daisy instructions for the day.

'This is a beautiful cottage, Cathy' He was gazing around the room at the furnishings and pictures. 'I love your pictures and paintings. I like this particular landscape in water colours and I notice it's signed C. Crawford. Is that you?'

'It is. I painted it a year ago.'

'It's very good.' He stepped forward to examine it more closely. 'I had no idea you were so talented! It's wonderful to be so gifted. I hope you're continuing with your art.'

'I am, but I don't get much time once school begins.'

He looked at her. 'You must miss your mother.'

'I do. I still haven't adjusted to the fact that she is no longer with me. I miss her companionship and the nights are lonely.'

'It will take time.'

They drove through the city centre on the way to find 'Come riding with me' following the directions Theresa had given him. It took some while but they eventually found it. The riding school seemed to be popular judging by the number of cars already parked under the trees. They could see that lessons were already in progress in the paddocks. Tom found a parking spot in the shade and they made their way to an office building adjoining the stables where they were greeted by a friendly grey-haired gentleman.

'Good morning to you! I'm Theresa's Dad, Fred Doyle. She asked me to welcome you as she's busy with lessons. You must be Tom and Cathy. We're happy to have you ride with us.' He shook Tom's hand and said Hi to Cathy. 'Come into the office and I'll take down your contact information and introduce you to the horses and grooms.'

'Thank you for taking us at such short notice. I'm only here for a week on business, but my friend Cathy and I would love a ride to explore this part of the 'Maritzburg outskirts.'

'A senior group will be leaving in fifteen minutes if you care to join them, or if you wish, you may like to go off on your own as you are experienced riders.'

'I think we'd better join the group today as we don't know this area at all, and could get horribly lost!'

Cathy nodded in agreement.

After noting their details he gave them a brochure of information about the school and then took them to the stables to meet Alfred and Amos, the grooms who were holding the horses in readiness for them, Duchess and Troy, two well-groomed horses. Tom looked them over and was happy with their condition.

'They both look good, Cathy. Put on your hat and we'll get

mounted and be ready to join the others.'

He helped her up and saw her settled and handed her the reins, then swung up on Troy, a fine dappled grey gelding. Alfred and Amos tightened the girths and adjusted the stirrups.

'The others are waiting for you outside the paddocks, sir.'

'Thank you. I'll have something for you later. Let's go, Cathy!'

They walked the horses to the far paddock, waving to Theresa as they passed her and she shouted back, 'See you when you return.'

There were four riders waiting for them, three girls and an older man who greeted them.

'Hello, I'm Roy Evans and the girls are Lucy, Megan and Jill. We're all fairly new riders, but very enthusiastic, never-the-less! Fred says this is your first visit to 'Come riding' so if you'd like to join us we'll show you where we usually take the horses.'

'That would be great. I'm Tom and this is Cathy.' They chatted a few minutes. 'You lead the way and we'll follow.'

They took a trail south-eastwards leaving behind the small plots and holdings as the land gave way to hills and valleys that made up the 'Valley of a Thousand Hills.' This huge valley is dominated at the western end by a plateau-topped sandstone mountain, some 660 metres high and geographically similar to Cape Town's Table Mountain. Its sides are precipitous and thickly bush-covered. From the summit you can see valleys and hills stretching endlessly around you. Natural bush vegetation covers the area where centuries ago thousands of wild animals roamed freely to graze where the grass was sweet and there were abundant green leaves to nibble on. The area is rich in flowering plants. Water is available from the many streams and rivers flowing down to the coast. Fish spawn in the rivers; animals from elephants, rhino, crocodiles to bush babies, vervet monkeys and mice live happily together. Here and there they could see isolated farmsteads dotting the hills and valleys.

'This was a natural paradise before the 17th century when people calling themselves the 'Nguni, led by a man named Dlamini, settled here on their move southwards from somewhere in central East Africa,' said Tom when they stopped for a short rest. 'From their many small clans grew the powerful Zulu nation into the many millions that occupy Zululand today.'

'It's a fascinating story,' said Roy. 'Their culture, like many African peoples, is rich in beliefs of the spirits of their ancestors and of the supernatural. Hills, rocks, rivers and waterfalls were said to be inhabited by ghosts and weird supernatural creatures. Witchdoctors are still highly regarded, some with awe, and play an important role in their lives. The Zulu kings were fierce warrior leaders and ruthless rulers. Their orders were unquestionably and implicitly obeyed. Near the Zulu village was the executioner's hill where offenders were put to death, if it pleased the king, sometimes merely for petty theft and minor crimes.'

The conversation changed to present day affairs and Cathy got to know the girls who worked in the city. They often rode together over the weekends.

'You should come and join us, Cathy, when Tom returns to Estcourt,' said Megan. 'I'll give you my cell number.'

They continued a little further and then it was time to ride back. By now the temperature was rising steadily. It was time to relax somewhere in the shade. Theresa met them in the stables as they were dismounting.

'Hello, I hope you enjoyed your ride and that you'll come again.'

'It was interesting to see more of this part of Natal, particularly on horseback, and to learn more of the history of the Zulu people. It was good to meet Roy and the girls. Thanks for giving us this opportunity. We'll certainly return. Your horses behaved well. I'll be in touch with you, Theresa.'

He drove her back to Hibiscus Cottage where they showered and changed.

'Stay for lunch, Tom. I have some cold chicken and bread rolls. I'll make a salad. It's all we need in this heat.'

He carried chairs and a small table outdoors, setting them up under a shady tree in the garden where there was a cool breeze blowing. He poured himself a beer and a cool drink for Cathy and took them outside. She joined him with their lunch-tray.

'This is perfect. Shall we repeat our ride tomorrow morning? I have some paperwork to do this afternoon ready for Monday, so sadly I must leave you after lunch. I would much rather snooze here on a rug under the trees with you beside me.' He patted the rug next to him and gazed longingly at her.

'It's very tempting, I know, but I also have things to attend to. I must clean out Peter's cage for one thing. Yes, please, I'd love another ride tomorrow if you have the time.'

'I'll be here at eight. Thank you for this lovely day together.'

Seventeen

A surprising visitor

Sunday promised to be another sunny day. Tom came for her at eight and they set off for 'Come riding.' Theresa was giving a young girl a lesson in the paddock but Fred was there in the office.

'Hello, Tom! It's good to see you and Cathy again.'

'We had a most pleasant ride yesterday and would like to ride Duchess and Troy again this morning if they haven't been taken.'

'They're ready to be exercised. Come with me to the stables. I'll have Alfred and Amos saddle them up for you.'

They waited a few minutes for Roy and the girls, but as they didn't arrive they decided to do some exploring on their own, setting off on the same trail before turning off in a more southerly direction.

They rode steadily for half an hour before taking a short rest. It was already very hot and humid, and Tom decided to return back to the stables in a circular direction.

'I think we've seen enough, Cathy, and it's too hot to continue.'

He took her back to the cottage, showered, but didn't stay long. She cooked him a quick snack and he left soon afterwards.

'I've been invited to lunch by the manager here, so I must leave you now. Thanks for today, Cathy. I'll call you during the week and I hope we can have another dinner together. I'm planning to drive home on Friday mid-afternoon.'

She waved him Goodbye and knew she would miss him and their rides. She had enjoyed his companionship. It was too hot to garden so she spent the afternoon watching a movie and later called Claudia, telling her how sad they all were when she left, and of Neil's generous cheque.

'Gosh, that was very good of him! He must have appreciated you.'

'I splashed out and bought myself a new dress to celebrate my good fortune, and I've decided it's time I bought some new clothes.'

'That's a good New Year resolution! I'm all in favour. Only one more week of holiday before we start the new term. Make the most of it and happy spending!'

She remembered she had to collect the portraits on Monday and after breakfast drove into the city. As she passed the boutique she glanced at the shop window and saw another pretty floral dress on a stand. It also was predominantly blue, but a different design and style from the first one. She went inside and the same assistant came forward to greet her.

'Hello! I wondered if you'd come back. That blue dress was perfect for you, and so is the one on the stand in the window.'

'I'm delighted with it. I wore it to dinner that evening and the family all remarked about it. Is this one also my size?'

'Yes, it is. Would you like to try it on? I'll get it down for you. There's another one on the rack here which you might like.'

She tried on both dresses. The material was the same, soft and cool, and drip-dry. She paraded in them in front of the long mirror. Both had touches of blue in the design and suited her fair colouring. She knew she must have them! She also ended up buying two new cotton blouses suitable for riding, and two pairs of jeans. It came to rather a staggering amount but she happily paid for them.

As she entered the art shop she saw her two portraits standing on easels in a prominent position in the front of the shop. He had done a wonderful job. They looked beautiful. Frans came forward when he saw her standing back admiring them.

'Good morning, Miss Crawford! They look wonderful, don't they? Do you wish to sell your portraits? I've had two offers already this morning, both running into four figures, and I think they are worth far more.'

'No, I won't sell them, Frans. I might do two replicas later on. I want these for myself. I know exactly where I'll hang them. How much do I owe you?'

He named a price and she paid him. Reluctantly he took them down from the easels and wrapped them up for her.

'I see you are already laden with parcels. Let me call my assistant to carry them to your car. Johannes!' he called and a young Coloured man appeared from the workshop behind the shop.

'Johannes, please carry these pictures to Miss Crawford's car.'

'It's not too far, Johannes. It's a blue Renault.'

'Yes, sir. I'll follow you, madam.'

She drove home feeling she'd won thousands of dollars!


After lunch she called Elijah to help her hang them in the sitting-room. He brought a small ladder and after she had positioned them side by side on the wall, the girls higher than the one of Neil and Mark, he hammered two small nails into the walls and hung them up. They stood back to admire them.

'You have done a fine job, Miss Cathy. These must be the people on the farm where you've been staying.'

'Yes, Elijah. I've been looking after these three children while their mother's been ill in a clinic. This is Mark, and the girls are Helen and Louise.'

'Is this their father? He looks a good man. I like his face. He must be strong and healthy to be a farmer and look after so many cows.'

'Yes, he's a good farmer and father to his children. Thanks for helping me. Now they will always be with me and I can see them every day.'

She put several Rand notes into his hand. 'Buy yourself something you are wanting.'

'I need a new shady garden hat, Miss Cathy. My old straw one is broken and I must wear a hat when I'm working in the garden. The sun is so hot. I'll buy a new one.' He was smiling broadly.

Daisy came to look at the portraits as Elijah carried out the ladder.

'My, you are so clever! What nice children! You must have been sorry to leave them. Will you see them again?'

'Maybe, Daisy, sometime in the future. The schools open next Tuesday and then I'll be busy with lessons to prepare and books to mark. I bought myself some new clothes today so I'll have some of my older ones for you.'

'Hauw! This is my lucky day!' She clapped her hands and did a little dance around the room. 'I'm so glad I'm not fat otherwise they wouldn't fit me. Thank you, thank you.'

Tuesday came and went quietly by. There was a brief call in the evening from Tom asking after her and to say he was back at the salt mines and missing her.

On Wednesday it was cooler after a good shower during the night and she was able to do some gardening. There were new red salvia plants that had seeded themselves from last year's flowers and needed thinning out and re-planting – a job she enjoyed doing. After lunch she had practically finished cleaning out Peter's cage when she heard a car coming up the drive. It came to a sudden stop at the cottage. Some-one got out, hurried up the path and banged loudly on the front door several times.

'I'm coming!' she called out.

Some-one's in a hurry, she thought as she went to open it wondering who the impatient person could be.

To her amazement she saw Neil standing there in front of her!

She knew something must be terribly wrong to have brought him to her. He looked extremely worried and upset.

'Cathy!' he said as he looked at her and took hold of her hands, holding them tightly together in his hands. 'Thank God I've found you!' It was a cry of relief.

'Whatever is the matter? Come inside and sit down and tell me.'

He sat next to her on the sofa and the story gradually came spilling out. She had never seen him so stressed. He had been angry when he was called out at night to find Celeste, but he was never as stressed as he was now.

He took out his handkerchief and wiped his face. 'It's Mark.'

'What has he done?' It must be something serious!

'He's had a bad accident and he was calling for you. He wants you. Now he's unconscious in hospital!'

'Oh no! What happened to him?'

'He was riding his bicycle and going too fast, as usual, coming around the corner of the sheds. He didn't see Sam driving the tractor until it was too late. He hit the tractor at speed and was thrown off his bike hitting his head against the cement wall of the shed. It happened so fast that Sam could do nothing – there was no time to move out of the way. He heard a loud crack as Mark hit the wall and fell down. Oh, Cathy, I'm so worried. There's a possibility he may have damaged his brain.' He stopped for breath. This was a long speech from Neil! 'I phoned Doc Kevin and he came over right away. He's been such a good friend, Cathy, I've known him since high school days and we played rugby together in the A team.'

She felt quite ill.

'Now he's gone into a coma.'

He looked at her in utter desperation. She was so upset she was at a complete loss for what to say.

'I've come to ask you to come back with me to the hospital. Cathy, please help me.' He took her hands again. 'I can't do this on my own. If I had phoned you with this news I wasn't sure what you'd say or do, so I felt it better if I came and explained it to you, and asked you myself. If you're coming, we need to get back right away. Joy has been marvellous and has taken the girls.'

What could she say? It was impossible to refuse this request involving one of the children that she already loved. She sat still and said nothing, her mind racing ahead, thinking of the awful possibilities this accident could bring.

'Mark needs you, Cathy, and I need you at the farm to help me get through this nightmare. Please don't say 'No.' I can't do it without your support ...... I realise that school starts next week and you're committed there. Could you ask for some extra time?'

'I'll have to tell Miss Thomas and see what she says..... I don't think she'll be pleased.......She hates these sort of disruptions to the normal running of the school, especially at the beginning of the year when she has everything planned........but she's very fair and I think she'll agree. She'll find some-one to take my class...Yes, I'm coming back with you........ I must go to Mark............. I love him, Neil.'

He did something then that she never expected.

He moved his hands to each side of her head, tilted up her chin, and looking at her steadily in her eyes, he kissed her, tenderly but firmly at first, and then with an urgent hungry desire.

He continued to look at her as a few seconds ticked by. Neither of them spoke. Cathy could feel her heart thumping.

She wanted to do what she would have done to his children in their trouble – put her arms around him to comfort him in his distress and tell him not to worry, it would soon be 'all better.'

But it might not get better!

'Cathy, I'm so sorry. Forgive me. I had no right to do that, but you're such a lovely person and I'm so relieved and grateful to you. I don't know how to thank you enough.'

'I think we both need a drink, or a cup of tea or something! What would you prefer?' She tried to speak calmly, but his kiss had unnerved her and shaken her more than she cared to admit.

'I'd like a strong cup of tea, please, and as I'm driving home, a drink is not possible. I'll wait until we've seen Mark and are home.'

She called to Daisy in the kitchen. 'Make us a pot of tea, please Daisy, and cut some fruit cake.'

She came running through to the sitting-room, and stopped when she saw a stranger with her. 'I heard a car and thought it would be your brother.'

'This is Mr Middleton, Daisy, from the farm. Mark has had an awful accident while he was riding his bike and is very ill in hospital. I'm going back to be with him. Please bring my case and I'll start packing.' She disappeared to the kitchen to switch on the kettle. 'The bathroom's down the passage on the right, Neil. I'll start getting some clothes together.'

All she could think about was Mark lying in a hospital bed, still and not moving. .

She felt the tears starting and brushed them away with her fingers. 'Oh, dear God,' she prayed, 'please help him to come through this ordeal and be a normal little boy again.'

Daisy carried in her case and she hurriedly threw in an assortment of clothes, her riding gear, and her little jewellery box which she took with her wherever she went. In a wild moment she packed her new clothes on the top.

'I might as well take them. I'll need the jeans and blouses, and I might need the dresses. Better take them and have them with me.'

Her cosmetics went in next with her alarm clock, hair brushes and the book she was reading. She closed down the lid, and pulled her case along the passage on its wheels to the front door. Neil saw her dragging it.

'Let me do that for you. Are we taking Peter with us?'

'Yes, please. He'll be lonely here and the girls love him.'

'Let's have tea first and then I'll load the car.'

As she was pouring the tea he said 'Cathy, I've been looking at the portraits you've drawn of my family and I'm absolutely astounded by their excellence and accuracy! I had no idea what a superb artist you are, and there's a watercolour here which I love and I see it has your name on it.'

She handed him a large mug of tea and a slice of fruit cake.

'Yes, I did the water-colour a year ago. My father was very artistic and I've inherited his gift. I was encouraged to draw from an early age, but that's enough about me. Tell me more of Mark. What did the doctor at the hospital tell you?'

'It's a matter of waiting till he comes out of the coma and that may take a few days. I'm scared to think that far ahead! Cathy, if you're ready I'd like to get back to him.'

'Shouldn't I take the Renault? I think it would be useful if I had my car there.'

'You're right. You drive ahead and I'll follow you.'

He stowed away her case, carried Peter's cage to the Renault and put it on the front seat beside her.

'Look after the cottage for me please Daisy.' She pressed some notes into her hand. 'Buy whatever food you want. See that you lock up the cottage before you leave each day. Phone Garth if there's any urgent trouble. You have his number. I'll phone you when I've seen Mark and give you news of him.'

'Don't you worry, Miss Cathy. Elijah and I will be here. I pray the Lord will make him better. You must go to him.'

Neil also gave her some Rand notes.

'This is for you and Elijah. Thank you for looking after Cathy. You are good people.'

She said Goodbye to them and they watched the cars driving away.

Halfway to Estcourt she remembered she hadn't phoned Garth.

'I'll phone him when I get there.'

Eighteen

An anxious time

The sun had set and the sky was darkening as they drove through the farm gates. Lights from the house beckoned them home. Betty had heard the cars and was there to meet them. Neil was the first out of the car, racing up the porch steps.

'I'm phoning the hospital and will help you later,' he called to her.

She nodded and went to say Hi to Betty.

'Everything's fine here, Miss Cathy, but the house is so quiet with nobody around. I'm glad you've come back to us. We have all missed you and Mr Middleton most of all. He comes in for his meals and I see him looking around for you. Please don't go away again!'

Neil emerged from the office and she was saved from answering.

'I've spoken to the Sister and there's no change, Cathy.'

'I didn't think there would be, but I want to see him to-night, Neil.'

'Let me get your things and Peter inside, and I need a drink. Have you cooked some supper for us, Betty?'

'Yes, I made a salad and a macaroni-cheese-and-mince dish for you. If you don't want it, I can freeze it.'

'Yes, we do need a meal before we see Mark. I'm hungry and I'm sure Cathy would like some too.' He turned to her. 'Come to the sitting-room and have a drink with me. You also need something. This has come as a shock for you. I'm pouring you a glass of wine.'

She watched him pour himself a brandy and water, and then her wine. It was beautifully cool and she enjoyed his choice of the light white wine for her. They hardly spoke.

Betty rang the bell to announce that supper was on the table. They enjoyed their light supper and left soon afterwards.


The hospital was a small red-bricked building near the town centre. Neil took her inside to meet the Sister in charge of the children's wards, a middle-aged lady who he had met previously.

'Good evening, Mr Middleton. We're watching Mark carefully and there's been no change as yet since this morning when you saw him.'

He introduced Cathy. 'Thank you, Sister. This is Miss Crawford who has been looking after the children for me. She's become very fond of Mark and she would like to see him.'

'By all means. Take her to his ward. Nurse Botha's on duty and will allow you to see him.'

He led her down a long passage and finally they came to Room 25. He knocked and entered as Nurse Botha rose from a chair to speak softly to him. Cathy followed behind and saw Mark lying on his back, his eyes closed. She moved to his bedside. He looked such a tiny, defenceless scrap in the middle of the hospital bed! Her heart turned over and tears blocked her vision, trickling down her cheeks. Suppose he was brain-damaged or that he should die? She stroked his forehead and moved his hair over to the side where he always wore it. His face was serene and there was no cheeky smile. She imagined he would look exactly like that if he was lying there dead. Her body was quietly shaking as she inwardly sobbed for him.

Neil saw her eyes swimming with tears. She felt an arm go around her shoulders.

'Here's my handkerchief. Don't cry, Cathy. He's going to recover. Be strong for him. Hold his hand and squeeze it so that he can feel you are with him. Talk to him, too. They often can hear you.'

She wiped her eyes, desperately trying to control herself. She covered his small brown hand with her hand and held it fast, squeezing it. This will never do – I must pull myself together. It was a huge effort for her to speak normally, but she swallowed several times, managing at last to find her voice.

'I'm here with you, Mark, and I'm staying with Dad and the girls to be near you, because we all want you to get better so that you can hear lots more stories and finish your Lego Star Wars fighter plane. Can you feel me holding your hand and squeezing it? I brought Peter with me. You love Peter, don't you? And I love you. I'll be here tomorrow to see you. Goodnight, Mark.'

She turned to give Neil his handkerchief and could see he was also emotionally moved. He took her arm.

'Come, Cathy, let's go home. There's nothing more we can do here for him. Thank you, Nurse.'

'I'll phone you if there is any change, Mr Middleton. Goodnight.'

She sat close beside him in the truck and left him to do the talking, what little there was. By the time they reached the farm she was in control of herself.

'I'm getting straight to bed, Cathy. It's been an exhausting day. I'm so relieved to have you here with me. I'll sleep easier to-night.'

'I intend to do the same, Neil. Goodnight. I'll unpack tomorrow.'

He watched her walk to the guest- room and close the door, then he switched off the lights and went to his room. It had been a long day, but he was pleased he had found her and seen where she lived, and taken her to see Mark. He thought about her portrait sketches. They were outstanding.......brilliant......uncanny......so lifelike. He had no idea she was so talented. He realised he was thinking more and more about her each day and wanted to have her with him.......

He fell asleep knowing he was falling in love with her..........

She opened her case and took out her nightie, toilet bag and her dresses to hang up. She set her alarm for six o'clock and climbed into bed. The rest would wait for the morning. To get into bed and fall asleep was more important, and all she wanted to do.

Six o'clock came all too soon, but once she was up and showered she felt a lot better. Neil was seated at the table studying the newspaper while he waited for her, but he threw it down when he saw her coming and stood up.

'You look rested this morning. Do you feel better?'

'Yes, much better. I slept well.' They sat down together. 'Neil, I realised I didn't tell Garth I was coming. May I phone him this morning? He'll be surprised that I've come back to the farm.'

'Of course. If you like I can also speak to him.'

'I don't think that will be necessary. I'll call after nine when he'll be in his office. What are the visiting hours at the hospital and what are the girls doing today?'

'Joy has offered to have them again today and the times for the hospital visiting are from eleven to twelve. If you go this morning while I'm busy here with the milking, I'll go this afternoon. Would you mind doing the shopping for me? Betty has made a list and it would save me the time. Charge it to my account.'

'I'll go after I've seen Mark. I'd also like to phone Miss Thomas.'

'Please go ahead. The phone is there for you to use.'

She couldn't believe the change in him! He was a different, approachable, polite person.

Betty came in with their porridge plates and the eggs and bacon. `
He had a good breakfast and left as soon as he had eaten.

'I'll be here all morning if you need me. See you at lunch-time.'

The new day had begun.


Garth was most surprised and not a little upset to hear she was back at Hartleyvale, but sympathetic when he heard about Mark.

'Do you think he has the chance of a good recovery?'

'We won't know until he comes round, and that might take days.'

'Do you intend to stay that long? What will you do when the schools open? You're committed there and Miss Thomas depends on your support and loyalty, Cath.'

'I'm phoning Miss Thomas for her advice. I can't and won't leave him, Garth. Perhaps I can get some extended leave.'

'Keep in touch and let me know her decision. Perhaps she can apply for a temporary replacement if she knows beforehand that you'll be absent a week or two. See what she says.'

She found Miss Thomas's home phone number in the directory, but when she called the maid said she was still on holiday and would only return on Sunday.

'Will you please tell her Miss Crawford phoned and that I'll call again on Sunday evening?'

Lastly she phoned Claudia, prepared for a lot of questions. She was lucky to find her at home and she picked up the phone.

'Hello, Claudia. It's me, Cathy. I have some news for you.'

'Good show! What have you bought now? A coat, new shoes?'

'I bought another two dresses, jeans and shirts for riding, but that isn't the news I was about to tell you.'

'What have you done now? Got engaged?'

'No, nothing so romantic.'

'Fallen off a horse and broken your leg?'

'No. I'm not injured....... Claudia, I'm back in Estcourt.'

'What? Back on the farm again? You're joking.'

'It's true. Mark's had a bad accident on his bike, hit his head on the cement wall of the cattle shed and is in hospital. He was knocked unconscious and he's now in a coma. Oh, Claudia, we're all so worried that his brain might be damaged! I can't imagine that lively, lovable little boy an invalid! Neil is terribly upset. He came to tell me and I've come back to be with him. I couldn't desert that child. I've grown so fond of all those kids.'

'What a tragedy! I'm so sorry. I can see him now, playing with the twins in the pool. Please let me know when you have more news. Mum, Dad and the boys will be upset to hear this news.'

She had a chat to Betty about the shopping and added a few more items to the list. She said Mr Middleton had taken her to see Mark the previous evening when she arrived and how seriously ill he was.

'What is a coma, Cathy?'

She tried to explain simply what it was and how it was caused.

'His brain has stopped working in its normal way because he hit his head so hard, and he can't do the things he would do before the accident. It's like fainting, but it's deeper and more serious and it lasts longer. It may be days before he recovers from it. We will only know then what has been damaged. It's a very worrying time, Betty.'

'Hauw, that poor child! I pray God will make him better so that he can ride his bike again. He should go to school in Estcourt so that he'd have friends here and not be sent to boarding-school; then he'd have boys to ride and play with him. He's a lonely child.'

'I know, Betty. It would be best for him to be home and to mix with boys of his own age, but it's difficult without a mother. At least he has boys there to be friends with and he is well looked after. Mr Middleton can't do everything.'

'He should marry again and have a proper wife.'

'How can he, when he's already married?'

'She has never been his wife. I can see he doesn't love her or want to be married to her.'

'I'll do all I can to help the children while I'm here. They're such good kids and I've grown very fond of them. I must go to Mark now. I'll be home before lunch and I'll bring the cold meat and salad stuff. We should start a vegetable garden and get the children to help.'

'That would be a good idea. I know how to make compost from the green leaves and skins I cut from the vegetables I cook.'

'I'll talk to Mr Middleton about it. Even if I'm only here a few days I could help to get it started.'

The more she thought about it on the way to the hospital the more appealing and necessary it became. She knew how much her mother had loved her herb and vegetable garden before she became confined to a wheelchair. She would spend hours pottering about in it and advising Elijah what to do and plant. And how satisfying it was to pick the green beans or cauliflower you have grown and cook them straight away for dinner! Or use the lettuce from the garden for a lunch salad.

She went straight to Mark's ward. A different nurse was on duty watching him. She got up when she saw Cathy.

'Good morning, Miss Crawford. Mr Middleton phoned earlier and said you'd be coming. There's no change, I'm afraid.'

'I'll sit with him to relieve you a while.'

'I'll be back in ten minutes.'

Cathy pulled the chair nearer to Mark where she could sit close to touch him and hold his hand. He looked very peaceful, so like she imagined Neil would look when he was asleep. She bent over and kissed him. She stroked his fingers and squeezed his hand in hers as she told him she loved him and that she had said a prayer asking God to make him better, just like the prayers he said when he went to bed.

'I'm staying at the farm and I'll come every day to talk to you. I'll stay with you when you come home, Mark. I have missed you so much. I know you'll get better soon and we'll make more crumpets for Dad. We all want you to come home to us.'

The nurse returned and they sat together watching him.

'I met two nurses from the hospital at a New Year's Eve party. Do you happen to know Jane and Emily? Jane's boy-friend is Ben. I can't remember their surnames.'

'Yes,' she said. 'I trained with both of them. I'm Tracey Lewis. Sometimes we work together in the same ward, but they're on night duty this week, in the women's ward. How did you come to meet them?'

'A friend, Tom Cathcart, and I rode with them after Christmas, and then we made up a party with them for the New Year's Eve Dance in the Town Hall. They were both good fun. I was here on holiday at the time and now I'm working for Mr Middleton to look after his three children.'

There was a knock on the door and a Sister entered with the Doctor who had come on his rounds to see Mark. They stood up and Cathy introduced herself.

'I'm pleased to meet you. Let me examine young Mark this morning.' They watched him as he first looked at Mark's chart, and then went to his bed to examine him, lifting up his eyelids. He shook his head. 'There's no change, I'm afraid.'

He said something to the Sister and then nodded to Cathy and they moved away to visit his other patients.

'He's the Neurologist in charge of Mark,' whispered Tracey.

She sat with him a while longer before kissing him Goodbye.

'I'll go now, Nurse. I'll come this evening with Mr Middleton.'

She drove to the supermarket and came out with a trolley laden with packets. With her own money she had bought chocolates, biscuits and biltong for the children. Betty helped her unpack and put everything away. She just had time to make a green salad before Neil came in for lunch.

'How was Mark?'

'The Neurologist who is attending to him came while I was there and examined him. There's no change, Neil. I sat with him for an hour and talked to him before the bell rang for visitors to leave. I did all the shopping. The supermarket was fairly quiet and I managed to get all that was on the list.'

'Thanks for doing that. I hate shopping!'

'Most men do. My father bought the first thing he saw, paid the assistant and walked out of the store with it!'

They sat down to enjoy the cold lunch, fresh bread rolls and fruit.

'How was your morning?' she asked, to break the long silence, expecting his usual brief reply.

'Very busy. The few problems which cropped up yesterday while I was away needed to be dealt with. I don't know what I'd do without Sam. He's been with me for several years. He's so reliable and takes messages for me. My Zulu workers have the greatest respect for him. Did you get through to Garth and Miss Thomas?' She briefly gave him the details and he went on. 'You must come and see Merry when you have time. She's growing steadily. The children come every day to see her.' He stood up and looked at her. 'I have some work to do in the office before I leave to see Mark and afterwards I want to check on a boundary fence. Would you like to ride with me? It should have cooled down by then.'

This was a long speech from Neil! She was taken by surprise that he had asked her to ride with him.

'I'd love a ride. I'll get changed and be ready when you return.'

'Good. I'll see you later.'

He left her to walk down the passage to his office. She sat at the table finishing her tea, thinking of the ride with him. He was an unpredictable character! She didn't quite know what to make of him.

He was so rude to her when she first arrived and now he was thoughtful and considerate. Was it Mark's illness that had changed him for the better? Recently he had shown her another side of his character that she thought didn't exist.

She decided it was a good opportunity to clean and tidy the girls' toy cupboard in the play-room while they were with Susan. They loved their dolls and teddies, and were always dressing them up in different outfits, or tucking them up in bed in their pyjamas.

She was changed and ready when he got back after four o'clock. Betty appeared with the tea-tray and a plate of crunchies which Cathy knew he had liked and she had included on the shopping list. He flopped down into a chair on the porch. She didn't expect there'd be any change in Mark's condition otherwise he would have told her immediately he stepped out of the truck.

'There's no change, Cathy. I managed to speak to the Sister on duty. Tomorrow is the third day and it's possible he may gain consciousness then. We have both seen him today – do you think we should go again to-night?'

'I'll go with you if you'd like to go.'

'Let's have tea and go for our ride. The horses need exercising and I must check that west boundary fence. It won't take me long to get changed. Pour the tea please, Cathy. I see we have crunchies today – how nice!'

He helped himself to one. Cathy smiled and handed him his mug of tea. He drank it down and got up to change.

'Would you like to wait in the truck for me when you've finished your tea?' She nodded with her mouth full of crunchie.

She put on her hat and climbed into the truck. He drove to the stables and called Jackson, a young Zulu boy in charge of the horses, to saddle them up.

'You are riding Starlight, the mare, and my horse is Captain, a stallion. I hope they'll produce a foal for Mark one day.'

Jackson brought out Starlight for her. She looked a nervous, spritely animal. Neil watched Cathy who was looking apprehensively at her. She was hoping for a less spritely mount.

'Looks are deceptive, Cathy. She's actually quite docile and has a gentle nature. Don't worry, she'll be fine. Let me help you up.'

He saw her comfortably settled and handed her the reins after Cathy had pulled up the girth and adjusted the stirrups. Then he swung up on Captain.

'We'll be away about an hour, Jackson.'

They walked the horses at first so that she could get used to Starlight, and then Neil changed to a trot.

'Are you OK?' he shouted.

'Yes, we're getting along just fine,' she shouted back.

Neil rode beside her and she noticed how skilfully he handled the big stallion. He stopped after a while to point out various features.

'Those peaks you can see straight ahead of us are the highest in the Drakensberg range. That's Champagne Castle in the far distance, Cathy. It's 3300m high, and Cathkin Peak and Cathedral Peak are the next two peaks to the right of it. Far below us in the valleys the gravel road winds through to take you to the holiday resorts. Can you see parts of the road appearing on the other side of those smaller hills?' He pointed down to them. 'There it is, zigzagging below us.'

Cathy was gazing at the sheer beauty all around her.

'This is a most awesome part of South Africa and there's so much here for me to sketch! I think you have a beautiful farm, Neil, an ideal place where children can grow up healthy and strong. It's not too large to control, you have sufficient water, and it's not far from a good-sized town. Did you inherit the farm from your parents? Did they farm here?'

'Yes, I was virtually an only child. I had two elder brothers who died in infancy. I inherited the farm from my father, Sidney Middleton, who married the eldest Hartley daughter, Sarah Ann Hartley. Her mother was Florence Dawson who married Charles Hartley, a descendant of settler emigrants from England. His family arrived in Natal and bought the farm. When he died Florence and Charles inherited it as there were no male heirs and Sarah Ann was the eldest of five daughters. Sidney named it after her. There were only daughters in her mother's marriage and five sons-in-law! My grandmother was a remarkable hard-working woman, who outlived her family and died when she was 92, working on the farm until the day she died.'

'So that's how Hartleyvale got its name! You have a wonderful family history. Florence must have been an amazingly strong woman to have worked the farm until the day she died! I wonder what happened to the other Hartley girls? It would be fun to find out. Possibly you have aunts living in this area. Have you any old family photographs? I would love to see them.'

'Unfortunately, no. Celeste wouldn't allow any photograph albums to be kept or photographs to be displayed, and she burnt a lot of them before I discovered what she was doing and stopped her. She had some weird ideas. I never understood her.'

'What a pity to lose those links of your family history.'

'We must ride on, Cathy. The horses are rested and I must inspect these fences before we can return home. I'll phone the hospital and then decide what we should do.'

The fence had been cut by poachers, but was not too seriously damaged and he managed to pull it together with pieces of wire that he had brought in a rucksack.

'That will keep the cows inside. They don't usually wander as far as this, and Sam and the boys will do a permanent job tomorrow.'

They returned by a different route, equally as picturesque. Jackson was there waiting for them and took the reins. Neil helped her dismount and she slipped easily down as his arms closed around her. He undid the strap of her hat and handed it to her.

'You have a good head of lovely fair hair, Cathy,' he said as they walked to the truck. She was surprised that he had noticed it and had commented on it.

'Yes, it has a natural wave and is easy to control. I spend very little time at the hairdresser,' she replied for something to say. 'Helen and Louise both have pretty fair hair, but Mark is dark, like you.'

He left her to shower and phoned the hospital.

She returned to the sitting-room to find he had poured a glass of wine for her and was watching the evening news.

'There's no change, Cathy. I think we'll stay home and have an early night. Come and enjoy your wine with me. You have heard my family history this afternoon and now I want to hear yours.'

This was so unexpected of him! And why was he suddenly so attentive and caring? Was this due to the seriousness of Mark's injury? There was no time to puzzle it out so she plunged into the life story of her parents and grandparents who were also emigrants from England.

'My family weren't farmers and lovers of the land, like yours were, but they did love their trees and gardens which were their pride and joy. They were townsfolk, a family of bankers, and settled in Pietermaritzburg, the capital of the new colony of Natal, after the British took over the Cape from the Dutch. They have lived here ever since. Garth and I were born in Chelmsford House and grew up there. When my father died suddenly two years ago, the upkeep became too much for my mother, and as Garth had left us to marry Julia, we moved into Hibiscus Cottage on the property and let the big house. I wish my parents had had more children – I would have loved a sister and another brother – but she wasn't a well person and relied heavily on my father. She collapsed with heart trouble after he died and was put into a wheelchair. Garth bought Peter for her, and he became her companion. My only grandmother, my mother's mother, now lives in England in a retirement home. She has two sisters, cousins and many friends in the village who live nearby and visit her.'

'I can see now why you love the farm and the open country-side where you can ride and sketch and paint to your heart's delight! This is where you should be, not in a town, or confined to a class-room....' He suddenly stopped, realising he had said too much. 'Forgive me, Cathy, my thoughts were running away with me.'

She looked down at her hands. 'You're probably right. I love the farm and I've been so happy here with the children, but I do have a career and I love that, too. I always wanted to be with children and become a teacher. I could never be happy confined to an office environment and work with a lot of women.'

They were both quiet, deep in thought. The shrill ring of the telephone suddenly broke the silence and Neil got up to answer it. She hoped it wouldn't be a call concerning Celeste. He hadn't mentioned her name recently. She wished he would do so and talk to her about his marriage! He came back to the sitting-room, looking worried.

'It's Tom, asking for you,' he said, flopping down into his armchair. 'He sounds very concerned about you.'

Tom! She'd completely forgotten about him! She went to the phone in the hall and picked up the receiver.

'Hello, Tom....'

'Cathy!' he broke into her sentence. 'I had no idea you were back at the farm! Why didn't you call me and tell me? Why are you back there? I have just phoned the cottage to ask how you are, only to learn from Daisy that Neil had come for you and that you went back with him!'

'I'm sorry, Tom. It's been a long, nightmare four days, believe me. Mark had an accident on his bike, and was asking for me before he went into a coma. He's been in hospital all this time. We were terribly worried, wondering if his brain was damaged. Visiting the hospital three times a day is exhausting enough without wondering whether he'll recover or not.'

'Poor kid! Has he come through the coma yet?

'No, there's still no change. We pray he'll come round any time now. I want to stay here with him, Tom. It might take another week or two. He'll have to have a head scan and all sorts of tests to determine the extent of his injury. After that I imagine a lot of exercises with physiotherapists will be necessary. The doctors will study all the reports before they are satisfied that he has recovered and only then will he be allowed to go home. This will all take time.'

'Do you intend staying there that long? What about your teaching? The schools re-open next Tuesday.'

'I've phoned Miss Thomas and I'm hoping she'll apply for a temporary replacement. I'll come home and take over my class as soon as I am sure he will be a normal little boy again. I cannot desert him, Tom. I've grown too fond of the children.'

'Well, you know what you're doing and it's your decision. Will you have any free time to ride with me while you're here?'

'I doubt it. It seems highly unlikely.'

'I'll phone again in a day or two and see how Mark is, and whether a ride is possible. I have missed being with you!'

'Let's see how Mark progresses. I must go, Tom, as the dinner bell is ringing. Goodbye.'

She joined Neil and they made their way to the dining-room. Betty had cooked a chicken casserole which was very tasty, served with brown rice, butternut, broccoli and peas. Neil enjoyed his meals and ate a good plateful. He worked long hours and needed sustaining meals to keep him going during the long working hours.

He waited until Betty had left the room and their meal had been served before he asked about the call.

'I presume Tom was displeased to learn that you were back helping me with the children.'

'I think he was very surprised when I said I intend to stay over to be with Mark after the schools have opened. It is very irregular.'

'I'm undecided whether to send him back to boarding school, or to try to have him here at home with the girls so that we can live as a normal family. If he went to the local school then he'd have friends in the neighbourhood. It would mean adjusting my schedule to take both Mark and Helen to school and back home, probably at different times, as he would have sports practices in the afternoons and have to be collected later.' He put down his knife and fork. 'What do you think?'

She was quiet as she thought about this arrangement and they continued to eat their meal. It would be better, but would it be possible for him to do, knowing how busy he was, and how inevitably a major problem could arise out of the blue?

He went on. 'I've already tried to tempt you to stay on at the farm, offering you a salary five times more than what you earn now, but still you have refused me.'

'I don't know what to say, Neil. I know what I want to do, but it's a difficult decision. Let's leave it until we have Mark safely home and hopefully by then I shall know.' She had finished her dinner but still sat at the table. 'I do think it would be better to have him here with you as a family, but I'm not sure if you could manage the farm and do all the fetching and carrying, plus cope with all the problems that are bound to crop up.'

'That's why I need you here with us, but it's not my main reason.' He stood up. 'Sleep on it, Cathy. I'll be waiting for you.'

He watched her make her way to the sitting-room door, turn to him and stop.

'I don't think I'll stay up for coffee to-night, Neil. I'd like to get to bed early. I loved our ride this afternoon; thank you for taking me. Starlight and I worked well together. When the time comes the girls must also learn to ride.'

'It was all my pleasure. Yes, the girls will definitely learn to ride, and love all animals. I enjoyed showing you more of the farm. We must ride together more often. Goodnight, Cathy. Sleep well.'

He watched her disappear down the passage and into her room. He got to thinking of the story she had told him of her family. He could see she had led a sheltered life in a good home. She had a quiet nature; she was a gentle person who had a great capacity for love.

He knew he had fallen in love with her and wanted her with him and the children. She was the one who could give him the kind of love he needed, but did she have any feelings for him? Or was it Tom she wanted? Could she come to love him as much as he loved her?

He tried to watch a TV movie for a while, but he found he couldn't concentrate and finally switched it off and went to bed, wondering how Mark was, and if the new day would bring the change they were hoping for.

Nineteen

Mark comes home

At breakfast the next morning Cathy suggested to Neil that she felt the girls should come home.

'It's so good of Joy to have had them but they have been with her three days and I'm here now to look after them. I can fetch them before we go to the hospital.'

'Yes, you're right. I shouldn't overstep her generous offer. Could you do that while I'm finishing off the milking? I'll give you directions to their farm. It's not too far away and the road's fairly good. I'll phone her now and tell her you'll come for them.'

The girls were packed up and ready waiting for her on the wide veranda when she arrived an hour later. They ran to meet her.

'Oh Cathy, I *knew* you'd come back to us!' cried Helen as she put her arms around her waist and hugged her.

'Please stay with us now, forever and ever. Don't leave us again,' said Louise. 'Daddy doesn't read the stories like you do.'

She was so touched. 'I was upset to hear about Mark and I've come to see him. Daddy and I will visit him this morning while Betty stays with you. You will be good girls for her, won't you?'

She went to find Joy to thank her and tell her about Mark.

'They're no trouble, Cathy, In fact, Susan is happier when they are here. She needs their friendship. I wish I'd had twin girls!'

'Susan must come over to us as soon as things are more settled with Mark. We'll make a plan and let you know.'

She drove back to the farm and left them on the porch making bead necklaces with Betty when she and Neil left to see Mark..

'We'll go in the truck, Cathy, as I must collect farm equipment from town on the way home.'

They went straight along the passage to his ward. The Sister came forward, smiling, to meet them, as if she was waiting for them.

'I have some good news for you, Mr Middleton! Mark has begun to come out of the coma! We noticed early this morning that his eyelids were fluttering and he has since opened his eyes. Dr Kennedy has been to see him. We'll watch his movements carefully and his speech. He'll be sent shortly for a brain scan to find out the extent of his injury.'

'Thank you, Sister, what wonderful news! Do you think he'll recognise us?'

'I think so. After each hour his mind will become clearer. His speech might still be affected. Don't be surprised if he mumbles something and you cannot make out what he is saying.'

They hurried to his ward.

He was lying propped up a bit against his pillows so that he could see more of what was going on in the ward around him. As they came to his bed he tried to put out his arms and said, 'Da....Da...' Neil strode across the room to get to him first, put his arms around him and sighed with sheer relief.

'Mark! Thank God you're alive!'

Then Mark saw Cathy.

'Ca... I... wan... you.'

She reached him quickly and took him in her arms, kissing him again and again as tears of joy and relief gathered in her eyes.

'Oh Mark, you've come back to us! Helen and Louise went to stay with Susan and now they are home again. We all have missed you so much, but every day you'll feel better.'

He gripped her hand. 'Don.. go. Sta.... by me.'

'I can't stay all the time, but I'll come every day and see you.'

He looked at Neil. 'My b....ike.......'and started to cry.

'Don't cry, Mark. It was an accident. I'll buy you another one, a red one, the same as your Christmas one.'

A nurse appeared.

'We're taking him to the physiotherapist now, Mr Middleton. Say Goodbye to your Dad, Mark.'

He clung to Cathy, not wanting to let her go, his eyes pleading with her to stay.

'Come a....gain, Ca....'

'I will – this afternoon. Eat up all your lunch and get strong. Goodbye, Mark.' She kissed him once more.

They waved to him as he was wheeled away. Cathy hated to see him so sad and on his own. Neil looked at her face and took her arm.

'We can't do anything further for him. They'll look after him, Cathy. Each day will see an improvement. He's a tough little guy. I'll bring you this afternoon to see him.'

They were quiet on the way home, each so thankful he had turned the corner and would be a part of the family again.

The days passed by. They were anxious days. He was taken to Maritzburg for a head scan. All kinds of tests and exercises with the therapist were done and his reactions were noted. He appeared to have recovered amazingly well, without damage to the brain. He still had a lot of daily physiotherapy exercises to do. The doctors would study all the reports before they were satisfied that he could go home.

Cathy had managed to call Miss Thomas on the Sunday evening before the schools opened. She sounded displeased, but after hearing Cathy's story she was sympathetic and said she would phone the Department for a temporary replacement and hoped Mark would soon be completely better.

'I'm sure you have been through a very trying time. I need you back on my staff, Cathy. You are one of my best teachers and I don't want to lose you! Please keep in touch and come back to us as soon as you are able.'

Cathy gave her the farm contact numbers and promised to do so.

Neil took an excited Helen to her Pre Grade class-room on the

Tuesday when the schools opened, and Cathy walked with Louise to the nursery school. She chatted like a little magpie all the way!

'I'll show you where the story books are kept, Cathy. We have a doll's house with tiny furniture inside and real curtains and carpets and pretty lights. And there's a sand-pit, swings and a merry-go-round. My best friend is Lena. She wears pretty pink tights and tops. Lena's Mom works at the chemist shop. She always says 'Hello Louise!' when she sees me. Here's the gate where we go inside to my room and see my teacher. Her name is Sandra.'

Cathy introduced herself and she could tell at once that she was a young, enthusiastic teacher.

'Hello, Miss Chatterbox!' she said, smiling at Louise. 'What did you find in your Christmas stocking?'

'A new Barbie doll and her name is Fairy Queen.'

'How lovely. You must bring her to show me.'


Neil said Helen was equally happy to be at *'real school'* and found she knew quite a few friends. She waved him happily Goodbye.

'Wait for me in your classroom. I'll come and fetch you there.'

He spoke to her teacher, a Miss Howard.

'She'll be fine, Mr Middleton. Don't you worry. I see she already has several friends.' The children were watching different kinds of fish swimming around the rocks and sea-weed in a large tank.

'That's a sea-horse!' cried one little boy.

'And that's an angel fish.'

'There are also tiny crabs crawling on the sand.'

'This big one looks very fierce!'


The principal of Mount Eagle had been most upset to hear about Mark's accident and that he'd be attending the local school in future.

'I'm so sorry to hear of his accident and to lose him. He's a bright, well-adjusted, confident little boy. He was popular with the boys. We'll all miss him.'

Neil had phoned Fiona to tell her that he had decided to keep Mark at home and that he would not be going back to Mount Eagle.

'I think he should be home now with us, as a family, and I'll be able to watch him. This accident has made me realise how precious our children are, Fee.'

'Yes, it would be far better to have him with you and his sisters, but will you be able to manage with all the extra fetching back and forth to school? Is Cathy staying on to help you?'

'I'm not sure. I've offered her a huge salary, but she's undecided. She has asked her Headmistress for extra leave until he has completely recovered. She's grown very fond of Mark and will stay for a while I feel sure. She's so capable and fits into my home so well, Fee, and the children love her. I'll have to be patient and wait for her answer.'

Fiona wanted to ask him how he felt about her, but thought better of it. Rather wait and see how things developed.

'We'll bring Don over for a weekend to be with him. Let me know when it's possible. It's amazing that he's made such a speedy recovery.'

'Tell Don I managed to buy Mark another red bike, but they will both ride a little slower in future!'

Fiona told the boys that Mark would not be continuing his schooling at Mount Eagle. Don was the one who was most distressed. He phoned Mark immediately.

'Why can't you come back to us? You're my best friend and now I won't have anyone to have special fun with. Please come back!'

'I can't, Don. I must stay on the farm now with my father and my sisters. We can still have holidays together.'

'But it won't be the same. You've let me down!'

'No, I haven't. You'll make other special friends. We don't live so far away, and I'll still be a special friend.'


Neil had been to see the Principal of their local school who was willing to admit Mark as a pupil whenever his convalescence period was over and he was well enough to attend school again.

'I'd like to visit his teacher and bring home a reader and some work for him to do, so that he's not left behind. I can also do some revisionary work, particularly in Maths.'

'That's very good of you, Cathy. How long do you think you can stay...... with Mark?' He was about to say '....with me and the children?'

'Until he's completely better.'

'That might be a few weeks, not days.'

'In that case I'll ask Miss Thomas to get some-one to stay for the whole of the first term. It would be far better for the children to get used to her and complete the first term's work, then I could take over after that.'

Whatever made me say that? she asked herself. I should be thinking of my teaching career. I should be there with my new class not here with Neil and his family. They are people I've only just met and I'm only staying with them because I care what happens to them.

After all, I've only known them six weeks, since Christmas!

Will I come to regret this decision?

It was a great day when they all went to bring Mark home. Cathy and the girls had had another cooking day and had made cup cakes for tea in his honour. Susan was with them and shared in the cooking of them and the excitement. Neil had had difficulty trying to buy another red bike for him as all the Christmas stock had been sold, but with the help of a sympathetic sales manager and a lot of phoning around to other branch stores, a red one his size had been located. Neil went to fetch it and it was standing on the porch waiting for him.

Betty, Jackson, Sam and the milking staff were all there, waving and dancing in front of the porch, as the big family car drove up. Mark waved back, a huge grin on his face. Sam was the first to open his door and help him out.

'Welcome home, Master Mark! You gave us a big fright, but we are so happy you are OK. Please don't go speeding around corners on your new bike! We don't want any more accidents.'

'I promise I won't go so fast and I'll be more careful. I don't like hospitals and I don't want to go there again.'

Everyone made a fuss of him. He got on his new bicycle and rode slowly around the garden to show them he could still ride! Betty announced that tea was ready on the porch and his eyes gleamed with happiness when he saw the iced cup cakes and Cathy's cream scones.

'I see you girls have been busy. What a lovely tea party! When I'm really better I'll make you my special crumpets.'

He polished off a cup cake and then got down from his chair.

'Where are you going? You haven't had a cream scone yet?'

'I'm going to see if Peter is still all right. I want to talk to him.'

He found him sitting on his perch, nodding his head. He looked at Mark and said, 'Hello, hello! Kiss-kiss!'

'Hello, Pete! I've come home to look after you. I've missed you.'

'Hello, Pete! Hello, Pete!' repeated Peter.

'I'll keep your cage nice and clean, and see you have clean water.'

'Hello, Pete! Hello, Pete! It's tea-time!'

How good it was to have him home with them again!

Each day saw an improvement in his mental ability. Doc Kevin came often to chat to him and check up on him. He spent time with Peter, talking to him and letting him fly around the room to watch him land on Helen's head. He taught him to say 'Crumpets for tea!' He asked Cathy if he could help her clean out his cage and put in his clean water and seed.

'That's a wonderful idea! I need an assistant. Thank you, Mark.'

Garth and Julia phoned to ask after Mark and wish them a happy New Year. They were still on holiday with Julia's parents at their beach cottage enjoying a relaxing time and good sea bathing and golf while the weather was sunny and hot.

Joy brought Susan over for another cooking lesson and this time Mark joined the girls. They made chocolate brownies, much to Louise's delight. Neil arrived as they were cooling from being taken out of the tray and promptly helped himself to one.

'No, Dad, they're still hot! You'll burn your tongue.' But the last mouthful had already been swallowed!

Fiona came one afternoon with the boys. Mark showed them the Star Wars fighter plane he was building which was now taking shape and looking like a fighter plane.

'Gee, this will be a great plane!' said Don. 'I wish I could make some Lego models.' He was admiring the other models Mark had made and were displayed on his desk and on a cupboard shelf.

'You could make one, Don. It's not really difficult if you read and follow the instructions step by step. Start with a small model, like a bus or a tractor, and ask your Dad or Colin to help get you started.'

'I'm going to save up my pocket-money and buy one. Now show me your new bicycle. Can I go for a ride round the farm?'

'Yes, but don't go through the mud puddles and watch out for cows and tractors!'

He took them to see Merry who was grazing with the young calves in the nearby field.

'Isn't she a little beauty? She's named after Catherine Meredith Crawford; Merry for short. Now we'll always have Cathy with us.'

Tom phoned again, asking after Mark

'He's doing well. I've started giving him a few Maths lessons, and he's reading to me. He'll soon be riding his new bicycle.'

'He's so lucky to have you there with him! Cathy, Mum has asked me to tell you about a Flower Show this weekend in the Town Hall and has invited you to go with her and Olivia. She thought you'd enjoy it. Would you like to go? Olivia and Roger Summerfield are spending the weekend with us. Roger, Dad and I have arranged a golf game. Have you brought your car?'

'Yes, I'd love to go and I could meet them there.'

'She'll call you and arrange a time. It would be nice if you could stay for a light supper at home afterwards.'

'I'm not sure about that, but it might be possible.'

She felt a little guilty that she had neglected to phone him. She had been so worried about Mark that she had completely forgotten about Tom! He had been very good about taking her riding and dining when he was in 'Maritzburg, and it would be good to see the Summerfields again. She liked Olivia and had enjoyed their company.

She told Neil about the invitation.

'You should go. It's an excellent show. My mother loved her garden and went every year. There's always some new exhibit to see or a new gardening tip to learn. I'll be here to watch the children.'

Tom's mother called her next morning.

'Hello, Cathy! Denise Cathcart here. I'm so pleased you'd like to join us at the Flower Show. We thought of going on Saturday afternoon at three o'clock. How does that suit you?'

'That would be fine. I'll meet you in the foyer.'

'Please stay for drinks and supper afterwards. David is making an Indian lamb curry which is his speciality.'

'That sounds most tempting. I love any kind of curry.'

'Good. We'll look forward to meeting you. Until Saturday then.'

Saturday dawned hot and humid. In the morning she phoned Claudia to ask if she could bring the children for a swim in their pool. The   family had been very concerned about Mark, phoning several times to enquire about him.

'Of course you may all come!' said Iris. 'Claudia's on the tennis court but they'll be stopping soon as it's too hot to continue. Come as soon as you like. I'd love to see the children again, especially that little chirpy Louise! She's such a character.'

Neil saw them off. 'I'd like to join you, but there's too much here to supervise. Watch Mark, Cathy. He shouldn't stay in the water too long.'

They waved Goodbye and Cathy drove off to the Dean's home. She was looking forward to asking Claudia about her new class and catching up on the school gossip.

The water was cool and inviting. She and Claudia joined them for a ball game and after half-an-hour Cathy got them out and dressed. Iris arrived with a trayful of cool drinks and a cake.

'I like coming to Claudia's house,' said Louise, her mouth full of chocolate cake. 'Mrs Dean makes the best chocolate cake in the whole world, Mark makes the best crumpets and Cathy makes the best apple pie. I make the worst pastry and Helen's scones aren't *too* bad if you put lots of jam on. What do you make, Claudia?'

'I make toffee and pop-corn.'

'Oh, goodie! Can you make some for us now?'

'Sorry, no. Go and look at Dora on the TV. I'm talking to Cathy.'

She told her about the staff changes in the new school  term, and her large class of  ten-year old girls and boys. They were a mixed bunch and sounded quite a handful.

'In some ways I envy you being at Hartleyvale, Cathy. You have no lessons to prepare and none of the administrative nightmares to write up each day. I can see how attached you have become to Neil's children and if I were you, I'd definitely stay on at the farm. Now that Mark is recovering well, what do you intend to do?'

'I'm still undecided, although Neil has changed and become a very different person since Mark's accident. He asked me to ride with him to inspect the boundary fences and while we rested the horses he told me about his early life and how he inherited Hartleyvale, things I've wanted to ask him for some time but it was not possible to ask then.'

'Does Tom know you're back? Has he called you?'

'Yes, he phoned the cottage and Daisy told him I was here. As a matter of fact, his mother has invited me to the Flower Show on Saturday and to supper afterwards, and I've accepted. I always took Mum when she was alive. She loved her flowers and so do I.'

She looked at her watch.

'It's time to collect the children and drive home for lunch. We must say Goodbye to Iris. Good luck with your teaching. I'll let you know what I've decided.'

Twenty

A warning

What shall I wear?

This was every girl's perpetual problem. Jeans or trousers weren't right or smart enough for this occasion. In all their hurry to get to Mark she hadn't brought any of her casual dresses, skirts or pretty evening blouses. All she had were her three new dresses that she had packed at the last minute. It would have to be one of those. She looked at them hanging in the cupboard wardrobe and chose the first one she had bought. All the family had said how much it suited her.

After lunch she read to the children and then left them to change. She used her light make-up, brushed her hair, chose a pair of aqua-marine ear-rings and put on her cream sandals. She looked at herself in the cheval mirror. Yes, she was pleased with her choice.

'Cathy, how pretty you look!' said Mark as she emerged from her room and walked into the sitting-room where he and Neil were watching a rugby game on TV. Neil turned to look at her and smiled.

'I love the blue dress, Cathy. It matches your eyes perfectly and you look lovely! I wish I was going with you to show you off.'

He walked with her down the front steps to where Pixie was parked, opened the door and saw her comfortably seated.

'Please come home before the stroke of midnight otherwise you'll change into jeans and shirts, Pixie will become a pumpkin and I will have to drive into town to rescue you!'

She smiled at him. 'I promise that won't happen. Goodbye, Neil.'

'Goodbye, Cathy. Have a good time.'

She started the engine and drove off down the drive. Neil stood watching her until the Renault passed through the gate and disappeared. Only then did he walk slowly back to the sitting-room.

He flopped down into his arm-chair and closed his eyes He knew he loved her very much and wanted her with him. The room seemed cold without her presence, and he was lost without her. He switched off the TV and dozed in the chair, no longer interested in the game.

After tea when it was cooler he took the children for a walk to a small dam below the sheds and they went to find Merry.

Cathy had difficulty finding a parking spot near the Town Hall. The car-park was full but as luck would have it, a car was reversing out. She hurried inside the foyer and saw Olivia and Mrs Crawford waiting for her.

'Hello, I'm sorry I'm late! I couldn't find a parking spot until the last minute.'

'Cathy, my dear, how nice to meet you! We've only just arrived. Please call me Denise. Olivia and Roger are with us this weekend. The boys left early for their golf game.'

'Hi Cathy. So nice to be seeing you again,' said Olivia, smiling.

'Yes, I was hoping to meet up with you again. I loved our visit to your stud farm and it was unfortunate that I didn't see more of the horses.'

'Shall we go inside? I've bought a plan of the various stalls for each of us.' Denise handed them out as they moved inside the hall which was crowded with people and noise. 'I suggest we start at the left and move around.' The girls nodded.

The Town Hall had been transformed into a glorious kaleidoscope of every colour of the rainbow. The huge floral arrangements were simply stunning. Each stall and nursery had its own theme using a special variety of flower. Cathy loved the rose bowers and standard roses, each one neatly labelled with its name. She moved on to admire the hybrid tea bushes and bent down to smell a particularly prolific red bush and heard a camera click. She looked up, smiled and the camera clicked again.

'Thank you,' said a man's voice. 'A beautiful lady and a beautiful rose. You go well together and I have a perfect picture. Are you a visitor to Estcourt? What is your name?'

She told him and he wrote it down in his note-book before moving away, happily clicking his camera.

It took quite a time to get round the hall. Some flower lovers would stay for ages gazing at a particular arrangement, holding up the general flow. There was a voting competition for the most cleverly arranged stall. It was hard to choose the best stall. They were all so different and so cleverly assembled.

Amongst the stalls Denise spotted a little restaurant adorned with feathery ferns, arum lilies, blue agapanthus and a water feature in a beautiful rockery. It looked cool and inviting.

'Let's have a break and stop for a cup of tea! I must sit down and rest my poor legs for ten minutes. I had no idea the show would be so popular and crowded with visitors. I'm sure there weren't as many entries last year.'

'We've had good rains this year which has made a huge difference, and it has been well advertised,' remarked Olivia. 'I've been watching the stall-holders writing down orders. I think it's been a very successful show.'

They enjoyed their tea and cake and continued round the hall. There was an excellent entry of bulbs from Holland. Their growth had been held back so that they opened during the weekend of the Show. Rows and rows of tulips and daffodils were displayed, the colours massed for effect. It made a magnificent display. A replica of a Dutch windmill  stood in the background, its sails going round and round while Dutch music and songs were played, especially 'Tulips from Amsterdam.'

'Do you want to see more or shall we go home?  It's after five and I think we've seen most of the stalls,' said Denise. 'If Olivia goes with you, she can show you the way, Cathy.'

'I've seen a great deal and I'm quite happy to stop now. You'll probably be there before us.'

It didn't take long and they were ushered inside to sit on the cool patio. The boys arrived soon afterwards. Tom immediately came to her chair bent down and kissed her cheek.

'You look lovely, Cathy, as you always do. What would you like to drink? A glass of white wine?'

'It's a beautiful dress, Cathy,' said Olivia. 'Blue is your colour.'

David and Roger came to welcome her and hand round snacks. She liked Tom's parents very much. They were a friendly, easy-to-talk-to couple. Tom, she discovered was the eldest of three married sons and a daughter. There were pictures of their four grandchildren displayed on the bureau. The Flower Show was discussed at length. Roger had won the golf game which they had enjoyed at the local course.

'Please excuse me. I must put the finishing touches to the supper. I hope you're all hungry!' David disappeared into the kitchen and ten minutes later called them to the dining-room. They took their places at the long table. David served them his curry and rice while Tom filled the wine glasses. The salads and poppadoms were passed around and then the feast began!

It was the most delicious lamb curry Cathy had ever tasted.

'There's plenty more. Please help yourselves.'

A trifle dessert followed, and coffee was served on the patio.

'I'd love your curry recipe, David. It was simply delicious. I enjoy any curry but yours is perfect. What is the secret?' asked Cathy.

'Long, slow simmering, and cook it the day before. It's always better the second day. You may have the recipe, Cathy, with pleasure. I'll ask Denise to give it to you. I'm glad you enjoyed it.'


She helped Denise take the empty plates and food platters to the kitchen and place them in the dish washer.

'Thanks for helping, Cathy. My maid is off-duty this weekend.'

As they were leaving to return to the patio, Denise stopped her at the kitchen door, closed the door and put her hand on her arm.

'Cathy, Tom's very much in love with you. He speaks of you all the time, but I'm sure you must know this. He hasn't had many girl-friends – I think he hasn't found the right one up till meeting you. He's worried about you being at Hartleyvale, as David and I are, worried about your safety there. Neil Middleton has a bad name here in Estcourt. He is known to have a filthy temper which he cannot control, and he takes it out on his children. The maids have seen him beating them. There are all kinds of stories about strange happenings at the farm, midnight visitors and noisy parties. Some say the old farmhouse is haunted. I don't know how long you intend to stay with them, but I want to warn you to be careful. If you are in any trouble whatsoever, please promise me you'll phone Tom or David.'

Cathy knew from the Deans, Tom, Rachel and Betty that these stories had been going the rounds for some time.

'I'm well aware of the situation at the farm, Denise. I think Neil has had an extremely hard marriage, and to bring up the children on his own as well as manage the farm has been a tremendously difficult undertaking for him, for nine long years. He hasn't had many friends to help him, either. I'm trying to show him that he can care for the children in a better way, and I'm succeeding.' She smiled at Denise. 'There's no need to worry about me. I'm perfectly safe with Neil at the farm. Come, let's join the others. They'll be wondering why we have taken so long.'

She opened the door and they joined the conversation on the patio on the recent food price increases. After coffee she felt it was time to drive home.

'Will you excuse me? I don't want to be late getting back.'

'Would you like me to follow you there? It's not far, but I'd like to know you returned safely.'

'Thanks, Tom. I would like that.'

'Good, I'll get a jacket.'

She said her thanks and goodbyes.

'Come with Tom and stay a weekend with us at Willowmore, Cathy. Then Roger will be able to show you what work we do. We'd love to have you.'

'I'm not sure how long I'll be staying. I do have a teaching post in 'Maritzburg, and the Headmistress has been fortunate to find a temporary replacement for me, but thank you for the invitation. I'll come if it's at all possible.'

Tom took her to the Renault and kissed her Goodnight.

'We've loved having you here to-night. Please take care. Call me if you are in any kind of trouble. You know I'll come.'

'I'll be quite safe, Tom. There's no need for you to worry. Neil has been a different person since Mark's accident. It has changed him and made him aware of his shortcomings. He has become a more loving father to the children.'

She waited for him to start his car and then drove to the farm. He followed behind her and saw her inside the gate and drive to the porch. Then he reversed the car and drove back home, satisfied that she was safely there.

Neil had heard her arriving and was there to open her door.

'Thank God you're here safely! I've been so worried about you! I should have gone to bring you home. I won't let this happen again. These are dangerous times and we shouldn't take any chances. Lock the car. We'll garage it in the morning. Come and have coffee with me. I've boiled the kettle and it's all ready.'

He took her arm as they walked up the steps and into the sitting-room. She didn't like to say she'd already had coffee.

'Tom followed me home in his car. He was also worried. I wasn't frightened but I must admit I was grateful that he was with me. Did the children behave well?'

'Yes, I took them for a walk to the dam after tea and we saw Merry.' He made her a mug of coffee and handed her a rusk. 'Betty gave us supper and saw that they were bathed. Louise chose the bedtime story, 'Hansel and Gretel.' She complained that my witch's voice wasn't at all like yours and proceeded to show me how to make a proper witch's voice!'

Cathy smiled at him. 'She's as bright as a button, Neil, and she certainly knows what she wants.'

'And she says I've got to make the witch laugh and cackle like you do because the story says she cackled. Apparently I'm not cackling.' She looked at him and smiled – it was hard not to laugh. 'Will you please teach me how to cackle like a witch then I will have passed the test to Louise's satisfaction? It will be a pleasure to come for lessons whenever you say.'

Then they both did laugh.

'By-the-way, Garth phoned asking after Mark. I told him how well he was getting on. They're having a quiet relaxing holiday and enjoying the swims in the sea. He'll phone you again. Now tell me about the Flower Show and your meal at the Crawford's.'

She described the various flowers stalls and the evening meal as they sat comfortably together sipping their coffee. He hardly took his eyes off her face. He longed to gather her up in his arms and kiss her.

'I liked David's lamb curry so much that he's giving me the recipe and I want to try it out. I'm sure you'd love it. You can use beef or chicken just as well. Which would you prefer?'

'I think I'd like the lamb or the chicken. Curry is also a favourite of mine. In fact I enjoy a stew as much as a roast. They're so tasty. My mother made a wonderful oxtail stew. It's delicious with mashed potatoes.'

The clock ticked away, but neither noticed the time. Ten o'clock chimed and Cathy stood up.

'Heavens, it's late! I must get to bed. Goodnight, Neil. Thanks for the coffee. See you in the morning.'

He watched her disappear down the passage and then checked that the doors were locked before he turned off the lights and went to bed.

Cathy showered and climbed into her cosy bed. It was too late even to read two pages of her book. Her eyes closed as she remembered the events of the day.

Twenty-one

The picnic at the river

She woke suddenly.

For a moment she wondered where she was. It was very quiet. Then she remembered it was Sunday. She glanced at her bedside clock. Heavens, it was seven o'clock! She'd forgotten to put on the alarm bell! She shot out of bed and headed for the bathroom, splashed her face, brushed her teeth and pulled on some clothes. There were no children's voices and the dining-room was empty. Where was everybody? She heard plates rattling in the kitchen and went to see who was there.

'Good morning, Cathy! Mr Middleton said I was to let you sleep. I gave them breakfast and he's taken the children for a walk. Sit down and I'll bring your porridge.'

'I over-slept, Betty. It was late when I got to bed last night. Sorry.'

'That's OK. I'll cook your egg and bacon now, and make your toast and tea. Sit down and have your porridge. It's a lovely day.'

She had almost finished when the family arrived.

'Hello, lazybones!' said Mark as they came inside. 'We've been to the dam with Dad. You know, there are quite a few fish in the dam, Cathy, and Dad's going to put in some baby yellowtails and sticklebacks so that they'll grow and we can go fishing there. They are good to eat.'

'I picked some wild flowers for you,' said Helen giving her a small bunch of short-stemmed dandelion weeds.

'And I picked some grass,' said Louise, not to be left out.

She looked up at Neil who was watching and smiling at her.

'How lovely! Thank you, I'll put them in a vase of water.'

'Have you recovered from your busy day yesterday?'

'Yes, I slept too well! I think it was all the wine we had with our dinner. Thank you for not waking me.'

'What can we do today? Can we have a picnic, Daddy?'

'Why not? Cathy must come, too. Would you like to come?'

'Yes, please, it's a lovely day for a picnic. I'll help Betty make sandwiches for lunch and the girls can help pack the picnic basket.'

'Where shall we go? There are lots of shady trees down by the river, Dad. Let's go there. I'll take my fishing net and catch guppies and sticklebacks.'

'What can we catch, Mark?'

'You can look for baby crabs and tadpoles and catch them with my net. Ask Betty for an old bottle to put them in. We'll bring them all home and put them in our dam.'

'That's a good idea. Helen, ask Betty if there's boerewors (spicy pork or beef sausages) in the freezer and I'll braai them.'

It was all arranged in a flash. Betty was given the day off and everyone was happy. Neil brought the double cabin truck round to the front porch and found the rugs and cushions. He packed cool drinks and a couple of beers for himself into the cool-box. Soon they were ready to leave. Neil locked up the house and they set off in fine spirits. They sang 'Old MacDonald had a farm' at the top of their voices and all the nursery songs they knew on the way. Cathy looked at Neil singing with them. She had never seen him so happy.

Mark found a good shady spot  under a large acacia for their picnic. It was near some large boulders and rocky pools in the river. They all helped to unpack the truck and put down the rugs. Mark put on his rubber boots and sunhat, took his fishing net and was soon busy looking for sticklebacks and guppies. The girls did the same. Cathy lay back on the rug and gazed up at the patches of blue sky through the acacia's leafy branches.

'Isn't this a heavenly spot? Are the children all right? There aren't crocodiles in the river, are there?'

'No, but bilharzia is prevalent in many South African rivers. The children know they have to wear their boots.'

He brought a cushion for her head and settled down beside her, lying on his side so that he could look at her. He pulled a long piece of grass from the ground and twisted it around his fingers. He was silent for a time, then he threw it down and took hold of her hand and bent over to look into her eyes.

'Cathy, when I asked you to stay with me and help me with the children I said that wasn't the main reason why I wanted you to stay. Do you remember me saying that?'

'Yes, I remember. I wasn't certain then what to do.'

'There's a far better solution, quite a wonderful solution. It's been on my mind for days and days, steadily and firmly growing. I've been wanting to tell you what that reason was, and yet I hesitated to tell you. Cathy, I can't wait any longer. I think you might know what I'm about to say.'

'No, I'm not all that certain, but I have an idea. Are you asking me to give up my teaching, and stay and live here permanently as a housekeeper and children's nurse?'

He took hold of both of her hands and held them together in his.

'No, there's this more wonderful solution. I have never been more serious about anything than what I am about to say now.' He looked longingly at her. 'Cathy, I have grown to love you very much. Yes, I have loved you for some time. At first I resented that you came to help me. I was so rude. Each day was a perpetual battle trying to keep up with my farm work, look after the children, do the shopping and see to all the problems that cropped up. I was always tired. I'm ashamed of the way I spoke to you and treated you, but you have changed me, taken away all the hatred I had in my heart when I first married Celeste, and made me see that gentleness and kindness are still possible to find. I have never been so happy as I've been these past days with you here at the farm. I watched how you taught the children so many things and how they love you. I wanted you to love me, too, and to stay with us forever. I found I had grown to love you. When I saw you reading to them on Helen's bed, all clustered around you, I knew for sure that I loved you.

'Celeste is my wife – in name only. I had only been married to her three days when I realised I had made a huge mistake. I was twenty-two and she was thirty-four, a woman of the world, a great fashion designer. I was so immature when it came to understanding women, let alone the 'wheeling and dealing' that went on in the fashion world! She took advantage of my youth. I had grown up on a farm and had little knowledge of the world and its wicked ways. I was flattered that she had singled me out to marry. She rushed me into a secret wedding at a registry office. I soon found out that she didn't love me. She tricked me into marrying her, Cathy. She had a string of other men, lining up each evening to wine and dine her and spend the night with her. She was selfish and cruel. She told me she had never loved me – she had chosen to marry me because I was a strong, healthy man who would give her little girls so that she could dress them up in all her fashionable clothes and parade them for all the world to see. She was furious when Mark was born and the doctor told her she had a son. She refused to look at him, or feed him, and he was bottle-fed immediately. She rarely saw him when he was growing up. For the first three years he didn't know he had a mother. She has a warped mind. Helen and Louise were more acceptable, but by this time she had started drinking large quantities of whiskey and I think had been introduced to most of the minor drugs.'

Cathy had gone quite pale. She shook her head. This news was far worse than what she expected to hear! What a horrible woman to refuse to acknowledge her own child!

Neil stopped to squeeze her hand and kiss her cheek.

'I was managing a farm in northern Natal after I had completed my degree at the Agricultural College and I took Mark there. Kevin found an excellent Zulu nanny for Mark. She loved him as her own child and he thrived. Celeste refused to live on the farm. She was overseas most of the years that followed, anyway. She would arrive with her little French  maid out of the blue in a taxi piled high with boxes of material and clothes. She would stay for a week and suddenly say she'd had a call to go to London to launch another show. It was a relief when she packed up and left us.

'My parents were farming very successfully here at Hartleyvale where I grew up. I was their only child. They were both old and I didn't want them burdened with the upbringing of my children. They had not been invited to the wedding party which Celeste arranged after the registry signing. All her fashion friends were there. I had no-one. I wasn't even asked to invite a friend. I was a fool not to have seen through her then. I had no brothers or sisters to advise me, no-one to turn to. My parents never approved of her and she had no time for them. She refused to have them visit the children, but when she was overseas I often took them to Hartleyvale so that they would get to know their grandparents. Mum and Dad loved the children. They died within a few months of each other and I inherited Hartleyvale when Mark was five years old, Helen was two and Louise a baby. I brought the children here. I had very few friends to help me. Kevin was my only friend. He found good maids for me and somehow we managed.

'Celeste used to pitch up out of the blue, she said to visit the girls. She ignored Mark completely. I built on a studio and workshop which she demanded for her work, and I enlarged the bedroom, bathroom and dressing-room for her and Solange. I had a divan in the office where I slept or in Mark's room, to be near the children. If the staff wondered about her peculiar ways and the taxis coming and going at all hours of the night to attend the wild parties she used to have, they kept their observations to themselves. Fortunately their quarters are some distance away from the main house on the other side of the property.'

She had never heard Neil speak for so long! At last she knew his story – or most of the sordid details – and some of the secrets of Hartleyvale Farm.

She reached up and put her arms around his neck to be able to pull him down so that she could cling closely to him and kiss him.

'I've been waiting and waiting for you to tell me about Celeste! I knew you must have been terribly hurt long ago to have made you so unapproachable, unreasonable and unpopular. I have longed to make you a happy person, so that you would enjoy your lovely children.

'When I first met Helen and Louise at the picnic I thought them delightful girls. I had heard terrible stories about how you treated them, and when I read your advertisement for a housekeeper I decided to apply and hoped that I'd be chosen. I was upset to think that you had no-one to help you. I had a few weeks free before the schools opened so I applied and you accepted me.

'It troubled me so much to see you punish them when you were unable to control your own emotions, and take out your spent-up hatred of Celeste on them. I have seen you change since Christmas. You have been a different man and shown me another side of your character which I thought must surely be there, but up till now has remained locked up inside you.' She stopped to smile and kiss his mouth. 'I love you as much as I love your children. I wasn't sure, but it has slowly crept up inside me. At first it was sympathy I felt for you, trying to bring them up with hardly anyone to advise you, and I wanted to help you, Neil, for the children's sakes. When you kissed me at Hibiscus Cottage I knew then that I loved you. I have grown to love you, too, Neil, as much as I love your children.'

He kissed her then, gently at first and then with a hungry desire of passions long unfulfilled.

'Oh, Cathy, my love, what are we going to do? I'm married to Celeste and therefore I can't ask you to marry me, as much as I'm longing to do so. I want you here with me always.'

'There's nothing we can do. I'll stay with you and help with the children. I love the farm and we'll be near each other. Let's just take each day as it comes. Something will happen sooner or later. She cannot continue to abuse her body much longer. Neil, kiss me again!'

It was such a happy day. Neil cooked the sausages for them and the sandwiches were quickly gobbled up. Mark and the girls came home with bottles of sticklebacks, guppies, crabs and tadpoles which they joyfully tipped into the dam.

'Looking for crabs makes you very tired,' said Louise yawning at bath-time. 'That was the nicest picnic we've ever been to, Cathy.'

'Was it better than the White Water Falls picnic that I took you to in the pony-cart at Christmas time?'

'Oh, yes, much better, because my Daddy came with us.'

'You love your Daddy, don't you, Lou?'

'Yes, he's the best Daddy in the whole world.'

'He certainly is,' agreed Cathy.

They listened to their bedtime story, 'The Frog Prince,' and it didn't take them long to fall asleep. Neil listened with them, hugged them Goodnight and saw them tucked into bed.

Mark said his prayers very earnestly before Neil switched off the light. He sat up in bed, put his hands together and closed his eyes.

'Dear God, please will you check up on those baby fish *every day* and see that they get bigger and bigger, so that soon we'll have lots of big fat fish in the dam. I worked hard to catch that lot.' Neil was smiling. 'I'll have my fishing rod ready to catch one. I'm glad I'm better and that I'll be going to school with Helen, and *please* let Cathy stay with us, Amen.'

He looked up at his father before snuggling under the bedclothes.

'That was quite a long one, wasn't it, Dad?'

'It was the best one I've ever heard and I'm sure God heard it.'

He joined Cathy for coffee in the sitting-room. She had showered and changed into her blue dress. She handed him his mug and a rusk.

'You look lovelier than ever to-night. Your eyes are bright and shining. I'm so happy that you are staying with me, and that you love me. Cathy, I'm so much in love with you! My life on the farm means nothing to me now, unless you are here, and I come inside to find you in my home.' He kissed her again and again.

'I want you to have a happier life. You have been through enough pain and hardship during the past ten years. You have missed so much loving and I want to give you all the love I can to make up for those lost years. We'll have a happy family life soon, I feel sure.'

Twenty-two


Swimming at the Dean's home


It was Monday, an important day for Mark who was going to school with Helen at their local Estcourt School for the first time. Neil had been given a list of his uniform requirements by the Headmaster and had bought him his summer uniform and brown sandals. He came to the breakfast table smartly dressed, his hair brushed and carrying his ruck-sack. Betty and Cathy had made up their lunch-boxes and cool-drink bottles.

'My, what smart children we have!' remarked Neil. 'It's an important day for you, Mark. I'm sure you'll be happy with Miss Godfrey. She's expecting you today. I think you'll find some of your soccer club friends might be in your class, and you'll soon make lots of new friends. I'll take you and Helen this morning and Cathy will walk with Louise to nursery school. Cathy will probably fetch you. We'll see how it works out. Sit down and drink your orange juice. Betty is bringing the porridge.'

They went off happily in the truck with Neil while Cathy and Louise walked leisurely to 'Happy Days.' Louise kept up a running commentary all the way as she usually did.

'Did you know that kittens are born with their eyes closed, Cathy? Lena's cat, Mischief, had six baby kittens before Christmas. They stay with their mother in a basket in the kitchen. I wish we had a pet. I'd love a little puppy.'

'Perhaps you could ask for one for your birthday present. When is your birthday?'

She had wondered why there were no dogs on the farm. Probably because Celeste didn't like the noise of them barking. She suddenly realised she didn't know any of their birthday dates!

'I'll be five on the second of April this year.'

'Are you sure? How do you know?'

'I asked Daddy and he told me. Next year I can go to 'big school.' Lena says you can't talk all the time at big school. You have to sit still and listen to the teacher.'

'Do you think you could do that? You might find it difficult not to talk too much, Louise.'

'I'll sit still and listen and only talk if she asks me something, and then I'll talk and talk and talk, until she tells me to stop.' Cathy had to smile. 'I hope I get a pretty teacher like Sandra. She wears earrings to match her dresses and lots of bangles. She says I'm the best singer in the group. Would you like me to sing 'London bridge is falling down, my fair lady' and 'Pop goes the weasel?' I know all the verses off by heart. I like singing. One day when I grow up I'm going learn to play the guitar. Lena says then I can sing with a pop group. Wouldn't that be great?'

She proceeded to sing 'Pop goes the weasel' until they reached the nursery school gate.

'Goodbye, Cathy. Thanks for bringing me.' She skipped along to her classroom door, waved to Cathy and disappeared inside.

That child will have a successful life, thought Cathy. There's no holding her down!

On her return to the farm she got Pixie from the garage and drove into town. That morning Betty had given her a long list of grocery shopping to do. She found early morning was the best time to shop before the crowds arrived. When Neil came up for his morning tea she was unpacking the last bag.

He came straight to her, took the bottle of marmalade out of her hand and put his arms around her.

'How wonderful it is to come home and find you here! I love you,' he said and kissed her. 'You made yesterday the happiest day I've had for years. I could climb to the top of Cathedral Peak and back ten times!'

Her arms crept up shyly around him. 'I love you, too.' She kissed him, delighting in their new-found love. 'How did it go with Mark?'

'Miss Godfrey met us at the classroom door, took him inside and introduced him to the children. 'This is Mark Middleton, your new class-mate and friend,' she said. 'He has recovered from his illness but still needs a little more time to be completely better. Say Good morning and hello to him.' Mark said 'Hi, guys!' and smiled. She showed him where to sit. I said Goodbye and left him. Three of the boys I recognised as boys from his soccer club team. Don't worry, Cathy. I'm sure he'll be fine.'

'He's such a sensible child who doesn't panic or get upset easily. He's had the boarding-school training and it won't take him long to settle down. It will be far better for him there to meet other boys and make friends locally.'

'I'm switching on the kettle for tea. I see Betty's coming up to make it. Leave the groceries and come and join me on the porch.'

He took her hand and they sat together on the sofa. While they waited for Betty she thought it would be a good opportunity to ask him about making a vegetable garden and getting the children interested in helping with the planting and watering.

'That's an excellent idea!' He was instantly interested. 'There's plenty of open ground near the garages which would be ideal. The soil is good and there's plenty of sunshine. I can get water laid on. Let me speak to Sam. He will arrange for the workers to dig over and prepare the soil for you.'

'Neil, you must advise me what vegetable seeds to plant and where I can buy them. I think the children should each have a plot of their own to look after, don't you?'

'Yes, and I've been thinking for some time now of starting a small chicken run for our own eggs and poultry. Fiona would be only too happy to advise us. Louise would love to feed the chicks and see them grow. I'll buy the vegetable seeds for you when I'm next in town. Let's get the ground prepared first. Ah, here's Betty with the tea and muffins.'

I must look up a recipe for a simple sandwich cake, she thought. It would be a change for afternoon tea and the children will be home to enjoy it. I could have a jam filling and icing on the top.

'I'll take the truck to fetch Louise, Cathy. It's too hot for you to walk there and back. I must get back to the sheds as Sam's waiting for me. Bye, my darling. See you at lunch-time.'

He kissed her and hurried away. Cathy marvelled at the change in him! He had been starved of love for years and years.

Neil also fetched Helen and Mark after school. Mark had home-work to do and she was happy to hear his reading and spelling. He brought home a library book which he had chosen, 'Jason and the golden fleece.'

'I want to start it right away, Cathy. Miss Godfrey says it's an old fable adventure story of how the children of the King of Thebes were carried off from their enemies on this skin from a golden ram. She explained to me what a fleece is. It's the coat of a ram sheared off by one shearing. You must be a very clever shearer to cut off the whole coat without breaking the wool or stopping! Jason and the Argonauts brought the golden fleece back with them to Thessaly. Have you time to listen to me read a few pages now?'

'Of course. I read the story when I was bit older than you but I've forgotten parts of the story. I'd like to hear it again. Let's sit on the sofa on the porch where it's cool.'

When Helen and Louise heard that he was reading a story, they crept up and sat next to Cathy.

'What's a fleece?' whispered Helen. 'Is it a kind of animal or some kind of treasure?'

'Stop reading a minute, Mark, and explain to the girls what a fleece is. They don't know.'

He did so and then went on reading to them.

'What a lovely story! I'm glad Jason brought the fleece back,' said Helen. 'What are we doing this afternoon, Cathy? Can we go to the Deans and swim?'

'I'm sure it will be fine but I'll phone Claudia and ask her. Put on your swim suits and get your towels.'

Mrs Dean was happy to have them, so they set off in Pixie after

Cathy had left a message for Neil. They were having fun in the pool when Claudia arrived back hot and tired from school.

'Hello guys! I'll be joining you in five minutes. It's lovely to see you swimming with us, Mark. You must be feeling better.'

'Yes. I went to school with Helen today, Claudia, and I like my teacher and the boys in my class.'

'I'm glad to hear it.'

She was soon swimming and splashing with them. After a while she and Cathy left them to sit on the edge, dangling their feet in the cool water, while the children played with the beach ball.

'Tell me the latest farm news. You look very happy. How is Neil?'

I'll have to tell her, thought Cathy, whatever she thinks or says, so she whispered to her.

'Claudia, be prepared for a shock! Neil has changed so much since I came back to help him with Mark. He's a different man. He's shown me a side of his character which I've thought all along was there inside him, but he had forgotten it existed.'    She paused......
'Claudia, he's told me he has grown to love me!'

She was taken aback, wondering what would be coming next.

'Am I hearing correctly? I can't believe you've just said that! What about Celeste?' She frowned and sounded very worried.

'He has told me how he was tricked into marrying her, how she has disowned Mark from birth and only wanted girls to dress up and show off to the fashion world. She refused to live on the farm and lived overseas except for an odd week when she came with her French maid. He had very few friends to turn to, except Doc Kevin, and has brought them up himself. I've never heard him talk for so long! I can't tell you the whole story now but I understand why he became so impossible, disliked and hasty with the children. He's not like that at all now. He's become a normal person and I've got to like him.'

Claudia shook her head. 'I don't know what to think. I'll have to wait to hear the whole story.'

She was  totally unprepared for the next shock!


Iris appeared from the family room door with the tea-tray and behind her walked Neil carrying a chocolate cake!

Louise spotted him first.

'Daddy's come to see us swimming,' she shouted, as Claudia and Cathy turned around to see him. It was hard to tell who was the most surprised!

'Look who has come for tea! Your Daddy phoned me and asked if he could come and here he is,' said Iris.

'When I heard there was chocolate cake for tea, I couldn't get here quick enough. Hello, guys! I've come to see you swimming.'

He put down the plate and sat in a vacant chair next to Claudia while Iris poured out the tea and cut the cake.

'Watch me diving under, Dad,' cried Mark.

'Look at us splashing!' shouted the girls.

'What a charming home you have, Mrs Dean, and I'm sure this pool is a great attraction in summer.' He was watching the children splashing about catching the ball. 'I think I must build one on the farm. I see how the children love it. I would love it, too.' He looked at Cathy and smiled at her. 'I used to have a swim-suit years ago, but it's horribly old-fashioned now and probably moth-eaten. I'll get myself a new modern one.'

'My whole family and their friends enjoy the pool.' She called to the children. 'Come out of the pool for tea and cake, children. It's your favourite chocolate cake, Louise.'

Neil handed Claudia her tea-mug and a slice of cake.

'Thanks, Neil. Cathy says Mark has joined our local school. I think it's a good move. He'll have more friends and it will be good to have all your family together. The girls need to grow up with a brother.'

'Cathy has taught us all so much. I look forward to seeing her in the house when I come up for tea and at lunch-time. And I'm learning how to read stories properly like she does, to Louise's satisfaction. I have to growl like a wolf and cackle like a witch!'

They all laughed.

'You're getting better, Daddy,' said Helen.

'I'm learning fast!'

Cathy had rubbed down the children and they were sitting on the grass with their towels around them. Their tea and cake quickly vanished and Iris offered them another slice.

'Swimming makes you *ever* so hungry,' remarked Louise, nibbling the icing off her second slice.

. He gave Cathy her tea and cake and sat down to enjoy his own.

'When I got your message, Cathy, saying you were all here, I felt so envious and decided to phone Mrs Dean and ask if I could join you. She very kindly agreed. Sam said he's supervise the milking so here I am!' He turned to Claudia. 'How are you enjoying your teaching this year, Claudia? Have you a large class?'

She told him about the children in her class and the school's plans to add three more classrooms. 'Our enrolment numbers increase every year.'

'Do you take afternoon sport?'

'Yes, tennis is my love. I'll be coaching tennis this term and also helping with the netball in winter.'

'What sport did you coach, Cathy?'

'Swimming and riding are my sport favourites. Last year Miss Thomas asked me to take the young ones for their first soccer games, believe it or not! I had to learn all the rules and also referee their matches. I soon got fit running up and down the soccer field.'

'Did you hear that Mark? Cathy will be able to help us at the soccer club. We need a good referee. Consider yourself duly hired, Miss Crawford!'

They were all pleasantly surprised at his easy friendly manner.


Charles arrived home from work, saw him seated with the girls and went to welcome him. The children were back in the pool.

'Hello, Neil. It's nice to have you with us. Why aren't you in the pool?'

'I came to see the children swimming. Cathy says they are doing well. Next time I come I'll wear my new swimsuit which I have yet to buy. The weather is so hot and the water is so tempting. I can see how the children love it.'

Charles was holding a folded-up newspaper in his hand.

'Look what I saw when I opened up 'The Witness' at the office this morning – a lovely picture in colour of Cathy at the Flower Show!

My dear, it's too beautiful! I simply had to show it to the office staff and tell them you are a friend of Claudia's.'

He gave the paper to Cathy and they all crowded round to see it. It certainly was a very flattering shot of her. The photographer had caught her gentleness as she bent down to look at the perfect bloom and smell its perfume. The caption read

*'A Pietermaritzburg visitor, Miss Catherine Crawford, like Robbie Burns, admires the beauty of the red, red rose, 'Mr Lincoln,' at the Estcourt Flower Show on Saturday. A record number of people attended this successful annual event to gaze with wonder at the rainbow floral entries and stunning flower arrangements.'*

'Cathy, it's a lovely picture of you!' exclaimed Iris.

'I must have a copy of it,' said Neil looking at her. 'It's excellent. I'll phone the newspaper office and ask them to send me a copy.'

He called the children from the pool to look at it.

'Can we have it to hang up in the sitting-room, please Mr Dean?' asked Louise. 'Then we'll always have her with us.'

'Of course. I'll try to buy more copies for you. You may take this picture home with you, Louise. Is there any tea left in the tea-pot, Iris? I see you've left me a slice of cake!'

They chatted on, delighting in his affability and charming manner.

It was a surprising discovery.

Cathy looked at her wristwatch.

'It's time we left, Neil. The children must be bathed and fed.'

'And it's my turn to read the bedtime story to-night. I hope there isn't a witch involved. I'm still not cackling to Louise's satisfaction!'

He stood up. He went to rest his hand on Cathy's shoulder and looked lovingly at her. Her eyes met his and she smiled at him. Claudia saw the look that passed between them.

'Right. I'll take Mark and the girls can ride with you.'

The Dean family saw them off and the girls waved Goodbye. They all remarked about the change in Neil, and his happy disposition and friendliness.

'I wonder what has changed him,' said Iris.

'Probably the fact that Mark has made a complete recovery. I hear the accident and his head injury frightened him and disturbed him immensely. He thought he was losing him. It's enough to shake you up to see your faults and do something to try to rectify them,' remarked Charles.

Claudia said nothing about Cathy's disclosures and kept her thoughts to herself.   Was it possible that they were in love? Certainly she could see that Neil was very attracted to her.

Louise carefully carried the newspaper home and Cathy cut out the photograph for her. She pasted it neatly on a piece of cardboard and drew a frame around it, painting it with gold paint. Neil hung it up for her on the sitting-room wall where she said she'd like it to be. It looked just like a real photograph in a gold frame. She stood back to look at it, very pleased that she had asked for it, and beamed with happiness.

'Now you'll always be with us, Cathy.'

All three children admired it, and no wonder – it was the first photograph they had ever seen hanging up in their home!

## Twenty-three

## Planning the building of the pool

Next day Neil phoned Charles Dean asking him for more information about the building of a pool. He had discussed it with Cathy that morning.

'It's been on my mind ever since I saw it, Cathy. I want to get started as soon as possible. I don't think Charles would mind giving me the name of the builder who built theirs. I'm phoning him to-night.'

Charles was only too delighted to help with advice.

'The sooner we get started the better, Neil.'

'I agree. I'd like the children to have the use of it this summer. Does tomorrow afternoon after work around five-thirty suit you to come and look at the possible position I've chosen? We can discuss it before it gets dark. I'd like to get your opinion. Please bring Iris with you. We'd love to have you both with us.'

The children were very curious next day when they arrived back from school to see Neil and Sam with the tape-measure rolling out the tape in front of the house.

'What are you and Sam doing, Dad?'

'We're measuring the ground to see where we should put a swimming pool for you and the girls. Would you like that?'

'Oh yes! Wow! It would be great to have our own pool, then we can swim every day and not just once a week when we go to the Dean's house.'

He ran to tell his sisters and they all came running to watch. Louise grabbed Neil's hand and kissed it.

'Daddy, what a lovely present! I love you.'

Helen did the same. He took each one in turn, threw them up in the air, caught them and kissed them.

'I thought you'd like it! I must buy my new swimsuit and then Cathy and I can also swim in our own pool. You'll be able to invite your new school friends as well and we'll have swimming parties. Won't that be fun?'


Tom phoned before lunch that morning. Neil took the call.

'Cathy, it's Tom asking for you.'

She was in the kitchen fixing a green salad for lunch for Neil and herself, while Betty finished off the potato salad and set out cold chicken and cold meat on a platter. The cheese, biscuits and pickles were already there for them.

She went to the hall to pick up the phone. 'Hello, Tom.'

'Hi, Cathy. Mum and Dad were so happy to meet you on Saturday and hope you'll come again for a meal. We only noticed your picture in 'The Witness' today. Mum was so surprised. It's a very good one of you. Did you see it?'

'Yes, Louise already has it hanging in the sitting-room.'

'Is there a chance of a ride one afternoon or at the weekend?'

'I doubt it. Now that the schools have opened I'm very involved with the children during the afternoons. Mark is no longer a boarder at Eagle Mount. Neil has decided to keep him at home since his accident. It's much the best for him to be with the family and attend the local school and make friends here.'

'How is he now? Has he fully recovered?'

'I'm not sure. He seems to be practically back to normal. Doc Kevin comes to check up on him. He's enjoying his new school.'

'I'm glad he's improved so quickly. It's a pity you aren't free to ride with me. I know you love a ride.'

'Saturday or Sunday would be the only time, and then it would depend on what the family has planned to do. We'll see what the weekend brings. Thank you for asking me. Lunch is on the table – I must say Goodbye, Tom.'

Neil sat waiting for her. 'I take it he wanted to ride with you.'

'Yes, he was hoping for a late afternoon ride, but it's impossible during the week, and I said the weekends are doubtful depending on the family's arrangements.' She looked at him as she sat down. 'I'd much rather ride with you, Neil.' He took her hand and squeezed it.

'And so you shall, my love. Betty can keep an eye on the children and we'll exercise the horses after tea.'

She had discovered an old recipe book in a drawer in the pantry. The pages were well-used and turning yellow with age, and in it, wonder of wonders, she found a sponge cake recipe. It was fascinating to read the old recipes in pounds and ounces! There were various sections for each course of the meal, as well as special cooking instructions for such things as jam-making and bottling, how to preserve fruit, how to cook an ox tongue, how to stuff a Christmas turkey, how to choose the best cuts of meat, how to make brawn (this she would definitely try out as it was a favourite of her mother's) tips on pastry and bread making. Desserts and cakes took up several pages. Obviously Sarah Anne had a sweet tooth! There were chapters on Italian and French cooking.

'This book must surely have belonged to Sarah Anne, his mother, the eldest of five daughters, who married Sidney Middleton and inherited the farm which was named Hartleyvale after Sarah Anne's father,' she thought. She turned to the first page and read the inscription written in a bold hand-writing :

*'To my dearest daughter, Sarah Anne,*
*May your married life be as happy as mine has been.*
*Feed Sidney well and he'll cherish you forever!*
*I've written out my favourite recipes for you.*
*They should serve you well for as long as you live.*
*Hand them down to your daughter and grand-daughter.*
*With fondest love,*
*Florence Hartley.*
*Hartleyvale Farm.*

She had tried out the sponge cake recipe that morning and iced it for afternoon tea. The cake had turned out beautifully.

'That's a lovely cake,' said Betty, watching her ice it. 'Next time you must add some cocoa and make it a chocolate one for Louise.'

'You shall have a slice, too, to taste it, Betty. I won't tell the children. Let's keep it a surprise.'

There were cries of delight from the children when Betty arrived with the tea-tray and cake.

'It's like a birthday cake!' said Helen. 'Is it your birthday, Cathy?'

'Where did that gorgeous cake come from, Betty?' asked Neil.

'Cathy made it for you.'

'No, I don't believe you!'

'It's true. She made it as a surprise for tea.'

'Wow! You're a star!' shouted Mark.

'Pour out the tea, please, Cathy, we're dying to taste it.'

It soon disappeared, pronounced 'Very, very good' by them all. Betty got her slice as well.

'Is this your mother's recipe, Cathy?' asked Mark.

'No, as a matter of fact it's *your* great-grandmother's recipe. I found an old book in the pantry in which she had written down her recipes for her daughter, your grandmother, Sarah Anne, when she first married your grandfather, Sidney Middleton. I'm sure she made this cake for your Dad when he was a little boy.'

'You must try out some of the other recipes, Cathy. I'm sure they'll be just as good as this one. My grandmother must have been a very good cook.'

When it was cooler Cathy walked over to the stables with Neil. He had told Jackson they would be riding and the horses were saddled up and ready for them. Neil helped Cathy up on Starlight, handed her the reins, then checked the girth and stirrups for her before he swung up himself on Captain.

'Where would you like to go?' he asked her as they walked the horses to the open fields.

'I don't mind. You choose.'

'Let's take the track westwards and watch the sun setting behind the mountains. I know you love those mountains.'

They set off at a steady pace enjoying being alone together. A cool breeze had sprung up. Cathy found the ride so exhilarating after the stifling midday heat. He watched her moving easily on Starlight and then changed to a canter. He reined in as they approached a small dam under some shady indigenous trees.

'Let's stop for a break and give the horses a rest. You can look at the sun slowly going down over the mountain peaks, and I'll look at you.............' A few minutes passed as she watched the ball of fire gradually descending behind those giant craggy peaks. It was an awesome, beautiful sight, but Neil didn't see any of it. His eyes were not on the mountains. He was watching her blue/grey eyes and her long lashes.

'Cathy, I want so much to marry you. Will you marry me and my tireless, exhausting, but wonderful, loving brood?'

'If only I could marry you! I'd love to marry you and your lovely children. I already feel they are mine and that they belong to me. Be patient a little longer, Neil. Have you spoken to Kevin about us and the possibility of divorcing Celeste? He may be able to suggest some-one who could advise you what to do.'

'I told him some time ago I had fallen in love with you and he was happy to hear it. He has the highest regard for you, my darling. He thinks you are so very talented and would make a wonderful wife for me. He said he would look into the legal possibility.'

'He's such a good friend. I'm sure he will be able to help us. We better return home now, Neil. It's nearly dinner-time.'

They rode home using another route equally as scenic. He helped her dismount and she slipped easily down into his arms. They closed firmly around her as he bent to kiss her waiting mouth.

'I can't get enough of you! You have completely bewitched me!'

They were showered and ready for dinner when Betty rang the bell. She had made a tasty casserole using the remnants of the chicken, some broccoli and a Mozzarella cheese sauce, served with rice, a meal the children loved. For dessert they enjoyed a fresh fruit salad and whipped cream.

Mark read the bedtime story that night. Louise had chosen 'The Three Little Pigs,' a favourite of hers. The girls sat on either side of him on Helen's bed, and Louise knew exactly when to turn the pages over when the time came. She knew it off by heart. Cathy and Neil said their Goodnights and Neil switched off the lights.

Neil had made a preliminary drawing of the probable size of the pool to show to Charles. It would be a similar size to their pool. It was to be a long rectangular pool with two steps going down at one end to a shallow area for little ones, and sloping down to a deeper end. It would have a tiled surround and then a grassed area. The pool would be enclosed with a low fence and be entered by a gate which would be kept locked and made completely safe.

Charles and Iris drove to the farm on Wednesday evening. It had been a hot day but once the sun had begun to set it had cooled down and a breeze ran through the trees. Neil had brought a tray of drinks to the front porch and Betty had helped Cathy to prepare plates of snacks. Mark wanted to help and carried out the ice-bucket.

Neil reached their car and opened the door for Iris.

'Good evening and welcome to Hartleyvale! We're sitting on the porch where it's coolest. Come and join us and the children.'

'Hello, Cathy, my dear. This is a lovely cool spot,' said Iris as she sat down. 'You have a pretty garden, Neil.' The children came to say Hello to her and Charles and then disappeared into the sitting-room to watch their TV programme.

Neil got them settled with drinks and cold beers, and Cathy handed round the snacks. The conversation turned to the farm management when Charles asked about his dairy herd and the milk production. Iris asked after Mark's health and offered Cathy plants and cuttings for the garden. Then Neil produced his plan of the pool.

'This is my proposed plan for the pool, Charles. It's just a rough idea of size and shape and we're open to suggestions.' He handed Charles the plan. 'I'd like to place it here in front of the house, but slightly to the one side, so that we can sit on the porch and watch what's going on. It will probably mean changing the drive and house entrance slightly. I also plan to extend the porch into a wide patio.'

Charles examined it, commented on various aspects and gave several suggestions.

'I like it, Neil. Let's go down and see where it could best be placed. Iris, you and Cathy must come, too, and give us your opinions. Claudia says you're a good swimmer and gained your Colours at high school for swimming, Cathy, so we would like to hear your ideas and suggestions.'

Neil raised his eyebrows but didn't comment. He had no idea she was such a good swimmer! He had so much yet to discover about this girl who he had fallen in love with.

They examined the pegged area. Space was left for the porch extension. One tree and three shrubs would have to be removed, but if they were lifted carefully they could be replanted successfully in another area of the garden. Charles gave him the name of the builder who had built their pool and his contact numbers.

'I'll get in touch with him tomorrow. Thanks, Charles, for your advice and help.'

'I'm only too happy to be of assistance. Phone me if there are any further queries.'

The building contractor, Fred Johnson, was eager to take over the contract saying he would be free to start in a fortnight's time. They discussed a price and Neil agreed to meet him the next day at his office with the plan so that further details could be discussed.

'I've started the ball rolling, Cathy. Isn't it exciting?'

He was like a young boy on his first visit to the zoo, so like Mark.

Tom phoned again, this time to invite her to go with him the next evening to the theatrical production 'Thank heavens for little girls' which he had previously spoken to her about.

'Please come, Cathy. I hear it's a most entertaining amateur production. Richard would like to ask Claudia. Do you think she would come? We could have supper earlier at Chez Suzette. It's short notice I'm afraid – I've just realised tomorrow is the final night.'

She had completely forgotten about the production! The invitation came out of the blue and she had to think quickly. She would have to tell him sooner or later about her love for Neil, but she didn't want to hurt him by bluntly doing so over the phone. She had planned on meeting him alone and telling him.

'Tom, I'm sorry to disappoint you, but it's not possible. My position here with the family has changed. Can I meet you during your lunch hour somewhere? I need to talk to you. Such a lot has happened since Mark's accident and illness.'

'Cathy, I'm worried about you.' He sounded so disappointed. 'Yes, I can meet you tomorrow. Can you come to Chez Suzette for coffee and a sandwich? I can be there at twelve.'

'I have the Renault. I'll be there, Tom.'

She put down the phone. Neil was still at the sheds and she would tell him about it at lunch-time.

She was in the kitchen finishing off a pastry fruit pie she was making for dessert that evening when he came bounding up the back steps and went straight to her, encircling her in his arms, trapping her and kissing her.

'I've missed you since morning tea-time! Have I told you today that I love you?'

'Neil, I'm full of flour and pastry, and you'll be covered in it, too!'

'I couldn't care less. Tell me you love me and I'll let you go.'

'I love you and love you and love you. Very much, flour and all.' She kissed him tenderly and planted a dollop of dough on his nose. 'Now can I please finish the pie? The oven's ready.'

She waited until Betty had left the room and they had started their lunch before she told him of Tom's phone call. He looked up and listened to his invitation.

'What did you tell him?'

'Neil, I couldn't blurt out over the phone that we have fallen in love. I wouldn't want to hurt him. He's a nice person and he's been a good friend. I said things had changed at the farm since Mark's injury and that I'd like to see him and talk to him. He sounded very disappointed, but he agreed to meet me at Chez Suzette tomorrow at twelve for coffee and a sandwich. Would you mind if I met him there and explained everything to him? The sooner I tell him, the better.'

'My love, I know you'll do what is right as you're such an honest person and you wouldn't hurt a fly! I won't mind if you'd like to see the show with Claudia and Richard. Go and enjoy the evening. Your friends are now my friends. I've had so very few. Please go and enjoy it.'

She leant over and kissed him. 'I'll see how it goes. Thank you for being so understanding.'

'There's one condition, though.'

'What's that?'

'You're not driving there by yourself at night. I'll take you and I'll come for you after the show to drive you home.'

What a different man he was now! She was continually amazed at the change in him. Each day she discovered more and more about him.

Twenty-four

Breaking the news to Tom

On Friday Cathy received a surprise call from Miss Thomas enquiring about Mark and asked when she was likely to be returning to 'Maritzburg.

'A Miss Lindsay has taken your class for this term, Cathy, but I would like you to continue with us for the rest of the year when she leaves.'

Cathy didn't like to tell her just yet that she wouldn't be continuing with her teaching career.

'I'm glad you've found a good replacement for me. Mark is progressing well, Miss Thomas. Doctor Wood, who is a friend of Mr Middleton's, comes to visit him every second day. He's started school and we're watching that he doesn't tire himself. I've been able to help him with the school-work he's missed.'

She asked about the enrolment figures and the possibility of getting more class-rooms before saying Goodbye

She had no sooner put down the receiver when Julia's voice came on the line.

'Hi, Cathy! How are you? We're wondering how you're getting on with the children and if Mark has fully recovered.. Garth has started work and is as busy as ever.'

'Mark has recovered well. He's started school here in Estcourt this week and has made friends with the boys in his class. Helen and Louise are enjoying their new classes. We're all getting used to the new school routine. How are you keeping? Only three more months!'

'I'm very well, getting larger by the day! Dr. Walters is pleased. When do you think you'll be coming home to the cottage?'

'I'm not sure. Miss Thomas has found a replacement for me for the first term so there's no rush. It depends on how Mark progresses.'

'Well, let us know and we'll arrange a 'Welcome Back' party.'

I think my family's in for a shock when they hear my latest news!

The children were settling well into their new classes. The boys in Mark's class discovered at break-time that he could kick a football accurately between two make-shift stones for goal-posts and they soon made him a member of their class team. Miss Godfrey told Cathy that his work was well above average, and that he had a good basic knowledge of Math, and the English language, and that his computer skills were exceptionally good.

Helen was slower to make friends. She sat next to Anna de Bruyn who befriended her and they became life-long friends. Anna's grandparents had emigrated from Amsterdam, Holland some forty years previously. She was the middle child amongst four brothers. Anna's father owned a well-known butchery in the town. It was always kept spotlessly clean. Rows of Dutch Delft blue plates decorated the tiled walls. The butchery catered for delicatessen meats and cheeses as well as many different kinds of sausages. He sold good cuts of meat beautifully packaged and presented. The girls liked to go there with Cathy to watch Mr de Bruyn slicing the cold meats on his machine. He always gave them a slice of ham or corned beef to taste. His bacon was delicious. Cathy had discovered his butchery when she did the family shopping and often shopped there for their quality roast joints and the huge variety of cold meats.

Louise had a gift of the gab and was never without friends. They flocked around her like bees round a honey-pot. She could always be relied upon to act out an impromptu scene from a play or to take the lead in a dramatic production. Nothing seemed to faze her friendly disposition. Everyone loved her.

Tom was waiting for her at a table for two when she arrived at Chez Suzette a little after twelve. He stood up and kissed her cheek.

'Cathy, how well you look! I've been anxious to see you. You've had me worried, wondering if Neil has been difficult and impossible as he usually is and if he has hurt you.'

She sat down opposite him and took his hand in hers.

'Tom, he's been just the opposite. He has changed so much, in fact he's become a very nice and loving person to us all, ever since Mark's accident. I think he had such a shock thinking he was losing him, that it woke him up to what a horrible person he had become.'

A waitress appeared and took their order.

'I can hardly believe how kind and loving he is now with the children - he's reading bedtime stories to them – he's never done that before! - and with Charles Dean's advice he's building a swimming pool for them in the garden!

'He has taken me riding around the farm, and talked to me about Celeste and his unhappy life. I've waited a long time for him to tell me. It was a marriage of three days, Tom. She never loved him. She was cruel and selfish. He was tricked into it. He was an immature boy of twenty-two, just out of College and flattered by her attention. When Mark was born and she was told the baby was a boy, she wouldn't look at him and refused to feed him and he was bottle-fed immediately – how can a mother deny milk for her own child? She only wanted girls for her own use, to dress up in her fashionable clothes and parade them at the fashion shows for all the world to see. She hated the farm and was rarely here. It was common knowledge in the fashion world that she had countless men friends who lined up every night to wine, dine and sleep with her. She could drink glass after glass of whiskey.' She stopped for a while.

'I have loved Helen and Louise from the day when you arranged a pony-cart ride for me, and I rode with them in the pony-cart to the picnic. Mark I love as my own child. They are lovely, delightful children considering they have missed so much, not having a mother. Neil has brought them up on his own with the help of good nannies. Doc Kevin is the only one who has helped him.'

He was looking at her intently.

'Last Sunday he told me that he has fallen in love with me..........
I know now that his temper and abrupt behaviour are the result of his
anger, frustration and hatred of Celeste. Deep down I've discovered
he is a gentle, friendly and loving person.' She stopped briefly.
'Tom,........I have grown to love him, too.'

There was a long pause. He looked terribly hurt. She could see that
her news had come as a great shock. He looked down and slowly
pulled his hand away from hers. The waitress brought their order and
placed it before them. .They both looked at their plates, but neither
made any attempt to sample it.

She waited for him to say something.

At last he lifted up his head and looked at her.

'Cathy, I'm naturally upset and disappointed because I too, have
grown to love you and I hoped you would come to love me, but I can
see it's not to be. You've been completely honest with me and I
thank you for that. The sordid story of Neil's life with Celeste will be
safe with me. It's not a story to be repeated through the town. We
knew he has had a difficult life with Celeste, but this is far worse
than anyone thought. He deserves a happier life, but are you sure that
it's love you have for him and not just sympathy?'

'Yes, it's love. I'm quite sure. At first I was sorry for the children
and what they had missed without having a mother, and I've tried to
make up for that loss. It has grown into love for them all.

'I have always enjoyed your company and friendship, Tom, and I
want it to continue. I liked your parents, too. You have yet to meet
the girl who is right for you and you will know then that she is the
one for you.'

They were quiet as they sipped their coffee. The minutes ticked
by. Cathy wondered what he was thinking about. At last he drained
his cup and looked up at her.

'I shall accept your love for each other and hopefully I shall also
find love one day.' He smiled at her. 'You're a lovely person, Cathy,
and we'll remain good friends. Have some of your sandwich.'

She didn't feel much like eating anything, but to please him she managed a few mouthfuls. There was a quiet spell while they tried to eat their sandwiches. After a while he put down his sandwich and looked at her.

'I've been thinking of the theatre show. Why don't we all go to see it! Why not? My sister arrives tomorrow for a week to see Mum and Dad and I'll phone Neil and ask him to come. Richard is asking Claudia to-night. Wouldn't it be good if we all got together?'

'Tom, that's a wonderful idea! It's time Neil led a normal social life. I'm sure he'd love to be included.'

'Right! I'll phone him and get more tickets. Most folk in Estcourt have seen the show so I don't think it will be a problem.'

Cathy drove back to the farm happy that she had told Tom. Neil was waiting for her and was there to meet her, taking her arm as she stepped from the car, and walking beside her up the steps to the porch sofa.

'How did he take the news? If you had done that to me, I would have been devastated! I knew he was in love with you.'

'He was hurt and disappointed, but he recovered well and accepted that we had fallen in love. I explained that your marriage to Celeste was a complete fiasco, that she took advantage of your youth and that she had never loved you, abandoning the children at birth. I told him of her licentious living and heavy drinking. He'll be discreet and keep what I briefly told him to himself.' She stopped to kiss him. 'Neither of us felt like eating, but we managed a few mouthfuls. I feel so much happier now that he knows about us.'

'We must invite him to ride with us and stay for a meal.'

'He's phoning to invite you to the Theatre Show party tomorrow. I think that's very good of him, don't you?'

Tom kept his word. They had finished their dinner when the phone rang and Neil got up to answer it. He came back to her with a big grin on his face.

'He's invited us to join the theatre party on Saturday night! His sister Pauline will be here for a week, and he says Richard has asked

Claudia and they're also coming. He'll get tickets for the six of us tomorrow. We'll have a light meal first at Chez Suzette's. I haven't been out to a dinner and show for years! My darling, you can wear another of your lovely blue dresses for me. Won't that be special?'

Twenty-five

The theatre show

Joy phoned early on Saturday to invite the girls to spend the day with Susan. Although she and Louise saw each other every day at 'Happy Days' they still liked to play with their dolls and make mud pies at Joy and Graham's farm 'Mountain View.' Joy came after breakfast to pick up the girls after she had made a quick visit to the supermarket. Cathy met her at the porch steps.

'I hear from Susan that Neil's building a swimming pool for you! How lovely to have your own pool. I expect Susan will want to come over more often in future.'

'You are all very welcome to come whenever you like. Has Susan had swimming lessons?'

'She started last October with Lindsay Forbes and is doing well. It won't be long now before she's swimming.'

'Helen is practically there, but Louise need more time. We've been going to the Dean's pool and she's becoming more confident. Thanks for having them today. You and Graham must come over for a braai.'

'We'd like to come. Graham says he met Neil in town this week and noticed a change in him. He was much friendlier and chatty. I think Mark's illness has had a profound effect on him.'

'Yes, he is far more relaxed.' Helen signalled to her that they wanted to get going. 'The girls are anxious to go so we must stop chatting. Have a good time with your mud cakes, girls!'

They waved Goodbye to her.

'What can I do this morning, Cathy? My new friend at school,

Andy Nixon, is coming after lunch to see my Lego models. I asked Dad and he said I could invite him. His Mom is bringing him. He also likes making Lego models.'

'I'm pleased you've made a new friend. This morning Dad wants to give you a riding lesson, Mark, as soon as he's free. He wants to give you more lessons now that you are home again, so that you'll be able to join us for longer rides. Won't that be great? And afterwards I thought you might like another cooking lesson.'

'Oh, yes! What will we be making this time?'

'I thought crunchies would be nice. I'll write out the recipe for you while you're having your lesson. I've bought enough ingredients for a double batch. They're handy to have if visitors arrive unexpectedly. Everyone likes them, especially your Dad.'

'Thanks, Cathy. I'm so glad I'm staying at home now instead of being at boarding-school. You don't get to have cooking lessons with a good cook at boarding-school!'

'Get changed now so that you'll be ready for your lesson.'

When he was dressed for riding in his jodhpurs, a clean white shirt, riding boots and hat he looked so smart - a small replica of Neil! He went off quite happily when Neil called for him. They were away for nearly an hour and were back at the farm in time for morning tea. Betty took the tea-tray to the front porch ready for them when they had changed.

'What's for tea this morning, Betty? Riding makes you very hungry and it's a long time since breakfast.'

'You children never seem to stop eating!' she declared. 'You may have  two biscuits now and no more until lunch-time.'

It didn't take him long to polish off his biscuits. Neil gave him another one when she had left them and Cathy wasn't looking.

After tea he and Cathy worked steadily together. He had to weigh out all the ingredients and have the square tray greased and ready before he could begin.

'Don't forget to switch on the oven, Mark. Crunchies need a lower temperature than a sponge cake. A moderate, cooler over is enough.'

It was a simple recipe which didn't require the usual creaming method of the sugar and butter. He followed the recipe carefully and blended everything together, then spread it over the square tray. Into the oven it went! He loved to watch whatever he cooked rising up in the oven. Triumphantly he lifted out the tray when the time was up.

'Leave the tray to cool for five or ten minutes before you cut them into squares.'

Neil came up to the house at twelve-thirty for lunch.

'There's a gorgeous smell coming from the kitchen! What have you made today, Mark?'

'Crunchies, Dad, especially for you. Cathy says they are a favourite of yours.'

'She's quite right. Can I sample one now?'

'No, they have to cool and set. Besides, it's lunch-time and Andy's coming this afternoon. We're going to work on my Lego plane. We'll have some crunchies for tea.'

Betty was quite happy to stay with the children that evening.

'I'll bring my crochet work. I'm making a large woollen blanket for my mother's bed, Cathy. She feels the cold in winter.'

She saw them finish their light supper and then Mark was reading the bedtime story to the girls. It was 'Cinderella,' another favourite. They never seemed to tire of hearing the stories again and again.

Cathy had showered and was wearing the blue floral dress the family had admired. She wore her pearl necklace and dropped ear-rings, applied more make-up than she usually did, sprayed on some lovely perfume Julia and Garth had given her for her birthday, and fluffed out her hair. She had only brought one other pair of shoes beside the sandals that she wore every day, a pair of high-heeled black shoes with an ankle strap, which she would have to wear. She strapped them on and decided they looked very elegant, and gave her the extra height she needed.

Neil was dressed and sat waiting for her in his armchair watching the evening news. As she walked to the sitting-room she felt like Cinderella going to the ball. She hadn't been out at night to a show for months! He heard her footsteps, looked up and saw her as she came through the doorway. For a minute he just sat and gazed at her.

'Cathy, my love, you are my beautiful princess!' He jumped up and went to kiss her and whispered in her ear 'and I love you!'

'I love you, too,' she whispered back. 'Neil, I think we must say goodnight to the children and be on our way. Would you put my small cosmetic bag in your pocket? We left in such a hurry I didn't think to pack an evening bag.'

'Sure.' He pocketed it and took her hand as they went to the girls' room where Mark was reading the final paragraph of the story............

........'and when Cinderella tried on the glass slipper, it fitted her foot perfectly. The ugly sisters were furious, stamping their feet and shouting with rage! It made not the slightest difference. Prince Charming lifted Cinderella onto his saddle and carried her away with him on his white horse to his palace where they were married and lived happily ever after.'

'I love that story,' said Helen wistfully. 'I hope one day a prince will come and take me away and marry me, and we'll live happily ever after.'

'I'm sure he will. Goodnight, kids. Be good  for Betty.'

'Cathy, you look so pretty,' said Mark when she kissed him Goodnight. 'Have a great time.'

'I like your  shoes,' said Helen, looking her up and down.

'I like your pearls and ear-rings,' said Louise as she kissed them.


Neil saw her seated in the large family car. 'No double-cab pumpkin for my Cinderella to-night. You shall ride in style to the prince's ball.'

She smiled up at him and sat as near to him as she could.

'I'm so excited. I feel like a young girl going to her first party.'

They were the first to arrive at Chez Suzette and were shown to their reserved table. Tom and his sister followed five minutes later with Claudette and Richard. Tom introduced them all. They chatted together, getting to know each other while Tom ordered their drinks. Pauline was the youngest of the Cathcart family, a lovely girl Cathy judged to be slightly younger than she was. She told Cathy she was a medical student and was spending a week with her family before the university opened and the new year commenced.

'What branch of medicine interests you the most?' Cathy asked her.

'I'd like to do obstetrics, and eventually become a paediatrician, but it will take years and years before I qualify and graduate.'

'I also love to work with children. They fascinate me with the things they say and do. Yours is a most noble profession and I wish you every success. It's been good meeting you, Pauline.'

A waitress appeared with menu cards and took their orders. Lasagne was by far the most popular dish. Pauline chose the chicken kebabs and Claudia the tuna salad.

'I'm sure you guys would like to join me and enjoy a juicy grilled steak plus all the trimmings, but we haven't the time to-night. We'll leave that pleasure for another occasion,' said Tom.

The lasagne arrived served with a fresh, tempting salad. There was time for a coffee mousse to complete a delicious meal on a hot night.

'We must be on our way. Here are the tickets for the four of you, Neil. Pauline and I have ours. I'll settle up and we'll meet up there.'

'Richard and I will sort out the bill with you later, Tom.'

It wasn't far to the Theatre Club. They had good seats and were settled when Pauline and Tom arrived. The final bells rang, the theatre lights dimmed, the soft music changed to the catchy main number as the curtains parted.

'Thank heaven for little girls!' was on its way! Neil found Cathy's hand and squeezed it.

'Isn't this just wonderful! My first musical for twelve years!' he whispered. He was so excited.

The show was an infectious ravishment, as item followed item in quick succession to become funnier and naughtier. The town had produced some exceptional local talent. A poultry farmer who they all knew made an excellent 'Maurice Chevalier!' The 'little girls' grew up gradually becoming more audacious, saucier, sexier and bustier to the delight of the audience. Each sketch brought gales of laughter and the dancing was excellent, especially a high-kicking number near the end of the show. Claudia glanced along the row several times, noticing that Neil was laughing and enjoying every minute, and that he kept Cathy's hand firmly in his.

'It must be true,' she thought. 'Those two are in love. I would never have thought it possible.'

'That was a great evening's entertainment,' they all agreed as they walked outside and said their Goodnights. 'Thanks, Tom, for insisting that we see it. We must do this more often'

Fee Mackenzie had phoned Neil to invite the family over on Sunday for the day.

'The boys want to see Mark and hear how he's getting on at his new school, and anyway, it's ages since you've been to spend the day with us, Neil. Is Cathy still with you? If so, please bring her, too. I liked her very much.'

'Yes, we'd like to come, Fee. Cathy is staying over until Mark is quite better. Her headmistress has found a replacement for her for the first term. We're so fortunate to have her. She's a very accomplished person and the children love her. I look forward to seeing her in the house when I come in from the milking. The house is empty and cold without her. She comes riding with me most afternoons.'

Fee wondered if he was also a little in love with her!

'Come early, Neil. We'll look forward to seeing you all.'

Sunday dawned sunny with clear blue skies, a lovely day to visit their friends. The Mackenzie homestead was an old farmhouse which Ian had enlarged and modernised since he had inherited it five years previously from his father and grandfather who were cattle ranchers. The children were up early, anxious to leave straight after breakfast. Mark was taking his cricket set, his fishing rod and his new red bike; the girls packed up their dolls and tea-set. Cathy had made a cake and crunchies for Fee; Neil had a can of milk and a can of cream.

They set off in the double cab, the children singing their songs and playing the 'I spy with my little eye ......' game. Cathy gazed all around her, loving the mountain scenery, the sheer grandeur of those lofty peaks, the rise and fall of the rocky terrain, the numerous mountain streams winding through the valleys, the wild flowers and grasses, the birds and eagles flying high above them – oh, everything was just perfect. She would remember and sketch them later.

As Neil drove through the farm-gate the three boys rode up on their bicycles to meet them, shouting to Mark. Ian and Fee were on the wide veranda watching for them.

It was a happy day.

They hardly saw the children – there was so much for them to do. Neil rounded them up for a braai lunch which he and Ian had cooked, and they were off again to fish in the dam.

When there was the opportunity Ian and Fee both remarked to Cathy about the change they saw in Neil.

'He's a different person,' said Ian. 'He's approachable and friendly. I could never get close to him because he always brushed me aside, but now I feel I can talk to him about anything and he will give me an honest opinion. How did it happen?'

'Cathy, I don't know how you've done it, but you have changed him into what we all would like him to be, a normal happy man.' She paused a moment. 'He's in love with you, isn't he?'

'Yes, I've loved the children from the beginning and I've slowly grown to love him, too. I want to stay with them on the farm, but it's an awkward situation. What can we do, Fee?'

Four o'clock came all too soon and it was time to say Goodbye.

'I miss you at school, Mark, but I have a new friend called Gavin. He's quite good at cricket, but he's not as good as bowling as you are. I hope I can come to you for the Easter hols. Ask your Dad.'

'I will. I'm sure he'll say it's OK. Goodbye, Don. Keep working on your Lego model. It's coming on well.'

'That was a lekker day!' was his comment when Cathy went to say Goodnight to him. 'Please stay with us, Cathy. Will you? Dad's so nice when you're here with us and we love you.'

# Chapter 26

## Intruders

The following week was easier for them all as they became more and more accustomed to the new school time-table and routine. Mark was doing well with his school-work, thanks to Cathy's guidance and tuition. Kevin popped in on Tuesday afternoon at tea-time to see him. He was pleased with his examination.

'Please stay and have tea with us, Uncle Kevin. Cathy has made us a chocolate cake.'

'I have another call to make, Mark, but Cathy's chocolate cake I can't resist! I'll stay for ten minutes.'

As he was leaving he caught hold of Cathy's hand and whispered to her as she stood at his car door with Neil.

'I'm absolutely delighted to hear your news and I have a friend who is helping with the legal tangle. Haven't you got a sister for me, Cathy?'

'Unfortunately, no, but I have some lovely friends. I'll invite them to the farm for you to meet.'

'I knew I could rely on you to come up with some-one! Goodbye.'

The rest of the week flew by and Friday came around again. Being the end of the week there wasn't much homework to do, so Cathy phoned Iris to ask if she could bring them to swim. Neil said he would come later on – he was dying to try out his new swimsuit! Claudia came home early and joined them in the pool. She was eager to hear more of Cathy's exciting news. She had managed to tell her snippets of Celeste's life-style but it really was hopeless with all the noise and interruptions.

Neil arrived so that put an end to their conversation. He pulled off his shirt and slipped down his shorts to show them his new swim-suit, then dived into the water, making a huge splash.

'Look out, everybody! Here comes the big yellowtail showing off his smart new swimsuit!' shouted Mark.

They had a lively time in the water before Iris appeared with the tea-tray. Neil was impressed to see how confidently the girls were swimming. Helen no longer needed her water-wings.

'Who taught you to swim?' he asked her.

'Cathy did. She's a champion swimmer. Didn't you know?'

Charles arrived home and sat with them, asking Neil if he had seen Fred Johnson and whether he was free to take on the building of the pool.

'Sorry I haven't phoned you this week. Work's been hectic.'

'No problem. Yes, he has an architect friend who is drawing up the plans. He'll submit these to the Council, and with a bit of luck they'll be accepted without any problems, otherwise the start could be delayed. Fred's willing to begin in a fortnight's time. He says there shouldn't be any trouble from the Town Council. They know the quality of his work. I can't wait for him to begin!'

When the children had eventually been put to bed, Cathy curled up next to Neil on the sofa in the sitting-room and they watched a movie which he had previously recorded. It wasn't one that she would have chosen, but she was happy to lie there close to him with his arm around her. After a while she felt her eyes closing. The swimming and excitement had caught up with her.

'I'm taking you to bed, young lady! You've had a busy week.'

It didn't take long before she was fast asleep.

She awoke some time later to hear a car coming at speed down the drive. It came to a screeching halt outside the porch. Car doors opened and there was a great deal of noise as several voices were shouting and some-one was banging loudly on the front door. Her bedroom door opened and Neil's grave face appeared in the torch-light he carried.

'Don't be frightened – it's me,' he whispered. 'I think Celeste and her friends have arrived at the front door and are demanding to come in. Stay in your room and keep the children with you if they wake up. I'll have to let them in. She's probably lost her keys for the outside apartment door.'

The light faded away as he disappeared down the passage to the hall. She looked at her bedside clock – it was one-thirty. By now she was wide awake and listening as the shouting and banging persisted. Then all at once the banging stopped and she heard a man's voice shouting loudly.

'It's about time! Let us in! This is her house! Celeste can't find the keys! Let us in!'

Neil must have unlocked the front door by this time. She heard heavy footsteps on the floorboards and over the carpet as they trooped inside the hall.

'Where's the whiskey you promised us, Celeste? We need a bottle or two, right now! We'll eat later.'

'Look in the drink's cabinet, you fool – where else would they be? I think you've had enough, Jake. Forget about the whiskey. I want you to take me to bed. You said you would have me to-night and not Rosie. She's had enough of you.'

'Not until I've had more whiskey. You promised me whiskey.'

'He needs more, Celeste,' slurred another voice, 'otherwise there'll be a fight, and he'll use his knife.'

Another voice in a foreign accent shouted out triumphantly 'I got ze whiskey bottle and anozzer one! We can drink all ze night!'

'Shut up and stop shouting, Louis! Bring them with you into my rooms. Come to bed with me, Jake. Don't give Rosie any more dope. She's had enough. Danny-boy wants her to-night. She enjoys his kind of wild love-making...........'

The loud voices faded away as they entered the passage. Neil must have unlocked the inter-leading door from the hall and let them into her apartment. Now she could only hear muffled voices rising and falling as they argued over who had the open whiskey bottle.

She was quite shattered.

She heard Helen calling her and crept out to her bed.

'I'm here with you, Helen,' she whispered, tucking her up with the sheet and kissing her. 'Go back to sleep. It's not morning yet.'

She stayed with her until she was sure she had fallen asleep again before she returned to her bedroom and waited in the dark for Neil.

After a while there was a gentle knock on the door and Neil came in. Cathy was lying on top of the duvet in her dressing-gown ready to go back to Helen if she called again. He sat down in her armchair and ran his fingers through his hair. He looked so despondent and dejected.

'Cathy, I'm so sorry this has happened! I've locked them in her apartment. At least we'll know where they are! I see the children are still fast asleep - that's a relief. I had to let the five of them into her rooms. She's escaped again and picked up a girl and three drunks, dreadful-looking characters. The one has a knife which I was told he won't hesitate to use if he doesn't get his own way. The girl is so young! She can't be more than fifteen or sixteen. I wonder if her parents know where she is? I think she's been taking drugs for some time. And I'm wondering if the car was stolen. The one side is  badly damaged and looks as if it's crashed into something.'

He paused and shook his head. 'It's not a pretty story, is it? I'm waiting a while until they have become totally incapacitated and then I'll phone the police. They'll be easier to handle then.'

She felt his heartache and despondency. She didn't quite know what to do or say to help him. Instead she put her hand in his and held it tightly.

'Helen called and I went to her. She's fallen asleep again. All is quiet. I don't know how to help you best, Neil. I feel so inadequate. Tell me what I can do to help you.'

'Just stay here with me and see that the children are spared from seeing this sordid charade. They must never see their mother like this! I need your help, Cathy, to get through this nightmare. God knows I've done all I can to help her. She's cured for a few months and starts designing again. Her work is so good and she's often called to Paris, London or New York for a fashion show. It isn't long before it starts all over again. She will never get over it. It's a heartbreaking disease of which very few remain completely cured.'

There were no sounds coming from the apartment. Everything remained silent for some time. Neil wondered if Celeste and her guests had passed out and if the rest of the night would be quiet. To go back to bed and try to sleep was impossible. He looked at Cathy. She was lying on her side looking at him.

Suddenly loud banging and shouting started up again.
'Open ze door! We go back to ze club. No more whiskey here.'
Neil quickly left to let them out. Better let them have their own way to avoid a fight and blood being shed. He'd phone the police as soon as they had left.

They swayed down the porch steps, holding each other up, continually letting out a string of obscene swear words at each other. Somehow they managed to crawl back into the car, pulling themselves up onto the seats, noisily arguing with one another as to who was sitting where, and where they were going. The one coloured guy, Danny-boy, wanted to go to a shebeen for beer and the others wanted to go back to the club to dance. The large coloured guy who had the knife, Jake, slumped into the driver's seat. He didn't check to see if they were all inside or not. He switched on the engine, let out the clutch and they shot forward like a bullet down the drive. Neil watched the car as it zigzagged towards the gate and somehow sailed through on its way to the club without touching it!

Neil phoned the main police station in town where he had been on other occasions to help take her back to the rehab clinic. The Station Commander was grateful for the information and sent out police cars to find them. Neil remembered the registration number of the car and gave it to him. He put down the phone and came back to Cathy to sit on the end of her bed..

'I've done all I can. The police will track them down. It's better that it happens there in town, than here at the farm.' He shook his head. 'I couldn't bear the publicity here on the farm, Cathy. I've been through enough over all these years. Thank God the children slept through all the noise.' He stood up. 'I'm pouring myself a drink. What can I bring you? What would you like?'

'I feel quite numb with shock. I kept expecting more to happen. It could have been so much worse. Suppose they had attacked you!' The very thought made her shiver. 'I think I'd like a nice cup of tea. I'll get up and make it.'

'No, stay where you are and I'll bring it to you. That's an order.'

It was no use arguing.

She was back beneath the bedclothes when he arrived with her mug of tea and one for himself.

'I decided to have some, too. A good cup of tea is the most welcome and comforting of all drinks, don't you think, Cathy?'

They drank their tea and Neil left her.

'It's four o'clock. Try to get a little sleep. There's nothing more we can do. Don't set your alarm. I'll ask Betty to see to the children's breakfast.'

He closed the door after him and she pulled up the bedclothes and tried to sleep, but the night's events kept coming back to worry her. She had led a very sheltered life and to come into contact with alcoholics, drug-users and prostitutes was unfamiliar, abhorrent and disgusting, a most disturbing revelation for her to witness first-hand..

Eventually she did fall asleep, only to be woken up by Louise climbing up on her bed and kissing her.

'I'm the Prince and I'm waking you up with a kiss! Get up, Cathy. We've had our breakfast and we've been to see Merry. Daddy says we can wake you up. Andy and his Dad came for Mark and he's spending the day with him. What can we do today?'

She looked at her watch – nine o'clock!

She felt better after she had showered and dressed. She had almost finished her toast and marmalade at the breakfast table when Neil came in from the kitchen. His face was grave. He looked terribly serious. She could tell Celeste and her friends had been found.

'Hello, Cathy. I'm glad you had a good sleep.'

'Have you heard anything further from the police?'

He looked around the room to make sure the girls weren't present. Taking her arm he gently pulled her up and kissed her.

'Come to the porch and sit with me on the sofa where I can get close to you and hold you.'

She took his arm and they walked together to the porch. He sat close beside her, held her hands in his and looked into her eyes.

'Cathy, the news isn't good.'

She expected him to say that Celeste and her party had been found and arrested, but she was totally unprepared for the report he gave her from the police.

'The Station Commander at the main police station called me early at seven o'clock. They have found their car..........'

'Where was it?'

'At the edge of the old quarry outside the town..........'

'Is Celeste alive?'

'There were five bodies lying around the car. Jake, Louis and Rosie were found to be alive, either drugged, stone-cold drunk or in an unconscious state, but both Celeste and Danny-boy were dead.'

'Dead! Oh, no!' She gripped his fingers, horrified by this news.

'They presume there'd had been a fight with Jake. Both bodies had several chest stab wounds and Jake was found unconscious with the knife in his hand. He had a bad head wound. He, Louis and Rosie have been arrested and taken to the police cells to sober up, and they are waiting to get some sort of story from them to try to piece together the events leading up to the deaths.'

'It's too horrible! What a tragic way for Celeste to die! Neil, I'm so sorry it had to end like this. What do you think happened?'

'We'll never really know the truth. When he finally sobers up and realises the position he's in, Jake will lie and make up some story to put the blame on one of the others. Perhaps Jake and Danny-boy were fighting over Celeste. Perhaps she preferred Danny-boy as a lover and Jake wouldn't let him have her so Celeste intervened and was also knifed. Who knows? It's anyone's guess.

'I don't think Rosie and the foreign guy, Louis, were involved. They were merely 'hangers-on,' out to get free whiskey and dope. But it's only guess-work.'

'Where were Celeste's parents, Neil? It worries me that they weren't around to help her overcome her drinking habit. They don't seem to have been at all concerned about her. Did she have brothers or sisters or anyone who could have tried to help her?'

'She told me she was born in Krugersdorp, an only child, and that her parents died in a light-aircraft crash when she was three years old. She grew up in an orphanage and later had several foster mothers. She won a bursary to an Art College where she studied dress designing, something she excelled at. Soon she made a name for herself and fashion houses vied with each other to display her designs. She made a lot of money. The only thing she demanded from me was the addition of rooms and workspace at the farm, but she was very rarely here. I think she only came from time to time to see how much the girls had grown, and take their measurements for the next set of clothes she was designing. She spent hardly any time with them; she couldn't bear any noise when she was working; she never read to them or interested herself in their dolls or what they were doing – she was the worst possible mother – quite hopeless. I tried to make up for the love she never showed them, but I haven't succeeded very well. There was so much work to do on the farm. I was always tired. I didn't give them enough of my time or my love.'

'You did all you could to bring them up without a mother. You were very hard on them at times, but they went on loving you. That's all that matters. Children are very forgiving. You brought them up on your own with only nannies to help you. You have three wonderful, lovable children, and I love you for it.'

He ran his fingers through his hair, a typical gesture he made when he was worried, and leaned back on the sofa. He had become very emotional. He was very near to tears.

'I keep thinking it's for the best, Cathy. It would have come sooner or later. She was a strange girl, so gifted, but she destroyed that talent by mixing with the wrong company and living a life-style that slowly took over her life and destroyed her. I was so immature and should never have married her. What does one know of the world when you're twenty-two? I only knew her three weeks and was flattered by her attention and that she'd chosen me from all the men who wanted to marry her. She said she loved me, but that wasn't true. She only loved herself.

'I had no older brothers who I could have turned to for advice and my friends were all my young College friends. I have paid dearly for my stupidity and for rushing into a marriage which for her was only a marriage of convenience. She wanted a man who would give her little girls so that she could use them as models in her fashion shows. She saw me, liked what she saw and went all out to trap me into marrying her. The only good that has come from the marriage has been my three children. I wouldn't *ever* have let her take them away from me. Now they will never be hers to flaunt for her own ends.'

The tears gathered in his eyes. 'Cathy, at last they belong to me alone. At last they are really mine.'

She could see he was choked up with emotion and the tears now ran freely down his cheeks. Reaching up she caressed his eyes with her fingers and kissed his cheeks wet with his tears. He enveloped her in his arms and she cried with him.

'That life is over. Once the court case is closed you can put it behind you forever. You can start afresh.'

'Cathy, I want you to stay with us. Will you? I need time to adjust and get over her death. There will be a court case. The children will ask questions. You will know what to tell them. Mark is better and has made a good adjustment to our local school. People will ask him questions about her. It will be a difficult time for them..... .... and most of all, I need you here with me. Every day I want you more.' He looked longingly at her. 'I no longer want to work the farm without you here with me. This farm will be dead without you and your love. You belong here with me.

'I can't believe I'm free at last! When all this drama is over, will you marry me, my darling? I've asked you before and I'll keep on asking until you say you'll marry me.'

'Neil, I said 'Yes' before, and I'll say it as many times as you want.
I will marry you. Today, if it were possible. I love you, and the children, and the farm. I want to be here with you always.'

He kissed her, holding her tightly to his chest.

'Hartleyvale Farm will become a greatly renowned farm, full of happiness and love. We'll have more children, I hope brothers for Mark. I'll open up her apartment rooms and enlarge the farm.'

He was kissing her gentle face when the girls saw them and came running up the steps.

'Kiss her again, Daddy!' cried Louise. 'It's just like what Prince Charming did to the Sleeping Beauty in my story-book, but your kiss is much better – your kiss is for real!'

## Twenty-seven

## Unlocking the doors

The Station Commander called during the next morning to ask Neil if he would come to identify her body.

'Cathy, as her husband I know it's something I have to do.'

Cathy kissed him and watched as he drove down the drive.

It had begun to rain softly, a welcome relief from the summer's heat. She sat on the porch sofa for a while, listening to their rhythmic sounds as the raindrops fell on the sun-baked earth, dry grass and parched flower-beds. She knew every farmer would be thankful for this heaven-sent gift. They had waited and prayed for rain for weeks.

As it was Saturday the children were home watching a programme about a lioness and her cubs. It was a fascinating story filmed with amazing photography. They were completely spell-bound.

'I'll feel better if I'm doing something. I can't sit here all day doing nothing! I'll make a cake and two banana loaves for the weekend.'

She had the cake in the oven and the loaves ready to follow when the phone rang. She picked up the receiver.

'Hello, Hartleyvale Farm, Cathy here.'

'Cath, we've just heard the midday news over the radio!' It was Garth's excited voice. 'Celeste Middleton has been found murdered outside the town! Is that Neil's wife or another relation? Did you know about it?'

'Yes, Neil has gone for the identification. Garth, I can't say any more as we are keeping it from the children. It's been a huge shock.

I'll phone you later to-night when they are asleep and we have more details. I expect there'll be more about it in this evening's newspaper. I have to stop. 'Bye.'

She put down the phone before he could ask any further questions.

Neil was back before lunch. Cathy heard the truck and ran to the porch to meet him. It was still raining. He stepped out, ran up the steps and took her hand in his.

'It's over,' he whispered. 'I was dreading it, but they had cleaned her up and she looked very peaceful. Let's have lunch. Where are the children?'

'Their programme came to an end so they've been watching me make banana loaves for tea. I'll tell Betty to bring in the lunch.'

He called the children and they sat down at the table. Betty had made a good vegetable soup, followed by buttered ham rolls and there was paw-paw salad and yoghurt for their pudding.

'I'll be in my office if you need me, Cathy. I need to do some phoning. Can you keep the children occupied for a while?'

She got the girls settled on the back veranda with their paint boxes and painting books. Mark was doing a new jigsaw puzzle.

'It's a lovely rainy day to paint,' said Helen as she was finding a picture to paint. 'I'm painting this picture of the twins at the Zoo.'

Louise was flipping over the pages of her book.

'I think I'll do this one about children playing on the beach. I can paint the sea blue and the sand yellow. What colour are buckets and spades, Cathy?'

'You can make them any colour you like. What about red or green or orange?'

'I like purple. My buckets are going to be purple.'

'Oh, yuk! That's an awful colour. I've never seen *purple* buckets,' said Helen, pulling an ugly face.

'Well, now you will see them. Mine will be *purple.*'

That little madam knew exactly what she wanted!

Cathy left them to their painting and went to the office to tell Neil about Garth's phone-call. She sat in a chair next to his desk while he continued his phoning.

'I'm calling Kevin, Joy, Fiona, Tom and the Deans to tell them of her death, if they haven't heard the news already. I'll tell Sam to get the staff together tomorrow and do likewise. They should know the truth. Reporters will come snooping around eager to get a sensational story, and ready to provide a cash payment for any snippet of news, and they must know what to tell them. I want to open up her rooms, but I can't do it while the children are awake.' He looked at her intently, his face serious. 'I think I should clean them up first before you see them, Cathy. You will find them so disgusting, but this is what I have had to live with, my love. I'll take you tomorrow evening when they are asleep, if you like. Do you want to come with me when I unlock the doors?'

She hesitated, knowing it would shock her, but it was something she felt she had to see.

'Yes, Neil, I'll come with you.'

She had wondered for weeks and weeks what lay behind those curtained windows and walls. Soon she would see it for herself.

Neil made his phone-calls and next morning had a meeting with all his workers. They were upset and deeply sorry for him and the children. Some of them knew a little of the sad history of his marriage; the nannies and domestic workers knew the most, having worked in the house and had seen for themselves how he and the children lived. On the whole they had been very loyal and supportive. They thought his marriage a strange one, which it was, but they accepted it. He expected them to work hard; he was very fair in all his judgement; he paid them well. It was not for them to question a white man's marriage. If that was the way he wished to live, well, so be it. It didn't concern them.

That evening on Sunday after the bed-time story had been read and the children tucked into bed, he took her arm and they walked to unlock the inter-leading door from the hallway.

'This will be an unpleasant shock for you, my love, but I'm here with you.' He smiled down at her and kissed her mouth. 'These rooms will be seen for the last time to-night and then they will be changed completely and made happy, bright living-rooms where the morning sunshine will shine into every room, and a fresh breeze will blow through the open windows.'

By this time they had walked to the end of the passage and entered a darkened room which Cathy presumed Celeste had used as her work-room. He found the light switch. Immediately they were transported into a movie scene of chaotic disorder.

The room was in complete disarray.

It hadn't been cleaned for weeks........probably months.

Heavy, dark green curtains hung down to the floor. A thick layer of dust had settled on everything. A revolting pungent smell pervaded the room. Cathy put her hand up to her nose to try to blot it out. Cardboard and papers, fruit skins, greasy take-away plates and paper-bags, half-eaten meals and left-over pieces of several pizzas, dirty cutlery, dozens and dozens of empty liquor bottles and dirty glasses littered the tables and floor. Patterns and cut-out pieces of material hung over the chairs. Open built-in cupboard doors revealed several unfinished garments hanging on hangers. She could see boxes of paper patterns, rolls of material, laces, ribbons and all kinds of sewing needs on the shelves. A sewing machine in a cabinet stood open in one corner of the room. There was also an ironing-board and two electric irons.

They moved forward a few steps and heard a scratching sound below them. Looking down they saw they had disturbed a nest of field mice. Cathy screamed and clung to Neil as suddenly two large grey mice scampered across their feet to hide underneath another pile of rubbish.

'Neil, this is too disgusting! How could she possibly have worked here in this dirty room?'

'It was cleaned up a little by her maid from time to time but she always left in a hurry to catch a plane, and locked the doors behind her. It remained as it was until she came again, sometimes months later. I couldn't ask my staff to see the rooms and clean them up.'

Cathy gazed at the once beautiful pale green carpet now full of stains – blood, vomiting, spilt liquor and food. The easy chairs which Neil had chosen so carefully for her were dirty and stained with food droppings. Her pictures in heavy black frames were odd surrealistic drawings that looked like meaningless scribblings a child of two years old would have drawn.

Neil was watching her. 'Do you want to go on into the bedroom, dressing-room and bathroom?'

She nodded and looked at him with wide eyes.

'It can't be worse than this, can it?' she whispered.

He said nothing, but took her arm, as if to steady her against what she would now see, and opened the door of the bedroom.

He switched on the lights.

The first thing she saw was the huge king-size bed. It looked as if a tornado had hit it. It was a rabbit warren of crumpled up, soiled, stained bedding which hadn't been changed and washed for months, maybe years. Then her eyes caught sight of the enlarged photographs on the walls around the bed – suggestive, sensuous, lewd, horribly disgusting pictures. She turned to hide her face in Neil's shirt.

'No! No! I can't bear to look any further! Take me back, Neil, take me back! Please take me away from this dreadful, obscene room!'

His arms closed around her and he guided her back to the passage and to their sitting-room. He put her down in an armchair and gave her a glass of red wine. She was horrified by what she had looked at.

'Drink this to blot out what you have seen. It's not worth thinking about, Cathy. Celeste and her friends became so hooked on drink and drugs that they lost their identity as human beings.'

She took three large mouthfuls of the dark red wine and felt its warmth as it slid down her throat.

'It's filthy and disgusting, but we'll clean it up, rebuild it into two more bedrooms, another bathroom and a small study. You will never know that it had existed.

'And I have a surprise for you! There's plenty of space in the garden for an additional room which I'm designing as an art studio for you, my love, so that you can continue with your sketching and painting. Your work is so good.'

'Oh, Neil, I shall love it!' She hugged him and kissed him.

She drank the rest of the wine more slowly and closed her eyes as she tried to picture the apartment as he wanted it to be rebuilt. It would be completely different and would become the new wing of the existing farmhouse.

He would make quite sure that there would be no more secret rooms and strange, night-time visitors at Hartleyvale Farm.

Neil tore down the photographs and all the pictures and burnt them himself. A team of workers came in and removed all the furniture. The curtains and bedding were sent to a laundry and then, washed and clean, were given to poor families. Then the vacuuming and washing began, from ceiling and walls to the floor. The carpeting was ripped up, the bathroom was scrubbed clean until it shone and the tiles glowed again. Her sewing materials were given away, her patterns burnt. Cupboards were washed and disinfected. All the windows were washed and polished until they gleamed and sparkled. They remained open all day.

The cleaning continued all the next week and only on the Saturday morning were the children allowed to walk into the new wing and see the rooms. Neil and Cathy unlocked the door and took them through to the empty rooms.

'What a lot of lovely empty space!' said Mark as he walked through the rooms waving his arms around. 'We can make a racing circuit and have fun riding our bikes round and round the room.'

'Forget it, Mark. When the builders have left, this wing will have two new bedrooms and bathrooms, a TV and playroom, and a small study. I'm adding on an art studio for Cathy, too.'

'Is Cathy going to stay with us, Dad?'

'It's highly possible, Mark. Would you like that?'

'Oh, yes! We wish she would stay with us forever, don't we, girls?'

They all ran to her, flinging their arms around her waist and hugging her. There was no mistaking the love they had for her. Neil caught her eyes and winked at her.

Little Miss Chatterbox had the final say.

'You're our Fairy Godmother, Cathy. Please wave your magic wand and make our wishes come true.'

'I will. Stand still and watch me, otherwise the magic won't work.'

She closed her eyes and waved her arm around, several times, very dramatically, above their heads while she chanted the magic words:

*'Ab-ra-ca-dab-ra, malinkly-loo,*
*Make all your wishes and dreams come true;*
*Ab-ra-ca-dab-ra, malinkly-loo,*
*Like they do in your story-books, they will come true!'*

About the author:

Una Halberstadt is a South African widow and retired Johannesburg primary-school teacher. She now lives on a farm in the tiny Kingdom of Swaziland, Southern Africa where her family has an extensive vegetable and flower seedling nursery. She enjoys reading, writing, music, cooking and gardening. Her children's stories for little ones have been well received and she has given successful story readings at several Primary and Nursery Schools in Swaziland.

Also by Una Halberstadt

## *Sally's Story*

*A group of four related novels telling the story of a young girl growing up in the last century, set in Kwa-Zulu Natal, South Africa*

Book 1 - 'Those hotel years!'
Book 2 - 'Sally at College 1941'
Book 3 - 'Sally and the Professor'
Book 4 - 'The Marriotts of Ridge View'

Stories for Luke          First Edition 2006
Stories for Luke          Second Edition 2008